RELAY

CHANGING LANES #1

LAYLA REYNE

Relay
Copyright © 2018 by Layla Reyne

Cover Art: G.D. Leigh, blackjazzdesign.com
Layout: L.C. Chase, lcchase.com/design.htm

All rights reserved. No part of this book may be reproduced or transmitted in any form or by any means, electronic or mechanical, including photocopying, recording, or by any information storage and retrieval system without the written permission of the copyright owner, and where permitted by law. Reviewers may quote brief passages in a review.

Second Edition
March, 2018
Print Edition

ISBN: 978-1-7320883-2-0

This is a work of fiction. Names, characters, places, and incidents are either the product of the author's imagination or are used fictitiously. Any resemblance to actual persons living or dead, business establishments, events, or locales is entirely coincidental. All person(s) depicted on the cover are model(s) used for illustrative purposes only.

ABOUT RELAY

Captain is not a title Alejandro "Alex" Cantu takes lightly. Elected by his teammates to helm the US Men's Swim Team, he proudly accepts the role, despite juggling endless training, team administrative work, and helping out on the family farm. And despite his ex-lover, Dane Ellis—swimming's biggest star—also making the Olympic Team.

Dane has been a pawn in his celebrity parents' empire from crib to pool, flashing his camera-ready smile on demand and staying deeply in the closet. Only once did he drop the act—the summer he fell in love with Alex. Ten years later, Dane longs to cut his parents' strings, drop his too-bright smile, and beg Alex for another chance.

Alex, though, isn't ready to forgive and forget, and Dane is a distraction he doesn't need on his team, until an injury forces Alex to accept Dane as his medley relay anchor. Working together, their passion reignites. When Dane's parents threaten reprisal and Alex is accused of doping, the two must risk everything to prove Alex's innocence, to love one another, and to win back their spots on the team, together.

For Tera

CHAPTER ONE

DANE SLAMMED THE wall beneath the starting block so hard the tips of his fingers bent back and pain shot down his knuckles. With Mo's wake a lane over lapping at his side, Dane hadn't let up, charging hard to the very end of the hundred-meter race. He pushed off the wall and broke the water's surface, gasping for breath as he tore off his cap and goggles. The crowd roared. He twisted to check the stadium's giant scoreboard and understood why.

He'd hoped that's what the ruckus was all about.

"You bastard!" came a laughing shout beside him.

Dane sloshed around to face his grinning mentor. Mo had finished two-hundredths of a second behind him, both of them shattering Mo's existing freestyle record.

"Not too bad yourself, old man. Madrid, here we come!" Dane clasped Mo's offered hand and held their arms aloft in victory, the crowd cheering louder. They'd done the same at countless other meets when they'd swum together at UNC, but this was their first time both competing at the Olympic Trials.

They climbed out of the pool, and Mo slapped him on

the back. "I'd say you're healed up just fine."

Not even a slight twinge of pain. It'd been a while now since Dane had felt any aftereffects of the injury that'd sidelined him during the last Games. "I've been back on the circuit for two years. Are you getting senile in your old age?" At thirty, Mo was far from old, but he would be the oldest member of the USA Swimming squad.

"You've been back, but now you're up to full speed. Better than." He pointed at the scoreboard as they finished toweling off. "That's what we need. Good job, Ellis."

Dane basked in the praise, until two swimmers strolled out of the tunnel. Lockstep, arms thrown over each other's shoulders, the one had a fly-stroker's massive upper body, much of it covered with tattoos, and blond dreadlocks piled atop his head. Sebastian Stewart, California native and the world's best at butterfly. The other swimmer was leaner in build, a backstroker, but no less ripped, his light brown skin and dark curls glowing under the arena's lights.

He'd been scarce since Dane's return, rumors flying about a sick family member, but there was no mistaking Alejandro Cantu. Dane would never forget that body or those deep brown eyes. Lifting and clashing with his, those eyes were no less captivating in the here and now, freezing Dane to the spot. He was caught, between the past and present, between jealousy and envy, between love and hate.

Bitterness stung the back of his throat, bile surging up on a rising tide of memories best left forgotten, *never* forgotten. Dane swallowed hard to force it all back down. Harder still when Alex paid him no further mind and returned to carousing with Bas. Thick as thieves, the best friends and former college roommates walked with the easy confidence of being themselves, not caring if Dane, the press, or anyone thought they were more.

Resentment bubbled, at their freedom, and at their nonexistent regard for the world record he'd just shattered.

Well, *eff that*.

For the first time in a long while, Dane didn't begrudge the horde of reporters bearing down on him, or his parents and publicist in the lead. They shouldn't have been allowed on deck, but "the country's minister" and home shopping's reigning TV queen had a way of getting what they wanted, rolls of bills always at the ready. Dane met them at the corner of the pool, close to where Alex huddled with Bas.

His mother, dressed in navy blue Chanel with an orange scarf around her neck, the colors of his home swim club, clasped his towel-covered shoulders in imitation of a hug. "We're so proud of you," she said, loud enough for the reporters. Then, on her tiptoes, for his ears only, "Five minutes before they shoo us off deck for the next event. Make it count."

Translation: always be selling.

She lowered back to her stiletto heels and stepped to Dane's side. His father, in his trademark three-piece suit, complete with red, white, and blue striped tie, gave him a firm handshake. "The good Lord was with you in that pool, son."

Dane bit back a retort. God had nothing to do with it. Twice-a-day swims with one of the country's best clubs, plus daily dry-land workouts and yoga, were why he was now the fastest swimmer in the world. No time to argue though, as reporters lobbed questions at him.

"How's it feel to be a first-time Olympian?"

He slicked back his wet hair, biceps flexing. Cameras clicked and spectators tittered. He hated his role as swimming's current poster boy, so much of the image a lie that turned his stomach, but it served his purpose in this instant. Alex canted his head toward him, listening.

"Great!" Dane replied. "I can't wait to represent Team USA."

"Do you think you'll win your other events?"

He smiled big and drew out his Southern accent, amping up the charm. "Well now, that's certainly the plan."

"We sure hope so," his publicist said. By *we*, Roger meant the sponsors, who counted on their wares being displayed as much as possible, and his mother, who would in turn feature those products on one of her many shows. A vicious cycle, always turning.

"Will you be team captain?"

Motion in Dane's periphery—Alex approaching.

"That's voted on by the team," Dane said. "But I'd sure be honored if they chose me." Truth be told, he hadn't even considered the captaincy, assuming it'd go to Mo or Alex, but he'd play up the possibility to get a rise out of Alex.

"Will you be swimming on the relay teams?"

Before Dane could answer, Alex joined their group, standing at the outer edge, and directly addressed the reporters. "Relay teams are drawn from the top six qualifiers in each event. Lineups will be decided after Trials and announced at Media Day. We'll look forward to seeing you then."

"Alex, are you going to win your races?" one of the reporters asked.

Alex glanced over their heads at Dane, barely concealed fury swirling in those bottomless brown eyes. "What was it you said, Ellis? Well now, that's certainly the plan."

He had the good grace not to mime the accent. Dane's manners, however, were lacking. "*Buena suerte*," he replied, snidely wishing him luck in diction-perfect Spanish.

Alex's nostrils flared and red streaked across his cut cheekbones, but before hostilities escalated further, event staffers surrounded the group, indicating their five minutes were up.

"Dane, honey," his mother drawled. "We'll see you in San Antonio." She tugged him down for a kiss on the cheek, pausing long enough for the cameras.

Roger stepped forward, handing out business cards. "Dane and Reverend and Mrs. Ellis will be available for interviews in San Antonio."

That sounded like more than just Media Day. Dane groaned internally.

"If you'll follow me," Roger carried on, "I'll get those scheduled."

Dane's father gave him another cold, hard handshake, then Roger and the staffers whisked the road show away, leaving only Dane and Alex locked in a stare down.

"*Do not* bring that shit with you to Colorado," Alex

gritted out.

"I don't control my parents."

Alex took two long strides toward him, and Dane's blood revved at his closeness, then chilled with his next words. "Oh, I'm well aware it's the other way around."

Dane's bravado waned. "Alex..."

"And that's not the shit I'm talking about. I know I'll never get the real you." Direct hit, right to the gut. "But at least leave the poster boy at home. Bring me the swimmer; anything else and we're going to have problems."

"Problems are unavoidable."

Alex's dark gaze swept his body, leaving a trail of fire in its wake. "Don't I know it."

"If I bring you the swimmer," Dane said, "am I on the relay teams?"

"Coach makes that call, not me."

"I want on medley." Team USA had lost the medley relay gold by the slimmest of margins at the last Games, and Dane had cursed from his recovery room an ocean away. If he'd only been there. Well, he was here now, and they wouldn't lose it with him swimming anchor.

Alex's eyes hardened, glittering. "We can't always get what we want."

"But we get what we need?" Dane retorted, unable to resist.

He should have.

"Not that either," Alex replied, an iceberg of anger in those three words. He turned on his heel and stalked back to Bas, leaving Dane to sink, shivering all the way to his soul.

"CANTU!"

Startled out of sleep by Coach's bark, Alex jerked up his head as his arms splayed out, sending stacks of papers flying. His laptop careened in their wake, sliding off the side of the desk, headed for certain death, but Alex's big foot and long arms saved it, barely. With a relieved sigh, he hauled himself upright, set the dinosaur back on the desk, then gave his boss and mentor his attention.

Coach Hartl was standing in the office doorway, shoulder leaning against the wooden jamb. His USA Swimming shirt was pressed, his whistle shined, and his black hair slicked neatly back. Dressed to impress for their first official team meeting.

"You sleep here?" he asked, dark eyes assessing.

Wrinkled clothes, check.

Pen imprint on his cheek, by the feel of it, check.

Puddle of drool on the desk, sadly, check.

No use denying it.

Alex rolled back his desk chair and slid out of it onto his knees, crouching on the floor. "I was just finishing up these training schedules." He waved a hand at the mess of scattered papers.

Coach crossed the tiny office and knelt beside him, helping collect them. "Have you slept at all since Trials last week?"

"Some."

Less than a little, if he were being honest.

Standing, Alex tucked the schedules into a red bucket file. Coach held up his stack, and Alex gestured at the desk. "Anywhere is fine." It was all a paperwork wasteland. He'd organize it later. At that mythical time in the future when he'd ever get ahead of his to-do list.

"Do I need to get another admin to take over some of this?"

Alex shook his head. "It's under control. Just a lot of predeparture prep." He could afford to lose sleep. He couldn't afford to lose income.

"I need you in top shape, Cantu, especially in the pool. If the job and training are already too much together, maybe we should reconsider the captaincy."

"No, I want it." Of that he was sure. His teammates, all but one, had voted for him to lead the squad, and he couldn't let them down. "I'll be in top shape by Madrid. That's what these next few weeks of training are for. The admin work will be out of the way by then."

After another bout of intense scrutiny, Hartl bought it, or at least decided to ignore Alex's bald-faced lies. "Let's go, then. Team's waiting."

"Everyone's here?"

Coach nodded. "Ellis arrived five minutes ago."

Versus Alex, who'd slept here overnight, buried in work and too afraid, if he'd gone home to sleep in an actual bed, that he'd get caught in traffic and be late for the meeting this morning. Which he now was, because he'd fallen asleep at his desk instead.

Fuck.

His gaze flickered back to the computer screen, catching on the man whose ripped torso and freckled right arm were lifted out of the water in victory. He snapped the screen shut. "I don't want him on my relay."

He and Coach had debated this decision all weekend, and now they had to make a final call, before going out there to the team. And Dane. After the show Dane had put on at Trials, and their confrontation afterward, Alex had lobbied hard for his exclusion from the medley relay. He just needed to sway Coach to his side, once and for all.

"He's swimming five other events. We can't risk another injury." Alex rested back on the desk's edge, fingers curled around the lip, nails digging into the underside of the worn wood. "After me, Jacob, and Bas swim, we'll have enough of a lead by the time Mo swims anchor."

"You sure about that? Dane's the fastest in the world at free. He all but guarantees gold."

"We'll be fine." Before Hartl could argue further, Alex added, "But you're the coach. It's your call."

"And you're the squad captain. You know these guys better than anyone. If you think Ellis will disrupt your relay team, then he's not on it."

Dane Ellis, with his too-bright smile and cult of personality, couldn't help but be a disruption—to the entire USA Swimming Team, to all the relay teams, and to Alex. It was like dropping Brad Pitt into an ensemble cast and asking him to play a supporting role. That shit only worked in the

Ocean's movies and only because Clooney was hotter. Alex was no Clooney. It wasn't going to work here. He'd take his victories where he could get them, and Dane off his medley relay was a win. Striding across the office, he yanked his spare ironed shirt off the hanger on the door hook. "Thanks, Coach."

"You gonna tell me what Ellis did to piss you off? You're a backstroker. You guys are the calm ones, and you get along with everyone. What gives?"

"He exists."

Alex shrugged out of his wrinkled shirt, down to his threadbare tee, and before he could get the fresh shirt over it, Hartl's hand wrapped around his biceps, wrinkled fingers pale against Alex's sun-darkened skin. "There's more to it than that."

"That's between me and him."

Black eyes stared back at him, hard as onyx. That stare was what kept a group of rowdy, adrenaline-fueled jocks in line. "Ellis might not be on the medley relay, but he is on this team. Of which you are the captain. You're *both* representing this country. Whatever's between you and him, set it aside."

Alex respectfully lowered his eyes. "Yes, sir."

Satisfied, Coach released his arm and started down the hall toward the pool. Alex finished changing, grabbed the training schedules off his desk, and followed, infusing his spine with the confidence his twisted insides lacked.

Set it aside.

Like Dane had set him aside.

The anger and hurt still lingered. So did the attraction and jealousy.
Set it aside.
Easier said than done.

CHAPTER TWO

TRANSITIONING OUT OF the paper-thin Colorado Springs air into the chlorinated soup of the US Olympic Training Center's Natatorium was a learned skill. As a local kid who'd taken swim lessons at USOTC, then as an Olympic trainee and US Olympic Committee employee, Alex was accustomed to the abrupt shift in air density.

Dane, however, didn't have a lifetime of practice here, and much to Alex's satisfaction, he was struggling. Chest heaving, their resident celebrity sat on the upper-most bleacher, closest to the circulation fans, with his eyes shut and his red-gold head lolling against the cement wall.

Alex savored another victory.

"Welcome to Colorado Springs and the US Olympic Team," Coach said, amid claps and cheers from the gathered swimmers. He launched into his welcome spiel, and Alex tuned out, having heard it before.

So did the other repeat performers on his squad. Mo, a three-time Olympian, tapped away at his phone, occasionally looking up to give the impression of attention. More than could be said for Bas, who drew on a waterproof graphics tablet, probably another tattoo for his personal or professional collection. Ryan, their individual medley ringer and Alex's backup, watched over his shoulder.

Only the noobs were listening, including their youngest teammate, Jacob, the nineteen-year-old breaststroke champ. And Dane, who, breathing marginally better, eked open his eyes. Slits of blue-gray mist swept the pool and coaches, trailing down the line to where Alex was standing at the end next to the women's team captain. A passing glance, then Dane's icy gaze floated back to Coach.

Alex's gut burned. Resisting the urge to curl his hands into fists, he shoved them in his pockets and focused on Hartl. Coaching staff introduced, a round of applause and chants of "U-S-A" broke out, followed by hugs and handshakes, greeting teammates old and new. The coaches let the reunion go on a few minutes longer before the women's team adjourned and Hartl called the men to order again.

"All right, lineups." He rattled off where everyone placed at Trials, then announced the tentative heats for Olympic prelims and finals. When he reached the relay teams, Coach turned the floor over to Alex.

Stepping forward, Alex started with the four-by-one-hundred freestyle relay, his gaze lighting on each member as he called out their names: "Mo, Kevin, Mike, Dane."

"Four-by-two-hundred free," he continued. "Sean, Kevin, Mike, Dane." No objections were raised to swapping out Mo, a sprint specialist, for Sean, one of their distance swimmers.

"Medley relay will be me, Jacob, Bas, and Mo."

A smattering of confused whispers rippled through the group, but the man atop the bleachers didn't speak. Auburn-stubbled jaw locked tight, eyes glaring daggers, Dane dug his too-white teeth into his full lower lip, biting back what was sure to be a torrent of privileged anger.

And he let it rip, as soon as Hartl left the deck. "Why am I not swimming medley relay? I beat Mo in the hundred-meter free at Trials."

Mo extended an arm and middle finger toward his protégé.

Dane slapped the hand away, gaze unwavering. "Well, Alejandro? Answer the question."

Alex prickled at Dane's use of his full name, accent perfect and dripping with condescension. Quite a contrast from the last time he'd heard Dane use it. Whispered in the dark, his honeyed Southern drawl wrecked by lust. Alex shook off the flash of damning nostalgia. "Because you're swimming five other events."

"I swam as many as eight in college."

"Four years ago, *and* you got injured," Alex replied. "This is the Olympics. Our goal is medals, as many gold ones as we can bring home. We stand a better chance if you don't get reinjured and we allocate our resources accordingly."

"This isn't an economics problem."

"Well, actually—" Jacob started, before Dane snapped, "Shut it, Pup," and the rangy first-timer shrank where he sat on the front row, curling in on himself.

"That's enough." Alex drew himself up to his full six and

a half feet and reasserted control over the deteriorating situation. "The decision's made."

"Who died and made you captain?" Dane challenged.

Mo reached over and swatted the back of his head. "The rest of the team, jackass."

"I didn't get a vote."

"Yes, you did," Bas said, not looking up from his tablet. "You couldn't be bothered to reply."

"Among those who voted, it was unanimous," Alex said, drawing Dane's deadly glare off the back of Bas's head. "Does anyone want to change theirs now? Throw in with Dane instead?" No one raised a hand or gave the slightest indication of wavering support. "So that's that."

"Aye, aye, Captain," Jacob chimed in a pirate accent, breaking the suffocating tension. Everyone laughed, except Dane, who slouched back against the wall in ill-tempered defeat.

"All right, then." Alex crossed to the starting block where he'd left the folder of training schedules. He passed stacks down the rows.

"Paper, Cap?" Mo's pitiful eyes shifted between the printed schedule and his phone.

Alex was beginning to think he was surgically attached to the latter. Then again, his wife was eight months pregnant with twins.

"Electronic copies will be emailed later today."

Mo sighed dramatically and tossed his paper schedule in the air, right into Dane's face.

Alex grinned. "Take the rest of the day off, and get adjusted to the time zone and altitude. Tomorrow we get started. We've got a week before domestic training moves to San Antonio. Let's make the most of it."

"Yes, let's," Ryan called from behind him.

Turning, Alex wondered when and why the team jokester had snuck behind him, until a blast of water from a pool hose nailed him in the chest. Sputtering, he batted uselessly at the spray of water. His other teammates piled on, grabbed more hoses, and chaos erupted.

When the impromptu water fight finally ended, all of them were drenched and smiling, and the paper schedules were ruined. Alex didn't care, his insides warmed by the first flickers of team camaraderie. This was his favorite part of competing in the Olympics, why he sacrificed sleep, his body, and precious time with his family for hours in the pool. He glanced around at each of his teammates, counting himself lucky to swim with such gifted athletes.

But the most gifted of all, Alex noticed with a passing chill, was nowhere to be seen.

DANE THREW THE paper schedule down on the desk in his private room and bolted for the attached bathroom, crashing to his knees on the hard tile floor and clutching the sides of the toilet bowl. By now it was only dry heaves, his stomach long emptied of its meager contents. Between the press interviews before he had left Charlotte, a layover in New

York for a *GQ* photoshoot and ESPN interview, and the overwhelming anxiety at seeing Alex again, he'd subsisted on airplane peanuts alone the past twenty-four hours. Once he'd arrived in Colorado, the altitude had gone to war with his stomach, and he'd had to ask the driver to pull over twice on the way here, making him late. His insides were apparently still set to expel, whether or not there was anything left in him. Only his injured pride was more miserable. Alex had banned him from the medley relay, from the freestyle anchor spot he deserved.

Dane had told him at Trials that he wanted it. He should have known from Alex's response then that he wasn't going to get it.

And the heck of it was, as much as he deserved that spot, Dane couldn't deny he also deserved Alex's retribution.

Memories filtered unbidden through his mind.

Dancing in the dark with Alex, smiling, as he hummed Van Morrison in Alex's ear, changing that one crucial word.

Chapped lips pressing together.

Pruned fingers gliding over sharp angles and sinking into hidden places.

Lanky limbs entwined, hard bodies grinding together.

Short, ragged breaths and muffled cries of release.

Alex's stricken face when Dane's parents and cheerleader girlfriend had arrived in a stretch limo on the last day of developmental training to take him home.

Dane heaved again.

He didn't move from his spot on the cool floor, curled around the toilet, too tall to stretch out and too exhausted to crawl to the bed, until a knock sounded on his door some time later.

He lifted his head and shouted hoarsely, "It's unlocked."

The door opened and closed, plastic bags crinkled, and the savory smell of takeout ramen wafted into the room. Dane's stomach cramped but failed to force his body upright. Heavy footfalls approached, and his mentor's deep chuckle rumbled above him.

"I thought this might happen."

"I haven't felt this bad since—"

"Squaw Valley," Mo finished for him, and Dane groaned, recalling their disastrous spring break in the Sierra Nevadas.

"You spent all week just like this." Mo knelt beside him and wrapped his big hands around Dane's shoulders. "All right. Up, you big baby." He hefted him up to seated.

Dane breathed deep and rested back against the wall, careful not to hit his head on the towel rack. "I can't help that my body rejects higher altitudes."

"We're here for a week. Your body's gonna have to get over it. Put that big brain of yours to use and get the rest of you in line."

"You gonna tell your wife that when she's pushing out your evil spawn? Spawns? What's the plural of spawn?"

"Spawn, and hell no, I ain't gonna tell her that. I'm not suicidal."

Dane couldn't help but laugh. Morris Mayfair may have been a towering black man, but his pint-sized, high school civics teacher wife put the fear of God in everyone, especially her husband.

"There he is," Mo said with an answering smile. "Think you can stand?"

Dane accepted the offered hand and used Mo and the towel rack to lever himself up. Halfway to standing, the metal bar gave, tearing from the wall. "Shoot!" He scrabbled for purchase against the glossy-painted wall as Mo shouldered the rest of his weight.

"There you go . . ." Mo clicked his tongue against his teeth, playfully chiding. "Breaking the fancy suite."

"I didn't ask for it," Dane grumbled back. They hobbled out of the bathroom and into his "performance suite." He wondered if his parents or his publicist had paid for his lodging in the exclusive private room, versus the dorm-style doubles where most of the athletes bunked.

Mo dumped him on the end of the king-sized bed. "Don't look a gift horse in the mouth. You could be stuck with a horrible snorer."

"Who's the unfortunate victim?"

"The pup."

Poor Jacob. Dane felt doubly bad for snapping at him earlier. To be the new kid and be stuck with the Slumbering-Morris freight train. He'd kept a box of earplugs on him whenever traveling or rooming with his mentor. He made a mental note to check his bag for spares—a peace offering, if Jacob needed them. "I don't know how Vanessa does it."

"Her dad snores. Her mom breeds pugs. We have two of the runts," Mo said as he unpacked the bag of food. "Nessa's immune to it." He held out paper-wrapped chopsticks and a quart-sized container of ramen. "Think you can stomach this?"

Noodles, broth, protein. Everything Dane needed, even if his stomach protested. "Have to, if I'm getting in the pool tomorrow morning."

Mo grabbed his own quart, opened his chopsticks, and dug in, bypassing the desk chair for the desktop. "You slipped out of the meeting awfully fast."

Dane cut his eyes to the bathroom. "Did you miss the part where I was curled around the toilet? I could have sworn you were just there."

"Silly me, I thought it had more to do with Cap."

"Look, no disrespect—"

Mo waved his chopsticks in the air, cutting him off. "You're the better, faster freestyler. Everyone knows that."

"Then why?"

Shoving in a mouthful of noodles, Mo chewed and swallowed. "Alex earned his spot as captain. He earned the right to make that call."

"But—"

"You can't deny you'll be a disruption on his relay."

"It's been ten years."

Mo glanced up, his gaze sharp and assessing, something he'd picked up from Nessa. "He loved you, and you turned your back on him. Not because you didn't want him, but because someone told you to. You're still turning your back—on who you are, and by doing so, on him."

Dane stared into his container of soup, wishing he could somehow dive inside and avoid the world. "Can we not have this conversation? It's all I can do to stomach these noodles as it is." There was no room left in his stomach, all the space taken up by a boulder-sized knot.

"All I'm saying is, Alex's decision is understandable. Because of your history, and because he's right about the possibility of injury. I might be getting old, but I'm still the second-fastest freestyler in the world. That was my world record you broke at Trials, and I was right behind you. We can win the medley relay without you."

"It's not fair."

"Life's not fair. Alex knows that better than most. Time for you to learn."

Indignation seared through him. "You don't think I know that?"

Mo bowed his head and sighed, deep and weary. Dane knew that sound, all too well. Lecture coming his way in five, four, three . . . Mo hopped off the desk, capped his soup and stood in front of Dane, staring him down with his mentor-face on. "Get your shit together. Be prepared for Alex to ride you, harder than the rest of us, which you'll soon learn is pretty fucking hard."

Deflated, Dane set his half-eaten noodles aside and folded his hands in his lap, cracking his knuckles. "What if I can't?"

"Can't is not an option. You brought your computer?"

He nodded.

"Good. You get frustrated, you don't take it out on Cap. You hack something instead. Take your frustrations out on someone who deserves it. Do not go after Alex, or you won't be on the team at all. We may not need you on medley relay, but we do need you."

"Gee, thanks, old man," he said, rolling his eyes and earning another slap upside the head for it.

"What the fuck am I going to do with you?"

Dane rubbed the spot where he'd been hit. "Give me a concussion, apparently."

Mo pointed to the soup he'd left on the desk. "Eat that one too."

"Yes, Dad."

Mo moved to whack him again, but Dane dodged, the contents of his stomach sloshing in a way that made him double over and groan.

Mo settled for sympathetic hair ruffling. "You feel up to it, some of us are going out later tonight. I'll swing by and check on you then."

The door clicked shut behind him, and Dane stood slowly, waiting for his insides to settle before making another move. Steadier, he retrieved his computer bag from the closet, pulled out his laptop, and set it up on the desk, plugging it in and powering it on.

He waded through the layers of encryption he'd installed on his personal files; the folder he was looking for was the very reason he'd started hacking. He'd wanted to protect the one precious thing he'd returned home with from developmental camp. At sixteen, finding a way to hide, and keep, that lifeline to his real self had seemed like the only thing he could do to rebel. As he became more skilled, his rebellion evolved too. From behind his hacker tag of *LBKnight16*, he skimmed funds from his parents' accounts each month—just enough they wouldn't notice—and anonymously donated them to LGBTQ charities.

And he had his own personal ways of rebelling every day too, including this one.

He located the folder labeled *Knights*, after the mascot of the college in Laurinburg where their camp had been held, and double-clicked. Pictures filled his screen. In the foreground, his favorite, a selfie of him and Alex, a decade younger, embracing and gazing at each other with every bit of desire he still felt for his captain.

CHAPTER THREE

DAWN WAS JUST beginning to brighten the horizon when Alex's alarm went off the next morning. He slapped the clock radio quiet, plunging the morning back into silence, and stared unseeing out the window at the open plains east of Pueblo. After a night spent tossing and turning, he wished he could lock his bedroom door and call in sick. But that wasn't an option. He was the team captain, and today was their first practice.

Maybe it wouldn't be so bad. Yesterday could have gone worse. Dane aside, the team was already gelling. They had three and a half weeks until Madrid. Plenty of time to renew bonds with returning members and form new ones with the rooks. Plenty of time to get their starts sharp and their relay exchanges down.

As long as everyone got in line.

Coach was depending on him. And Alex was depending on Mo to wrangle Dane. But who was going to wrangle Alex, if his buried anger at Dane—or the even deeper buried desire—got the better of him? It was going to be a daily exercise in self-restraint not to wipe that thousand-dollar smile off Dane's face, one way or the other.

An exercise he wasn't physically or mentally prepared for, already stretched too thin. School was out for the summer, so substitute teaching was off his plate, but then so was another source of income. To make up for it, he was working overtime at USOC, banking every spare cent so his family could hire extra farm help while he was in Madrid. When he wasn't in the office, he was in the pool or gym training, or making the long drive back and forth from Pueblo. He'd been offered on-campus housing with the rest of the athletes, but Pueblo was closer to the family farm in Vineland. At least traffic was light at six in the morning and ten at night, just him in his beat-up Ford Ranger and the long-haul semis making the drive up and down I-25.

The silent morning didn't last but another minute, his sister double-tapping his bedroom door. "¡*Levántate, levántate!*"

"I'm up, I'm up." He threw off the sheets and stumbled out of bed.

Carla was the other reason he kept an apartment in Pueblo. Five years his junior, she took year-round classes at the community college, trying to finish up her accounting degree in record time. The apartment provided a place close to campus for her to study and crash. And hide. She was as bad, if not worse, than him about getting roped into chores and obligations at home, taking on more than she could handle. As it was, she went out to the farm after classes each day, stayed there on her days off, and drove their mom back and forth to chemo treatments.

Another swift knock as she coasted past again in the hallway. "Breakfast in ten." She cooked for him too and straightened the apartment each morning. He'd told her she didn't have to, but since he paid all the rent, she'd insisted.

By the time he showered and dressed, eggs, turkey bacon, sliced avocado, and wheat toast were laid out on the table. At home, they'd get shit for the healthy pickings, but Carla took his training diet seriously.

Thank God she still let him have his coffee, though. She sat an extra-large mug next to his plate and claimed the mismatched chair on the other side of the dumpster-find card table. "You look surlier than usual and like you didn't sleep. What's up?"

He shot her a narrow-eyed glare. "You're getting worse than Mom."

She shrugged, sipping from her mug, then nibbling a piece of toast. "You didn't show at the farm this weekend, and you haven't called since getting home from Trials. She's just going to hound me, wanting to know what's up with you. If I have answers, less hounding for both of us."

"Sorry I missed Sunday dinner. I was with Coach, putting together training schedules and heat seedings."

"*Está bien, hermano.*" She reached across the table and squeezed his forearm. Her skin was shades darker than his, more brown than tan. Either she'd been studying outside or she'd picked up some of his farm chores on top of hers. "So, dish," she said, but it was faint over the roaring guilt in his ears.

"How's Mom this week?" he deflected.

"Better." Carla folded her toast around slices of bacon and avocado. "It's an off week between treatments. She's weak but holding down solid food again."

"That's good," he replied, his next bite tasting like ash in his mouth.

Alex hoped like hell this round of post-operative chemo, following her second mastectomy, would be the last of it, but the same treatment plan had failed before, since the cancer had come back. Three years, two major surgeries, and countless rounds of chemo and radiation later, his vivacious mom was worn down and the rest of the family along with her.

His sister most of all. Her curly black hair hung dull and limp, smudges darkened her under-eyes, and she'd lost weight. An unhealthy lot. He needed to do more, he couldn't do more.

Fuck.

"I promise to get out there before I leave. I want to check the swather and baler, in case anyone has to use them before I get back."

"Rafe's better with the farm machinery, and you know it."

Because his younger brother had gone to the local vocational school, practically for free, and earned two associates degrees in farm management and automotive technology, all while continuing to work on the farm. Versus Alex, who'd gone away to USC for four years and come home with a trunk of swimming medals and a degree in education. Admirable, but not useful for the farm, nor very lucrative.

He didn't have the smile or charm to turn his medals into dollar bills like Dane, and his substitute teacher's salary was shit, but all he could manage with training. He supplemented it with USOC admin work, but all those extra hours meant less time for the farm.

Double-checking the equipment wasn't much, but it was the least he could do before disappearing for two months. "For my own peace of mind," he said, meaning it in more ways than one. God forbid anything happen to his mom, or any of his family, while he was gone; he'd never forgive himself if he hadn't said goodbye.

Carla shrugged one shoulder and rose, collecting their dishes and carrying them to the sink. Alex followed with their empty mugs, dropped them into the basin of soapy water, and grabbed the dish towel from where it hung over the fridge handle.

His sister let the silence carry for a single plate. "So, back to my original question. What's up with you?"

As persistent as their mom. He had to give her something. "Team shit," he said.

"It's been one day, and you know most of the guys. How is there *shit* already?"

He swiped the towel over the plate. "There was some . . ." he considered his words carefully, falling back on his habit of downplaying things, "debate about who should swim the medley relay. Odd man out wasn't happy."

"You're the captain. Did Coach agree on the lineup?"

"Yeah." He shoved his clothed fist into a washed mug.

"Then what's odd man out's problem?"

"He's used to getting what he wants. And he's the fastest."

A slow, knowing smile spread across her face. "Ah, the poster boy." She handed him the last plate, unplugged the sink, and dried her hands on the end of his towel. "Red hair, big smile?"

"That's the one." He avoided her gaze, hoping his cheeks weren't as red as they felt. "Dane Ellis."

"He's a looker." She bumped his hip with a snicker. "You gonna hit that?"

He nearly dropped the stack of plates he was putting away in the cabinet. While his family knew and accepted he was gay, they didn't know about his decade-ago summer fling with swimming's biggest star. He'd kept that piece of heaven that had devolved into hell to himself. "I'm not his type."

"His loss." In the living room, she levered the futon where she slept back into a couch. Another dumpster find. "If he's the fastest, why isn't he on your relay team?"

"He's swimming five other events. Mo's only swimming three others. Fresher arms and legs and more senior leadership."

"Makes sense to me." She folded her sheets and blankets and dumped them, along with her pillow, into the leather footstool that tripled as a coffee table and storage.

He needed to check again with the complex's main office to see if any two-bedroom units had opened up. He could work more hours at USOC, maybe pick up an extra teaching period or two in the fall, if it meant Carla got her own room.

He startled out of his thoughts when she laid a hand on his forearm. "You tell Big Red who's boss." She looked up at him with the same brown eyes they'd both inherited from their mom. "I'm gonna hit the shower. You set?"

"I'm good. Thanks, sis." He dropped a kiss on the crown of her head. "Plan on me for Sunday supper, and have Mom call me for an update."

"Because you'll answer, right?" Just a jest, the wink she threw over her shoulder indicating it was said in good humor.

Alex drowned in guilt all the same.

THE GUILT LINGERED through Alex's early morning swim in the deserted pool, eighty laps, alternating strokes. Through two hours of office work, making sure each swimmer's passport was valid. Through the phone call with his mom, her breath labored and energy fading after only ten minutes. By the time he trudged into the locker room and observed the three-ring circus underway, it was all he could do not to channel his sour mood into anger and aim it directly at the big top's ringleader.

Smile bright in his auburn scruff and chest bare but for a light smattering of hair, Dane, decked out in the latest performance jammers, stood at the end of the second row of lockers, holding court for a group of reporters. While some athletes came off model smarmy in these situations, Dane exuded boy-next-door charm, easily engaging the press in conversation about advancements in swim gear. Standing on one side of him was his publicist and on the other a swimwear rep, dropping well-timed remarks about his company's research in cooperation with SwimMAC, the prestigious club in Charlotte where Dane swam.

No one mentioned the money Dane made every minute he stood there.

Or every dollar Alex lost while staring.

But Dane wasn't his only problem.

Ryan, dressed in last year's jammers, was standing across the aisle with Mike, snapping their biceps, futilely trying to get the reporters' attention. And one row back from them, Jacob was straddling the bench, forearms pressed to the wood, head resting on his clenched hands. He looked sleep-deprived and nausea-tossed, with one half of his shaggy blond hair shorn off.

Maybe Alex should have taken that room on campus.

And maybe Dane distracting the reporters wasn't all bad.

But as Jacob turned a sickly shade of green, Alex realized Dane's distracting charm wouldn't hold much longer. They didn't need the press catching on to the fact their youngest teammate had been hazed and was hungover on the first day of practice.

Running both hands over his hair, smoothing down the unruly curls, Alex straightened his USA Swimming shirt and approached the peanut gallery, positioning himself to draw their attention away from Jacob.

"Good morning, everyone." His smile was nowhere near

as bright as Dane's, but he looked official, if nothing else. "I'm sorry to cut this short, but we've got a practice to get to."

Official attire didn't matter. But his skin tone did. Like vultures, the reporters descended, pouncing on the line of questioning they hadn't had time to get to at Trials. "Alejandro," one of them called, even though everyone used his nickname, Alex. Even the television title cards read *Alex Cantu*. Less opportunity for misspelling. "How does it feel to represent the Hispanic community at this year's Olympics?"

One of the other reporters chimed in. "In Madrid too? That must be special."

And another. "Will the team be looking to you to translate?"

Never mind that the pasty-white swimmer beside him spoke fluent Spanish. Never mind that he had more in common with Dane than anyone in Madrid. Never mind that his family had been in the States for three generations, descended from Mexican immigrants, many, many generations removed from the Spanish conquistadors.

Never mind all that.

He smiled and gave his canned response. "I'm not the only person of color on the team. We've got other Latina and African American swimmers, two Latino ball players, an Asian American gymnast, and many more. We're a diverse group, just like our country, and we're all proud to represent the US and its many faces, wherever we compete."

"You're representing the LGBTQ community as well," the first reporter tried to redirect.

"Yes, I am." He didn't make a big deal of his heritage or his sexual orientation—his prowess as a swimmer and USA team member were more important to him—but he didn't hide those other vital parts of himself either.

That was Dane's specialty.

And by the barely there flinch only a few people would know to look for, the reporter's question had hit Dane right where it hurt. But an expert at hiding and covering, he clapped Alex's shoulder and smiled big. "Anyone here would be honored to be captain, regardless of their heritage or sexuality, and we stand behind Alex."

"Why aren't you the captain?"

Dane's fingers dug into his shoulder. "Alex was elected by the team."

"Speaking of, who's swimming medley relay?" the same reporter from Trials asked.

Dane's hand dropped from his shoulder, as another tagged on, "Will you be bringing home the gold this time?"

"Gold is always our goal," Alex answered. "As I said last week, final lineups will be announced in San Antonio on Media Day."

"How many events are you swimming, Dane?"

"Five," Dane answered without hesitation, and Alex bit back a curse.

Brows furrowed and notebook pages flipped. Before the reporters could put it together, Alex ushered them toward the door. "Like I said, we've got a practice to get to. We look forward to seeing you all next week."

The team's PR rep met them in the hallway and led the

reporters the rest of the way out. Unfortunately for Alex, that meant he had to handle Dane's very irate swimwear rep. "He's only swimming five events?"

Alex spread his legs shoulder-width apart and crossed his arms. "Yes."

"He's the face of our brand. We need him out there as much as possible."

"We'll sort this out," Roger said.

"We expected him to swim six," the rep insisted.

"You're welcome to take it up with Coach Hartl," Alex said.

"Don't worry, I will." He stormed off, Roger on his heels, and Alex rounded on Dane, his earlier rage boiling over. "You just had to say something, didn't you?"

He shrugged, nonchalant and entitled as hell. "They asked; I answered."

Closing the distance between them, Alex put two hands to his chest and shoved, hard. "You backed me into a corner."

Dane shoved back. "You backed yourself there when you didn't put me on the relay."

Kevin approached, hand out toward Dane. "Let it go, man."

"He's the one who jumped all over me."

"Because you can't keep your damn mouth shut." Alex stepped into Dane's space again, ready to shove, but then a tattooed arm sliced around his chest and yanked him back.

"Cool it," Bas warned.

Not a moment too soon, as Coach's voice boomed off

the locker room walls. "What's going on in here? Why aren't you fools in the pool?"

Alex shook off Bas's hold and shouted over his shoulder. "On our way, Coach."

"That's right," Dane sneered, leaning forward. "Hide behind Hartl."

If Dane was going to give him such an easy target... Alex cocked an arm.

Bas grabbed his elbow, diverting the punch he'd intended for Dane's smug face.

"Freestylers in the water first," Alex said instead.

"Thank fuck," Jacob groaned from the bench where he was now laid flat out, clinging to the wooden plank like it was a life raft.

Alex shrugged out of Bas's hold, glaring at Dane. "Did you do this?"

Dane brushed past him, shoulders knocking hard. "Maybe you should be here watching out for your teammates more."

As Bas held him back, all Alex could think about, beyond blinding fury and crushing guilt, was that after ten years, the first time he'd touched Dane again was in anger.

So much for setting hostility and the past aside.

CHAPTER FOUR

DANE WAS SITTING by himself on the bottom bleacher, arms hanging like limp noodles between his legs, goggles and cap dangling from his pruned fingertips. He'd swum and trained with the best, SwimMAC was at the top of every professional club list, and he was the fastest in the world.

None of that had prepared him for the past three days.

Mo had warned him that Olympic training was hell. First, there was the altitude to contend with. While his stomach had finally stopped rejecting food, there was no help for the thinner air. He felt the reduced oxygen in his muscles, legs, and head. Everything hurt and burned, forced to work twice as hard with half as much. Taxing his body further, Coach rode them hard, three times a day. He blew his shiny whistle every time someone missed a start or switch, ordered extra laps if anyone dared make a whale turn, and if a swimmer's eyes drooped during tape review, he assigned the entire team more tape duty.

And then there was the biggest challenge of all—Alejandro Cantu.

Head bowed, Dane watched through his lashes as Alex's

arms cut through the air, a perfect arc of droplets following each trailing limb, splattering his broad chest breaking the water's surface. Coach and Ryan shuffled down the deck alongside him, the former timing the run with a stopwatch, the latter shouting and clapping. When Alex tapped the wall, Ryan slapped the starting block and reached out for a high five.

"You just broke your own record, Cap!"

Coach went to mark down the time in his books as hoots went up from the rest of the team gathered around the pool. Victorious, Alex yanked off his cap and goggles, smiling wide. The late-day sun streamed in through the overhead glass, reflecting off the water and warming his deep brown eyes.

Dane's body tightened, tension rippling out from his chest to his fingers and toes. He still wanted Alex as much as he had the first time he'd laid eyes on him. Only then, a decade ago, neither of them had had their names splashed across the headlines. They'd been tucked away at an obscure little college in an obscure little town, with no prying eyes except their fellow trainees', most of whom were too wrapped up in their own dramas to notice the quiet roommates who'd become fast friends. And inside their dorm room, more. It'd been the first time Dane acknowledged his attraction to men, the pull between him and Alex too strong to resist. He'd never been happier, before or since.

There'd been another critical difference that summer. Alex had been flipped the other direction, swimming freestyle. He only swam backstroke and relay now, but he used to compete in all four strokes, a gifted all-around swimmer. He'd honed his specialties in college, but here in practice, there were days he gave Bas and Jacob a run for their money swimming laps of fly or breaststroke. Never free, though, at least not when anyone was watching.

Or so he thought.

That morning Dane had arrived early, still on East Coast time. On deck before anyone else, standing unseen in the shadows, he'd timed Alex's freestyle laps. He was a solid third behind him and Mo. Together with his other times against Bas and Jacob, he could certainly qualify for the second individual medley spot behind Ryan. But he chose not to, sharing the wealth with his teammates instead.

Dane had no frame of reference for such selflessness. He'd only ever been taught the opposite, his parents and Roger shouting in his ear to hog as much of the spotlight as possible. Alex's easy relinquishment of attention and his effortless team spirit made Dane envy all the things he couldn't have, Alex most of all. Being around him here, he'd seen the swimmer and man Alex had become. Confident, reliable, a leader, a friend. Dane could have been in his sphere, in his life, and learned from that example the past ten years, if he'd only made a different choice. But there had been so many obstacles, his own fear the biggest, and it was torture, knowing everything he'd missed out on. And that torture bred anger and resentment, two ugly emotions Dane clung to desperately to keep from acting on the desire that wouldn't go away.

His emotional crutches propelled him to his feet. He

wasn't nearly as good a man as Alex, but he was still a better swimmer. "Bet I can beat you," he said.

Alex's eyes shot to his, and Ryan's head whipped around. "At backstroke?" Ryan said.

"At all the strokes." His gaze never left Alex's, which turned dagger-sharp.

Bas sat up from where he'd been splayed out across the adjacent starting block. "IM?"

"That's right." He glanced at Bas, then back to Alex. "You've been practicing with the other swimmers, and you've been swimming free in the mornings." Alex's eyes widened before narrowing, irate surprise at being caught and called out. Dane added fuel to the fire. "Two hundred meters; you're good for it."

Bas stood and inched closer. "Except for the fact he just swam three two hundreds, on top of two fours."

Two-handed, Alex pushed out of the water and onto the deck. "I'm good. Let's do this."

"Hey." Ryan slapped Dane's shoulder. "Is this just the two of you or can anyone play?"

They'd all finish behind their individual medley specialist, but that wasn't Dane's concern. He only needed to beat one person. He donned his cap and goggles and held his arms out wide. "Come one, come all. It's open IM day."

"What are you fools doing?" Coach hollered.

"Just a little friendly race," Ryan shouted back.

Coach waved them off and returned to his books.

Bas stepped to Alex's side, whispering something Dane couldn't hear. Alex nodded and Bas slapped his ass, sending a bolt of jealousy searing through Dane. After three days together, Dane knew there was nothing more than friendship between Alex and Bas, but the casual touches and easy bromance was something he could never get away with. His parents or sponsors would find out, they'd put two and two together, and he'd be finished.

"We gonna do this?" Alex said, claiming the Lane Five block.

Dane shook out his arms and took the block a lane over, Bas and Ryan on either side of them, and Sean and Mike in the outside lanes.

"Two lanes open," Dane said to Mo, who stood off to the side next to Jacob. "You want in, old man? Pup?"

Mo rolled his eyes, while Jacob, looking like a deer in the headlights, furiously shook his ridiculous, half-shaven head.

"Your call, then," Alex said to Jacob. "Grab my whistle."

In his starting stance, Dane glanced right, catching Alex's gaze through clear goggles. Fiery anger stared back at him. Better than the other kind of heat.

Dane refocused forward, the whistle blew, and he reacted on instinct, diving off and hitting the water clean. Arms in a V, legs dolphin kicking, he surfaced fifteen meters later, his head, chest, and arms lifting out of the water, mouth gulping in thin air as he swam fly. He didn't have to look right to know Bas led after the first lap. In his periphery, he spotted Alex ahead of him too, and his lead grew in the backstroke lap. But Dane pulled even in breaststroke, and by the splash of water on his other side, Ryan was right there with him. Ryan understood the pacing of this race best, whereas he and

Alex were running on rage-fueled adrenaline. On his last lap, Dane zoned out everything but the curl of his arms overhead, the alternating kick of his legs, and the gulp of air every fourth stroke. When his fingers hit the wall, he broke the water's surface, every muscle burning. Ryan was a half breath ahead, Alex and Bas a half breath behind, and the rest of the field was still hitting the wall.

Entertained applause filled the natatorium, but Dane only had eyes for Alex. He ripped off his cap and goggles and grinned smugly. "How's third place feel?"

"How's second feel?" he shot back, that beautiful tanned chest heaving.

"I wasn't racing Ryan."

Alex tossed his cap and goggles on deck. "Then I'm happy with the silver." His flashing eyes, however, told a different story. He'd only deferred to tick Dane off.

Dane rubbed the unspoken truth in. "Victory lap?" he said to Ryan.

They leisurely swam to the other end of the pool and back, cooling down. Alex was nowhere in sight when Mo gave him a hand out of the water. "I said get your shit together. Not stir more up."

"Needed to get it out of my system." The anger, the resentment, the jealousy, and most of all, the boiling desire.

Dane was merely simmering as they entered the locker room, his emotions dulled by the adrenaline of the win. "How about we continue the victory lap back at the dorm?" he said to Ryan. "I've got enough airplane bottles left for a decent celebration."

"Aww, yeah."

"Pup?" he offered Jacob.

"What the fuck do you think you're doing?"

Dane turned and tried his hardest to ignore the fact that Alex was dripping wet from a shower and dressed only in damp boxer briefs. "Celebrating."

"By getting drunk? Aren't you having enough trouble with the altitude?"

"You worry about you. I'll worry about me."

"And you just offered booze to Jacob, who's underage and barely recovered from the last round of hazing. So yes, I'm going to worry about my team, which you are also on."

Simmer heated to boiling again—anger, resentment, jealousy, and desire blazing—and Dane leaned into his captain's face, inciting him. "Bet you wish I wasn't."

Showing more restraint than he had the other day, Alex pressed his lips together and clenched his jaw, holding in whatever he wanted to say.

Dane bent to pick up his bag. "Ever the self-sacrificing diplomat."

A strong hand gripped his arm and hauled him back up. "You're right," Alex spat. "I wish you weren't on my team. You might be the fastest, but you're a privileged ass who thinks he owns this place when all you do is cause trouble. Between the press in our locker room, the sponsors telling us how to do our jobs, and you hazing other teammates, you are not worth it."

"What'd you say?"

"You. Are. Not. Worth. It." Alex punctuated each word

with a shove to his chest, harder than before, backing Dane into the corner of the lockers.

Dane seethed and a rare curse rolled off his tongue. "Fuck you, Cantu."

Alex wore a grin smug enough to match Dane's earlier one. "You wish."

Truer words had never been spoken. And Dane reacted to erase them.

With a fist to Alex's face.

Knuckles met jaw, and pain radiated up Dane's arm. He barreled out of the corner and landed another hook to Alex's chin before the other man fought back, swinging hard and giving as good as he got. They traded hits and jabs, moving their brawl into the main aisle as shouts echoed around them.

A violent minute later, Bas and Mo yanked them apart. Dane struggled in Mo's hold, and on the wet floor, with both of them barefoot, they tumbled backward, over the bench at the end of the nearest row.

A terrifying crack rent the din of noise, and once they hit the ground, Dane rolled off Mo and quickly assessed himself for injuries. Feeling no pain, he scrambled up and turned to check on Mo.

And almost lost his lunch.

His mentor lay on the floor, leg at an unholy angle, bone protruding through the skin.

Behind him, Alex gasped out a horrified "Fuck me."

He couldn't have been more right.

Eff them all indeed.

CHAPTER FIVE

THE CURRENT IN the endless pool stopped without warning, and Alex lurched forward, flexed palms slamming the wall. Torso lifting out of the water, he swiped at his eyes and pushed back his hair, not having bothered with a cap or goggles in his haste to forget the scene in the locker room.

It'd taken half a second to realize Mo's leg was not supposed to be at that angle, and the rest of that second to realize how badly he'd fucked up. Bas hadn't let him dwell. His best friend had pushed him forward, and with Dane's help, they'd staunched the bleeding around the protruding bone and arranged Morris more comfortably until the medics arrived. Coach had entered on their heels, disappointment etched in every wrinkle of his weathered face.

Alex had run from that look and from his teammates to the training pool, punishing himself with endless laps. He'd pushed through the body aches from the fight with Dane and tried to blank his mind with the repeated strokes, but it didn't work. He couldn't block out what he knew was his fault. *Dios mio*, is this what Bas had felt like four years ago, thinking he'd let down the team? Except Bas's relationship drama at the last Olympics had nothing on Alex's present mistake. They'd lost focus then, versus losing a teammate today. Four years from now, would Alex be blaming himself for lost medals too? He'd been the one who said their goal was medals, as many as they could bring home, and he'd just gone and cost them as many as four. Four events Mo could no longer swim. Because Alex had let his emotions get away from him, had failed to act like a captain. He'd cost the team their senior member and cost a friend and mentor his chance at more medals.

Squatting at the edge of the pool, Coach looked ready to lay into him too. "You want to tell me what happened?"

Alex levered up and landed like a beached seal on the deck, his jellied arms giving out. Years past embarrassment around Coach, he rolled over and dragged himself upright with his core. "You haven't heard it from the rest of the team already?"

"I want to hear it from you."

He prodded his torso and face, checking bruises. "I fucked up."

"Ryan said you were justified."

"Dane offered Ryan and Jacob drinks in his room. I told him to cut it out."

"That's what you're supposed to do. You're the captain." He shifted back on his haunches. "How'd it turn into a brawl?"

"I was tired of him prancing around like he owns the place and using his sponsorships to get what he wants. I told him as much."

"What else?"

"Why the fuck does there have to be something else? He acts like a privileged ass. I told him so." Alex didn't check his words or tone, the same anger that drove him to blows with Dane breaking through the cloud of guilt.

"This isn't like you, Cantu," Coach said, brow furrowed. "There's more behind that hair-trigger temper lately, and I think it goes back to our conversation earlier this week. I checked your schedule. You've picked up more than a few extra office shifts."

He tried to hold Coach's stare, to bluff as he'd done the other day, but Coach was onto him. What was the use now? The damage was done. Exhaustion catching up to him, fight bleeding out of him, Alex fell backward onto the deck, wincing as he scrubbed his hands over his tender face. "I'm gone this summer when they need me most at home. I have to bank the extra money so they can hire someone for the farm."

"I don't remember there being an issue last Olympics."

"Mom wasn't sick then, and Carla's only around part-time now because she's in school." He waved a hand in the soupy air above him. "And I'm not sleeping or eating much with all the Dane shit going on."

Coach stared down at him. "The Dane shit? You mean more than the press and sponsors?"

"Yeah, there's more, and it's not good. We were at the same developmental training camp as teens. Didn't end well there either." While Coach knew about his sexual orientation, it wasn't Alex's place to out Dane. But he felt it only fair that Coach understood there was a history of bad blood between him and Dane. And that Dane wasn't the only one at fault in the fight today. "I baited him in the locker room. It was my fault too."

"How are you going to make this work?"

Alex righted himself again, groaning as a wave of pain rolled from his head down. "Avoid each other as much as possible."

Coach shook his head. "Impossible with him on your relay team."

He whipped his head to the side, making the sledgehammer inside it worsen. His rising voice also didn't help. "What about Ryan? He beat both of us."

"Because he was rested and because IM is his event. He's *your* backup, not Mo's. You know as well as I do that Dane's our best freestyle anchor and our best shot at relay gold."

Hope circling the drain, Alex clutched desperately for any excuse. "But he's in five other events already."

"He can swim one more." Coach stood. "I'm overruling you, Cantu. I want gold for medley relay this time, not silver. Now, back to my original question, can you make this work?"

Alex pushed to his feet. "I guess I don't have a choice."

"Good. Mo's asking for you."

"He's in medical?"

"For about another hour." Coach clapped him on the back. "Don't make me sorry for nominating you as captain."

"I won't, sir." The last thing Alex wanted to do was let Coach down.

More than he already had.

ALEX RODE THE elevator up to USOTC's medical facility. While not a full treatment center, it had everything needed for emergency triage. An injured athlete could be treated, stabilized, then moved to the appropriate hospital or care facility to be seen by a specialist. The elevator doors slid open, and Alex stepped out. Halfway down the hallway, Dane sat in a row of blue plastic chairs, elbows to his knees, head hanging in his hands.

Alex knew the position well, having spent more than a few hours like that outside the chemo treatment room, waiting on his mom. He cleared his throat, making his presence known.

Dane dropped his hands and turned his discolored face to him, looking roughed up and utterly devastated. Alex's first instinct, despite his lingering pain and anger, was to run to him. To take Dane in his arms and chase away that ravaged look. As the oldest of four kids, Alex was a de facto third parent. Care and protection came naturally, and with Dane, his first love who would always hold a piece of his heart, those instincts were amplified, despite their rocky past.

He'd seen Dane like this once before—the night before summer training camp had ended. Alex had returned to their room and found Dane huddled on the end of his twin bed—shoulders slumped, chest heaving, face blotchy and wet with tears. Alex hadn't understood or cared why he was upset. He'd just gone to Dane, and they'd spent their last night together lost in kisses and tangled bodies. The next day, Dane had turned his back on him, and Alex had been too hurt and furious to put it together then. The truth had later sunk in, but the rejection still stung.

That remembered burn, and the lingering aches from their fight, throttled down Alex's instincts. He stuffed his hands in his pockets and approached slowly. "How is he?"

"Tibia's broken in two places. Muscle damage too, though they won't know the full extent of it until he's seen by a specialist."

"Shit." Alex collapsed into the chair next to him.

And Dane shot out of his, as if he couldn't stand to sit next to him. But then he began to pace the width of the hallway, cracking his knuckles, nervous habits of his that Alex had forgotten. "He still won't get his gold," Dane said. "All he's ever done is look out for me, and I just knocked him out of the Olympics and robbed him of the one thing he doesn't have yet."

"He has gold medals, Dane. A cabinet full of them."

Dane stopped in front of him, arms hanging at his sides in resignation. "But not a medley relay gold." Eyes more gray than blue under the fluorescent lights, they swirled like heavy storm clouds, blame and misery churning.

Weak, wanting to help, Alex looked away. "How do you do it?"

"Do what?"

"Go from being a total asshole—"

"I believe the term you used was 'privileged ass.'"

Alex startled at the curse, even if it was a quote from him. He'd been too riled up to be surprised earlier, but now that things were calmer, the rarity gave him pause. As far as Alex knew, Dane only cursed during sex, when he forgot to be a famous preacher's son and let himself feel and say anything. *Fuck me, please* and *fuck yeah* had been his favorite phrases that lost summer, growled in a sex-roughened drawl.

"You were saying?" Dane prompted, jerking Alex out of his memories.

Rewinding the conversation, he picked up where he'd left off. "How do you go from being a privileged ass who was ready to fight Mo for the relay spot, to this guy?"

Dane sat back down, angled toward him. "This guy?"

"One who cares so deeply about other people."

"Problem is," Dane said, holding his gaze, "I don't know how to put the people I care about first when they should be." It was clear in his stormy eyes and gravelly voice that he wasn't only talking about Morris.

"Then change that," Alex urged.

As awful as Mo's injury was, if it was the thing that woke Dane up, that shattered the self-centered shell his egomaniacal parents had built around him, then maybe some good would come out of it.

"I can't."

Or he could continue to live in his gilded cage, always too afraid to make a stand against those who'd locked him inside. Were the perks really worth it?

Disheartened, Alex tore his gaze away and stared at the

bland white wall across the hallway. "'I can't' is what privileged asses use as an excuse."

"Cantu, that you?" Mo called from inside the room.

"I'll be there in a sec," he shouted over his shoulder into the room, then turned back to Dane. "You're on the relay team."

"Thank you."

"Don't thank me. Thank Coach. I lobbied for Ryan."

Ignoring Dane's sharp inhale, Alex stood and entered Mo's room. And inhaled sharply himself. Mo's leg was wrapped in a full temporary cast, held aloft in a sling, and he was hooked up to at least half a dozen monitors and IVs. Painkillers, if Alex had to guess, judging by the glassy look in his eyes.

"Fuck, Mo, I don't know what to say. Sorry doesn't seem enough."

"Don't be so hard on yourself. Dane's the one that took me down. Heavy motherfucker." He waved a hand dismissively, and Alex thought it weird to see without a phone in it. The device was on the bedside table, and Mo hadn't even glanced at it.

"Yoo-hoo, Cantu, where'd you go?"

He was zoning out again; he needed sleep. He sat on the edge of the chair next to the bed. "You're injured because I baited him."

Mo's eyes cut to the door and back. "You baited him again just now."

"What can I say? He brings out the worst in me."

Mo's gaze sharpened. "And you bring out the best in

him." Not so drugged, nor so clueless to his and Dane's history, after all.

Alex relaxed back into the chair, arms hanging loosely over the armrests. "I don't know about that."

"Trust me, you do." Mo lowered his voice. "Don't let up. That boy's come-to-Jesus moment is long overdue."

Alex chuckled at the ironic choice of words.

"I've been waiting to use that line for years." Mo smiled, satisfied. "I've tried to get through to him, Alex, but I'm thinking it's got to be you."

"How are you even smiling right now?" His eyes made another sweep of the traction setup, and he winced in sympathetic pain. "You seem surprisingly okay with all this."

"Hospital tonight, then they fly me out to DC tomorrow for surgery. I'm going home, two months ahead of schedule."

Ah, home, and Mo had a lot of good to get back to. "Nessa's happy?"

He smiled wider. "Thrilled doesn't begin to cover it."

But was that enough? "Your shot at the gold, though? We fucked that up for you."

"You're young still—"

"Only four years younger than you."

Mo talked over him. "You'll realize soon enough that medals aren't everything." He held up a hand, forestalling Alex's objection. "Yes, you know better than most already, after the scares with your mom, but you still get tunnel vision sometimes. But do you know what I see down my tunnel? My twins, two baby girls coming into this world soon, and I'll get to be there for the birth this time."

Excitement lit his eyes, a stark contrast to the anxiety-stricken guilt Alex remembered from four years ago when Nessa had gone into labor as they marched in the opening ceremonies.

"You'll be teetering around the delivery room on crutches."

Mo swiped the phone off the bedside table, brandishing it. "Better than following along on this damn thing."

"I was beginning to think you were surgically attached to it."

"I'm attached to my wife." He laid the phone on his chest, atop his heart. Alex longed for a love like that someday. "I get to see her, tomorrow. And I get to help her take care of our new babies, even if I'm a little wobbly."

Smiling, Alex stood and placed a hand on his teammate's shoulder. "For what it's worth, I really am sorry, Mo. More than I can say."

Morris covered his hand. "I know you are, Cap. But not nearly as sorry as he is." He jutted his chin toward the door, toward where Dane was sitting in the hallway. "For everything."

CHAPTER SIX

DANE WAS A fool for thinking anything would be different after the night Mo went down. He was a bigger fool for not realizing things would get worse. While he'd revealed a little of himself, of his regret, to Alex, they hadn't called a truce. Alex's last words had been to call him a privileged ass, *again*, and when he'd left Mo's room, he hadn't spared Dane a glance or word.

In the days following, Alex hadn't let up in practice either, pressing himself and everyone harder. Dane could handle it, physically, but emotionally, he was worn thin. It'd be one thing if he had his team to commiserate with, to blow off steam with after a grueling day in the pool. Like joining the nightly runs the guys took around USOTC's campus or hanging out with them in the dorm lounge where they watched reruns of old TV shows. But the cold shoulders and death stares made it clear he wasn't welcome; they all blamed him for taking out Mo. No mentor, no friends, no team. Dane didn't have much in the way of a social circle back in Charlotte either, but at least people spoke to him at his home club. Not even Ryan was speaking to him here anymore.

Taking his mentor's advice, Dane channeled his frustration into hours of nightly hacking in his room alone, skimming a little more than usual and doing some freelance coding work he'd picked up online under an alias.

Maybe a change of scenery—one that wasn't Alex's home club and that wasn't the scene of the crime, so to speak—would help smooth things over. That had been Dane's hope, with domestic training moving to San Antonio for ten days before they headed overseas, first to Vienna for international training, then onto the Games in Madrid. But things got off on the wrong foot before they'd even left the San Antonio airport. While Media Day wasn't for another forty-eight hours, they were treated to an unscheduled trial run at arrivals. They weren't caught totally unaware—the earlier arriving women's team had called with a heads-up—but an ambush was an ambush, all the same.

Stepping out of baggage claim, Dane barely managed to suck in a gulp of hot, humid air before the press—local, national, and sports—converged. None too pleased with the scene outside the front doors, TSA ushered them into the oversized vehicles lot where their team bus was supposed to pick them up. And was late. There was no place to hide, no place to flee, and no shade in the wide-open space. Heat shimmered off the black asphalt as reporters relentlessly shouted questions.

"What are the team's chances for medals?"

"What're the final relay lineups?"

"How has training been so far?"

"What training adjustments will you make here and in

Vienna in preparation for Madrid?"

Almost all of their questions were prefaced with "Coach" or "Dane." For the questions addressed to the swimmers, Coach pushed Alex forward instead. After a handful of general ones, they drifted to Alex's heritage and sexuality, and then back to Dane. He smiled and tried to throw goodwill toward Alex and his teammates whenever the opportunity presented itself.

His efforts were ruined, though, when a gleaming black limo drove into the lot and his father climbed out of the back, fully suited despite the triple-digit heat. The local and sports media were slow to catch on, but two of the national reporters directed cameras and microphones his way. It wasn't every day they had access to the country's most popular evangelical minister.

"Reverend Ellis, saying any special prayers for the team?"

"Reverend Ellis, will you preach from a church here on Sunday?"

Only if the church had a dressing room, private studio, and all the trappings Reverend Patrick Ellis required "to put his best foot forward while spreading the Word of God," and to line his pockets. His father pushed a pair of designer sunglasses into his dyed brown hair, and the blue-gray eyes Dane had inherited squinted briefly against the sun. Once adjusted, he buttoned his suit coat and straightened his tie, like he was about to start a sermon. "Each one of these incredible coaches and gifted swimmers will be in my prayers tonight and every night until they win gold and return safe from Madrid. As for this weekend, I'm not here to broadcast.

I'm only here to support my son and his team."

Dane bit back a scoff. Five more minutes and his father would be in full sermon mode, making more of a scene and furthering his mythical stature. His father was never not sermonizing, in one form or another. Dane imagined he had come out of the womb preaching, even if his wails had been unintelligible then. So were most of his sermons now, in Dane's view, no matter how fancy the words.

"Son, Coach Hartl, we can give you a lift to the hotel," his father said.

Tension radiated off Alex beside him. It radiated inside Dane too. This was the last thing he needed, separated enough already from his teammates. His father's offer threw that separation into sharp, ugly relief. Now was when he needed to try to be a part of the team, not torn further from it.

"It's fine, Dad," Dane said.

"We appreciate the offer, Reverend Ellis," Coach added. "But we'll wait for the bus."

Not if his mother had anything to say about it. She rolled down her window and flashed her former beauty queen smile. It was a toss-up who was more widely televised, but there was no question Kimberly Ellis was more dangerous. "Dane, sweetie, get in the car."

She said it only loud enough for the team to hear, but if she had to repeat herself, it'd be loud enough to reach the reporters. Dane didn't relish the prospect of public emasculation.

"You better go," Bas said. "Before mommy dearest gets

angry." He stepped partway between Dane and Alex, whose hands were shoved in his pockets, dark eyes glittering.

"We'll see you at the hotel," Coach said diplomatically. There was a measure of understanding in his expression, but the rest of the team stood stone-faced behind him, dripping sweat.

Any shot at team acceptance gone, Dane acted to minimize collateral damage. He aimed his winning smile at the press, praying his charm was distraction enough from the obvious tension among the team.

"We appreciate you all coming out for us," he said. "We look forward to seeing you at Media Day. Until then—" he stood in the open limo door "—we'll practice hard so we can bring home the gold."

He ducked into the limo, and his mother slammed the door shut, the loud noise and dramatic shift in temperature causing him to shiver. The car pulled away—from his team, from Alex—and Dane twisted in his seat for one last glance out the tinted rear window. His shiver became a full-body quake, a chill to the bone, when his gaze landed on Alex. Hands fisted at his sides, beautiful face twisted in a menacing snarl, Alex was angrier than Dane had ever seen him, worse even than that day a decade ago when Dane had gotten a similar last look at the boy who'd given him the best summer of his life.

Sullen and anxious, he rotated back around and slumped in his seat, cracking his knuckles. "You're not doing me any favors."

"We saved you from standing out in the sun," his mother

said.

"I'm not going to melt."

"But you will burn, and how will that look on camera?"

She'd know, better than most. With the same freckled skin and red hair as him, she lived her camera-ready life under an umbrella, never exposed to the sun. No wonder she was so cold.

"Northside is outdoors," Dane said, referring to the national swim center where they'd be training. "There's no chance of that not happening."

"There's a welcome basket from Tropicana in your room. I featured them in a prime-time spot last week." She crossed one leg over the other and drummed manicured nails against her Chanel-skirted knee, this one a pale blue number. "Be sure to drop their name."

"Great, another reason for them to hate me."

Her whiskey-gold eyes widened. "What are you talking about? The sponsors and media love you."

"I meant my team." He leaned forward and glared across the narrow space. "Nothing breeds resentment like hopping into an air-conditioned limo while they wait outside for the bus in this fucking heat."

"Language," the Reverend scolded.

Dane talked over him. "Or getting my mentor injured."

"That worked out for everyone," his mother quipped brightly.

"How the hell do you figure that?" He didn't check his curses or the volume of his voice. "Mo's at home in DC, the rest of the team fucking hates me, and you are not helping matters."

"Enough!" his father barked. "What's done is done. We need to discuss how you'll conduct yourself here at training."

Dane fell back in his seat and threw open his arms. "Yes, by all means, lay out the ground rules for your grown-ass son."

"One, no more cursing. You're picking up those boys' bad habits." *Men*, but Dane didn't bother correcting him. "You were taught better manners, and it doesn't befit our image."

"Our image," he muttered, rolling his eyes. He was so tired of this farce of an "image." The cracks in his perfect poster boy persona were starting to show, which was exactly why his parents were here, giving him this lecture. They'd seen the cracks too.

His father lectured on. "Two, you're here to practice, to swim and to show up when and where the sponsors want you."

"And where you want me. Tell me something new." His gaze drifted out the window. Better to direct it there than to say or do something that would make his parents look closer. See that the cracks were fast becoming canyons.

"We needed to remind you of your priorities," his mother said.

"I'm twenty-six. I don't need a reminder."

"You gave up your spot on the relay team. We think you do."

His gaze cut to her. "It wasn't my call to make."

"You didn't fight hard enough for it."

"Well, I'm on the relay team now. I'm swimming six events. You and the sponsors got what you wanted. Happy?"

Her Mary Kay painted lips turned up in her closing-the-sale smile, and Dane wondered if she'd ever genuinely smiled in her life. Always a show, always fake. "Keep up the good work," she said. "And we will be."

Good work, yeah right. Felt like the devil's work to him.

COACH BLEW THE final whistle on day three of practice in San Antonio, and Alex couldn't get out of the pool fast enough. Even for someone who spent a good deal of time outdoors, his rapidly darkening skin was proof the sun burned hotter here. They'd coordinated practice schedules with the women's team to avoid peak hours, but it was still more exposure than most were used to, especially Dane, who despite smelling like he showered in Tropicana, was more than a little pink.

He looked good with color to his fair skin. Alex wasn't about to tell him that, though. After the debacle at the airport, Dane was at the top of his and everyone's shit list. It'd been another hour before their bus had arrived, and it'd cost them a half day of practice. Arriving late to breakfast the next morning after a call with his mom, Alex had found a single seat saved for him, and Dane on his way out with a tray of food. Banished elsewhere for that and every meal since.

As captain, Alex knew he should make an effort to bring Dane into the fold—his teammates were unfairly holding Dane solely responsible for losing Mo, when half that blame rested squarely on Alex's shoulders—but he was still fuming himself over the incident at the airport. Seeing Dane smile pretty for the cameras, then disappear into his parents' limo had resurrected all his old memories. And his old heartache. Dane had turned his back on him again, and this time on the rest of the team too.

Alex took his anger out on Dane in the pool, riding him harder than anyone else. Dane met every demand—swimming clean, following orders, and staying out of trouble. Because he was a team player or because his parents had come down on him to put on a good show? If the latter, which Alex suspected, he had little pity for him. That was the bed Dane had made. He could sleep in it with all his lies to keep him company.

"That's all for today," Coach said, interrupting Alex's thoughts. "Gather up for a sec."

Exchanging his cap and goggles for the towel in his on-deck cubby, Alex strode over to the bleachers. Toweling off as he climbed the stairs to the shadowed third row, he claimed the spot next to Bas and a row down from Ryan. Eyes on his phone, Dane headed for his usual solitary spot at the top, in the sun. Like with breakfast, he sat apart at every team meeting.

Only Jacob made the occasional approach. Cautiously, never too close, but close enough Dane wasn't completely an island unto himself. After the initial hazing, Alex had been impressed with the charmingly awkward kid. He kept his head down, worked hard, and improved daily, despite already being a national champion at nineteen. Their secret weapon who'd come out of nowhere at Trials and hadn't swum on the international stage yet. He was like a sponge, picking stuff up without being asked or told. He was also uncommonly good at reading his teammates and modifying his behavior to suit. A skill Alex had been taught in educational training and which Jacob either came by naturally or had already learned. Perhaps it was his age, his quirks and habits not yet set in, but that sort of hyper-observation and adaptation made Alex think there was more behind the pup's big green eyes.

"All right, everyone," Coach said, and Alex returned his attention to the front. "Media Day's tomorrow."

A collective groan went up from the peanut gallery.

"Open practice first. We give them a show like the one we put on today, that'll go good."

Alex hoped Coach was right. That the reporters would be too distracted by the times on the clock to notice the fissures, to notice the team's ostracized star.

"Be on your best behavior, and use your good sense in answering questions." Coach eyed Ryan. "You hear that, Nichols?"

The jokester lifted a hand, three fingers raised. "Best behavior, Scout's honor."

"My ass if you were ever a Boy Scout," Bas countered.

"I'll remember that when our plane crashes on a deserted island, and I'm the only one who can build a fire."

Alex chuckled. "Someone's marathon-watching *Lost* again."

"As long as there's a hatch that leads to a bunker of rum, I'm good." Bas lifted a hand, and Ryan gave him a high five, the slap ringing in Alex's ears.

While everyone laughed, Ryan leaned forward and jostled Bas's shoulder. "Rum and somewhere warm to stick your cock."

Bas swatted at Ryan's head like a fly.

"None of that tomorrow," Coach said, reasserting order. "For those of you who are new—" his black eyes bounced to each new team member, landing last on Jacob "—Media Day can be overwhelming. Stick close to a vet. After practice, we'll head back to the hotel to change for the press conference. Cantu, Stewart, Ellis, you're on the dais with me for the official Q and A portion. Full dress."

Ryan laughed as Bas groaned. "Definitely no rum for you."

Alex couldn't decide which was worse—donning his one thrift store suit in hundred-degree heat, or sitting on a panel with Dane, no doubt dressed in a four-figure getup, answering the usual inane questions and pretending everything was grand. Not that he hadn't expected it. Dane, with his sponsorships, his looks, and his world record, was the big draw. And truth be told, Alex would rather it be Dane than him facing the reporters, but it had to be both. Resentment bubbled, just beneath the surface.

Shushing Ryan as an excuse, Alex glanced up the bleachers, surprised to see Dane anxious, looking as if a spot on the dais was the last thing he wanted. Surely it hadn't come as a surprise to him either. Worried blue eyes clashed with his, but only for a second. Dane ducked his head, hiding the worry away, and resumed tapping at his phone.

Before Alex could further consider Dane's strange reaction, Coach sprung on them the welcome surprise that they'd have the Sunday after Media Day off. "Take a break and rest, see the sights, but stay out of trouble. Be back here bright and early Monday morning, ready to work."

Coach dismissed them to a round of applause, and Bas hauled Alex up and out into the aisle. They waited on deck for Ryan and Jacob, Bas pulling the youngster into a chokehold. "Don't worry, Pup." He knuckled the shaved side of his head. "I'll protect you from the big bad reporters." Said in jest, but a strategy Alex had worked out with Bas. They would shield Jacob as much as possible from the media, for their own advantage and for the pup's well-being.

"Start by fixing his hair," Alex ordered. "Tonight."

"Party pooper," Ryan said, then jutted his bottom lip out in a mock pout. He got over it fast, turning excitedly to Jacob. "You going to show us around town on Sunday?"

Jacob deftly slipped Bas's hold, heading off with Ryan to the locker room, reciting a litany of places to visit and things to see here in his hometown.

Bas started after them, then turned back when he realized Alex hadn't followed. "You coming?"

Alex's gaze drifted to Dane again. Head down, attention still focused on his phone, Dane hadn't budged, even though the sun was shining directly on him now, lighting his hair that was turning more amber-gold than copper each day. It had to be hot and uncomfortable. Yet . . .

He was waiting for everyone to leave.

"Cantu," Bas said.

"Go. I'll catch up."

Once Bas left, Alex cleared his throat, and Dane's head shot up. "You're getting as bad as Mo with that thing," Alex said, nodding at the phone in Dane's hand. "You that popular?"

Dane hesitated, obviously reticent to leave his perch. Alex leaned a hip against the cement stair post and crossed his arms, making it obvious he wasn't budging either. Caving, Dane rose with a sigh and descended the stairs. "No idea," he said. "I haven't checked my email since we got here."

"Games, then?"

Dane shrugged and sat the device facedown on the post. "Something like that."

"Your lap times are getting better."

"That's the point of training, isn't it?"

Impassive, Dane gave away nothing, and Alex's hackles rose, frustration challenging his nascent peacekeeper. He battled the warmonger back, reminding himself why he'd stayed behind. "Listen, I'm so—"

"Now you want to act like a captain?" Dane's eyes flashed, anger seeping through the cold shell. "When everyone else is gone?"

"You're never at meals or meetings."

Hurt crowded anger in his icy glare. "Because no one

wants me there."

Alex's chest clenched, like it had in the med facility when he'd wanted to go to Dane and comfort him. Dane was trying to pull off an air of indifference, but between the worry Alex had glimpsed earlier, and the hurt and anger on display now, something more was going on.

"Dane," he said, taking a step forward.

Dane lifted a hand, and Alex froze. "Say what you have to say, Alejandro."

"I'll speak to the team."

"No, you won't," he snapped. "I don't need you fighting my battles for me."

Alex stepped closer, meeting him snarl for snarl, hackles rising the rest of the way. "Tomorrow's Media Day. We have to at least appear to be on the same team."

"So that's what this is really about?"

"We're representing Team USA, together."

Dane scoffed and turned away again. "You just want to pull the strings too."

Alex grabbed him by the arm and forced him back around. "What the hell is that supposed to mean?"

"Don't worry about me tomorrow. I've been dealing with this my entire life."

"Oh, poor you," Alex spat and rolled his eyes, hard.

Dane wrenched his arm free and bellowed in his face. "You have no idea!"

"About how good you've had it?" Sure, the team and he had been hard on Dane this week, but life was harder on the rest of them. Anger, frustration, jealousy all unleashed, he stalked Dane back toward the stair post, arms flailing as he shouted. "The media wanting to talk to you. Sponsors making sure you get the spotlight. Riding off in Mommy and Daddy's air-conditioned limo while the rest of us sweat it out."

Dane grabbed his wrists, holding him back. "I didn't ask for that."

Gazes locked, chests heaving, Alex's voice came out a hoarse whisper. "You still got in that fucking car."

Both times.

Unsaid but said, thick in the space between them.

Space that grew narrower when Dane's grip became a caress, his eyes strayed to Alex's mouth, and his voice cracked on a strangled "Alejandro."

For an interminable second, Alex considered giving in to the tension—stepping over that thin line from hate to what they used to be, indulging in a kiss he missed more than any since—but then the fear, the *absolute certainty*, Dane would get back into that car a third time drove him out of his former lover's grasp.

"No," Alex said, rocking back on his heels. "You made your choice, and you keep making it."

"What about tomorrow?" Dane asked. "How are we supposed to act?"

"Keep on pretending. Nothing new for you."

CHAPTER SEVEN

KEEP ON PRETENDING.

No trouble there. Dane's life was one giant pretense, and the frightening accuracy of Alex's indictment continued to ring true over the next twenty-four hours.

After Alex had left him there on the pool deck, he'd grabbed his cap and goggles and dove back into the water, swimming hard laps and pretending their conversation had never happened. The words spoken and not.

Through the night, he'd pretended to sleep, but each time he'd closed his eyes, Alex's words, the nearness of his body, and the kiss Dane had dreamed about for years only a breath away, had kept him awake. Regretting. Wanting.

Despite his lack of sleep, he'd pretended to be on his game at the open practice, smiling wide, chatting with reporters and sponsors and standing close enough to his teammates not to raise any eyebrows. No schism to see here.

Yes, Dane was good at pretending, but after twenty-six years of it, he was so damn tired of it. And *fuck* his father's no-cursing rule too.

By the time he returned to his room to change for the

press conference, all Dane wanted to do was stop pretending for five minutes and collapse facedown on his bed. An impossibility, he quickly realized, when he crossed the threshold and found his father practicing a sermon, his mother on the phone by the balcony door, and her stylist fussing over a makeup counter's worth of crap spread out across the king-sized bed.

Dane let the door slam shut behind him. "How did you get in here?"

His father paused midscripture and tore his gaze from his own reflection in the mirrored closet doors. "Who do you think paid for this single room? It certainly wasn't the team."

"Did you pay for the one in Colorado Springs too?"

"One of your sponsors," his mother answered, hand cupping the speaker end of her phone. "Shower, dear, then Nicole will fix you right up."

Nicole, in her early twenties, gave him the same schoolgirl heart-eyes she always did whenever they were in the same room. She was pretty enough—blonde and blue-eyed, his "type," according to the rags. Another deliberate pretense on his part. He didn't have the heart to tell her she was as far from his type as possible, and even if she were his type, she didn't meet his mother's bank account or last name standards.

Dane escaped to the bathroom, standing under the shower's hot spray and letting his father's familiar rise and fall cadence, his practiced fire and brimstone, lull him to near standing sleep. So much for only being here to support Dane and the team. He was clearly rehearsing for a sermon tomorrow, on pride and team unity. Two things Dane sorely lacked at the moment.

He hid from the truth in his steam-filled bubble as long as he could, until his mother's every-five-minute countdown reached twenty. He toweled off and slathered on sunscreen, shooed his father out from in front of the closet long enough to retrieve boxers and an undershirt, then surrendered to the emasculation he'd avoided earlier in the week.

His mother finished her call and gestured for him to take a seat on the end of the bed. "We'll have to trim that awful beard," she said to Nicole. "He's too sunburned to shave it."

Nicole went to work, first restoring his dreadfully pale skin above his play-off beard in progress, while his mother grilled him from over her stylist's shoulder.

"Who else is on the panel?"

"Coach—"

"I meant swimmers."

He resisted the *Let me finish* on the tip of his tongue. "Alex and Bas."

"Not the kid?"

"Jacob?" Dane asked, and she nodded. "No," he replied. "They're keeping him under wraps, for now."

She hummed, satisfied. "Good, he'd steal too much of the spotlight, and between those other two, you'll look the most professional."

He jerked his chin out of Nicole's too-tender grasp and glared up at his mother. "*Those other two* are also world record holders."

"Yes, but they don't compete with you for the camera.

The one's a tattooed California hooligan and the other wears a perma-frown."

Because, as Dane was coming to understand, Alex carried the weight of the world on his broad shoulders.

"Shame too," his mother carried on, while Nicole trimmed his beard into revolting hipster fashion. "He's quite attractive. I could use him to connect with the Hispanic audience. Then again, he's gay, so that wouldn't do."

No, it wouldn't do for her Bible-thumping legion of home shoppers. His father strolled in from the hallway. "Didn't you go to developmental training with the Cantu boy?"

Nicole noticed his physical jolt, even if his parents missed it. She patted his cheek, probably assuming his father's booming voice, right behind them, had surprised Dane, but Nicole's gentle touch did nothing to calm his racing heartbeat. He'd never mentioned Alex to them. How did his parents know they'd been at camp together? In the next second, he answered his own question. *Of course they knew.* They'd probably paid someone for a roster of all the attendees. He didn't go anywhere without them knowing the who, what, when, where, and why of it all. If it didn't suit their purposes, they'd find something else that did. That summer, his father had been on a televised global ministry tour and his mother had gone with, to be by his side and to pitch international rights for her shows. They'd needed a summer-long babysitter for him, and developmental training camp had fit the bill.

With his parents an ocean away, Dane had thought himself safe to be with Alex, at least within the confines of their four cinder block walls. Outside of their room, they'd been discreet, never appearing to be more than friends and roommates. And once home, he'd taken steps to protect the only tangible proof they'd been more, storing his photos of them together on an encrypted drive he updated regularly. Despite all his diligent efforts, had his parents still found out about him and Alex somehow?

He hoped his voice didn't crack when he answered, "Yes, we were roommates."

"Use that," his father said. "Turn him around to God's path. Lead by example, son."

A wave of relief crashed through him, followed by an even bigger one of anger. He shoved his hands between his knees. Cracking his knuckles would be a dead giveaway. As would grabbing any of the makeup items beside him and hurling them in a fit of rage.

He forced his voice level, diplomatic. "I don't think Alex would be interested." He didn't specify whether about an impossible change in his sexuality or an equally impossible change in his anticamera stance. His father didn't care either way, no longer interested in the conversation and returning to his rehearsal.

His mother clicked her nails to refocus his attention on her. "Your answers are ready?"

The same answers he always gave. "Yes."

Nicole set aside her scissors and stood, stepping out of the way so his mother could inspect him, like a fucking show dog. Her nails bit into his skin as she rotated his chin, checking both sides of his face. Back to center, she leveled him with an imperious glare. "And don't deflect so much this time. I saw the footage from the airport presser we arranged."

Alex jerked out of her grasp. "You set that up?"

"Of course," she said, as if what they'd done hadn't caused a hassle for his team and days of hell for him. "We leaked the arrival times to the national media, and they leaked them to sports and local."

"You wanted them to see you there?"

"And you. Now, don't waste the opportunity today. Don't deflect, and don't be so deferential."

"Alex is the captain."

"Yes, but you're the star. Act like it."

ACT LIKE IT.

AKA, back to pretending.

Dane was so good at it he doubted his teammates, the press, or the average viewer at home had any idea how much he hated Media Day. Practiced smile and lines, all lies that made his stomach churn.

Never more so than today, sitting on the dais between Alex and Bas and pretending to represent the US men's swim team. He was a team member in name and job only, a pariah in every other way. Part of him resented Alex for allowing the team to cast him out, but he couldn't blame them or him. He'd given them every reason to believe he was the privileged ass Alex claimed. Or rather, his parents had, but Dane hadn't said no. Just like he hadn't said no the other time he'd turned his back on Alex.

Bas nudged his shoulder, and Dane snapped back to the present. Coach was finishing his introductory remarks, preparing to open the floor for questions.

Once he did, questions flew. The most at Dane, some to Coach and Alex, and a few for Bas too. Dane didn't want to give the impression of hogging the spotlight, but he also didn't want to raise any more red flags with his parents. He deferred when the question obviously called for Coach or Alex to weigh in and answered diplomatically when it didn't.

"Dane, how's the team gelling after losing its eldest member?"

"Alex can answer that one on behalf of the team," he replied.

Curls tamed and dressed in an attractive if well-worn suit, Alex leaned toward the mic. "Morris Mayfair was our senior statesman, that's true, and it was a tough loss, but we've got a lot of other repeat Olympians on the team. We miss Mo, but we're managing fine without him."

Managing.

Fine.

Dane smarted at the backhanded insult. That's the best Alex could say about him? They'd already shaved several hundredths off their relay time.

"Dane, why weren't you swimming in the medley relay to begin with?"

Alex's shoulders tensed, and had he not been tilted forward, Dane was sure he'd have seen those brown eyes piqued with aggravation. Dane's position, or not, in the relay lineup had never been confirmed, despite the scene in the locker room. Someone had leaked it. His parents, presumably, seeing as they were a virtual information sieve these days.

"That was my call," Coach answered. "I wanted Ellis in the best possible shape for the five other events we have him slated for."

"Dane, how are you adjusting to the extra event?"

I swam eight in college was on the tip of his tongue, but he withheld the remark. While indignation lingered over Alex's insult, Dane's anger over other matters, over the mistakes of his own making, outweighed his anger at Alex.

"Coach and Alex are working us hard," he replied. "We'll be ready for Madrid."

"Coach, why wasn't Dane captain? Not the best outing for Alex so far."

Beneath his jacket, Alex's shoulders jerked, tension radiating out and down his spine, his entire body noticeably tightening, and Dane shoved his hands between his knees for the second time that afternoon. The question was rude and patently untrue. Anything that had gone wrong to date was his fault, not Alex's. He shifted forward to address the slight, at the same time Coach pulled a mic closer.

Bas beat them both. "The captaincy was voted on by the team," he said, tossing loose dreads out of his face. "Alex was on the Olympic team four years ago, so he knows the drill. He also works for USOC and is the steadiest guy most of us know. If we didn't have Alex at the helm, things could have gone a lot worse after losing Mo. He's held us together."

It was an impressive front by Bas, even if it wasn't entirely true. But decked out as he was, in a tailored gray suit that accentuated his huge upper body and a blue paisley tie that brought out his striking blue eyes, the fly swimmer smiled wide and effortlessly charmed the crowd. Dane bet his mother was seething.

"Any response to the rumors you two are involved?"

Dane jolted, harder than he had in the hotel room, as fear lanced his chest and stopped his already racing heart. But then Bas laughed, and Dane realized the question was directed at his teammates. He prayed no one had noticed his reaction.

"Alex is my best friend," Bas said. "Has been since we roomed and swam together at SC, but he's not my type."

"Because he's gay?" one reporter asked.

"Because he's Hispanic?" said another.

The opposite of affronted, Bas laughed louder. "Now you're just being silly. I don't care about either of those things. I'm bi and live in California where almost half the population is Hispanic. Sexuality and heritage have nothing to do with it. I'd never date Alex because he's too damn bossy." Bas playfully shoved Alex's shoulder, and the crowd laughed with him. With them.

As Dane silently raged.

To be that easygoing, to be that carefree, to focus so little on what other people thought, to live and love as they pleased . . . The jealousy nearly strangled him.

"Alex, anyone special then?"

Rage and jealousy instantly banked, all of Dane's attention snapped to his captain. He shouldn't care about the answer—there was zero chance for him with Alex, regardless of yesterday's spark—but he still held his breath, waiting on the edge of his seat for Alex's answer.

"No one at the moment."

Dane exhaled slowly through his nose and clenched teeth, not letting the crowd see his immense relief.

"Any team issues with your sexuality?"

"No, it hasn't come up," Alex answered.

Dane was impressed at how much a nonissue it was with the squad. He hadn't heard or observed a single slur or askance look from team members or coaches. Then again, Alex and Bas had hit the swimming scene together in California, where one's sexual orientation wasn't as big a deal as in North Carolina. They'd never hidden their sexuality, and those who'd been on the team last go-round wouldn't think twice about it. Romantically together or not, Alex and Bas presented a united front that anyone would be crazy to challenge.

"It must be an honor, representing America's Hispanic and LGBTQ communities?"

Alex was more gracious with his answer than in the locker room last week. "It is." He smiled and threw an arm around Bas's shoulders. "We're going to make this country and all of our respective communities proud." As much as Dane knew Alex hated the cameras, his captain could turn it on when needed, and the heck of it was, Alex was still one hundred percent real. Same with Bas.

"Dane, how's it feel to be part of such a landmark diverse team?"

"It's great." A practiced line but not a lie. "It's important for kids, athletes, and adults to have role models who represent them, in all forms."

"Like yourself?" Not a complimentary tone, nor a reporter Dane recognized. "Living at home with your parents, a serial dater, a broken engagement. Your high school sweetheart, was it?"

Alex's spine went rigid again as he dropped his arm from around Bas's shoulders. Mouth dry as the desert, Dane racked his brain for the canned answer. There was often a gossip-mongering pap in the crowd, looking for dirt on him or his family for the tabloids. This wasn't the first time his abysmal love life had been brought up at a press conference. But it was the first time with Alex sitting by his side. The person Dane had hurt most with that particular lie. Fitting, then, that Alex's back was to Dane as he answered. And thank God since Dane didn't think he could deliver the lie if he had to look into Alex's eyes and do it.

He searched the crowd for the reporter who'd asked the question, gaze catching on his parents at the back of the room. Their faces were calm, not the least bit concerned. They expected him to be the good son, their puppet, and dispose of the problem. He found the reporter, met his eyes, and answered as practiced. "We were young and in love. She went to Harvard, I went to Carolina, and long distance didn't work out, not with our academic and athletic commitments. With so much of my time and energy devoted to swimming, I'm a terrible boyfriend. Nothing, no one, has ever stuck."

Except the man beside him, but he couldn't say that. Couldn't even look Alex's direction for fear of giving away the truth.

The pap opened his mouth to follow up, but another reporter jumped in and the conversation moved on, Coach and Alex answering team questions again. Dane, however, struggled in the mire of paralyzing fear, lingering anger, and mounting jealousy for a life he couldn't have.

Alex's words rattled around in his brain. *"'I can't' is what privileged asses use as an excuse."*

He was right. Dane *could* have the life he wanted. He just had to cut the strings. Say no to his parents and turn his back on the only life he'd ever known, save for one summer a decade ago when another path, another life, had presented itself.

A life with a boy he'd wanted so very badly then.

The man he still wanted so very badly now.

"This could be the last Olympics for all three of you. What comes next?"

"Swimming professionally and running my tattoo shop," Bas answered. "I've got a tablet full of sketches back in my room, if anyone's interested."

The crowd laughed, then quieted when Alex leaned toward the mic. "I'll swim as long as I can, then it'll be double duty for me as a coach and teacher."

"I'm trying to talk him into moving to California and

joining my club," Bas put in. "Get the gang back together more than just every four years."

They hammed it up for the excited crowd, then looked over their shoulders at Dane, waiting for his answer. Like his parents, their expressions were bored, expecting the same ole canned response. That he'd either join his father's ministry or his mother's company. He'd been hocking himself and swimwear for years; nothing new there. Looking out at the press, they wore the same bored expressions. Even his parents had tuned him out—no prideful gleam in his father's eye, no camera-ready smile on his mother's face, about an answer that should make them happy.

An answer they already knew.

But Dane didn't know it any longer. Not with two men beside him who had carved their own paths, who were living the life they wanted. Who were real. By contrast, Dane had only ever followed the path set out for him. He could choose to follow a different one, if he wanted it bad enough. If he wanted to be real, like them.

And he did.

"I don't know," he said quietly.

"I'm sorry," said the reporter who'd asked the question. "What was that?"

"I said, I don't know."

His parents pulled an immediate one-eighty, no longer bored. His father fumed, his mother glowered. And Alex . . . Dane didn't know what that look was on his handsome face—pity, pride, surprise, a mix of things it hurt to even consider.

Dane spoke directly into the mic. "I have no idea what I'm doing with my life. Some role model that makes me, huh?"

A wall of sound hit him, his name shouted from all directions, but the blood rushing in his ears, the pounding of his racing heart, drowned it out.

"I'm sorry. Excuse me." He stood and bolted toward the stage stairs.

One step down, Alex grabbed him by the arm. "Dane, wait."

He shrugged out of the grip. "I'm sorry," he said, not meeting his gaze, afraid of what he might see there. "I gotta get out of here." As fast of his trembling legs would carry him, he hustled the rest of the way offstage, out of the room, and toward the emergency exit at the end of the hallway.

His hand was on the door's push bar when his father's booming church voice rang out behind him. "Son! What in God's name was that?"

Dane rounded on him, fury lighting. "Careful, Dad. Don't want anyone to hear the country's minister taking the Lord's name in vain."

"What part of 'act like it' didn't you understand?" his mother admonished, catching up to his father's long strides.

"All of it," he snapped back.

"You have a script to follow. One that's been approved by us, Roger, and your sponsors."

"I'm tired of living my life according to your fucking script."

"Language!" his father bellowed, while his mother glared up at him like she was seven feet tall, far scarier than her five-two-with-heels let on. "You wouldn't have this life, including your sponsorships and trust fund, if not for our *script*, so you better think long and hard before you go off it again."

"Some life," he muttered.

"What was that?"

"I said, yes, ma'am." There was no use arguing when she was on a tear. He'd seen his father lose too many of those fights.

She stepped back, satisfied.

"Get back in there and clean up your mess," his father added.

"Yes, sir."

"Everything okay here?" Roger called from several feet behind them. Without a second's hesitation, Dane's parents turned their backs on him and rushed to assure his publicist. Not a care for their son who'd finally acknowledged the life they'd created for him was a lie, the last thing he wanted. He was just another tool in their empire, a puppet to perform according to their script.

Fuck the script.

They wanted to turn their backs on him? Well, he'd do the thing he should have done years ago. The thing they couldn't even imagine.

He waited for them to make their grand reentry into the event room, so sure he'd follow, then did the opposite of what they expected.

Shrugging out of his coat and tie, he tossed them on the ground and slammed out the exit door, emergency sirens wailing behind him.

CHAPTER EIGHT

ALEX HID IN the shadowed corner, out of sight, as Dane's parents stormed past and back into the press room. While Dane had bowed to their wishes, Alex's old friend fury was tempered, coming to understand Dane's choices were far from freely made. Given the threats the Ellises leveled against their twenty-six-year-old son, he could only imagine what they'd used to leverage a teenage Dane back into his camera-ready, conservative life. Back into the mold they'd created for him—*the script*, which it sounded like Dane had grown to hate. Had he wanted Dane to stand up to his parents a decade ago? Yes. Would Alex have done differently, if his family hadn't been so supportive? He couldn't say.

When Dane didn't trail past him in his parents' blustering wake, Alex poked his head around the corner and was greeted with a familiar sight—Dane's back, walking away from him. At the same time, the picture was wholly unfamiliar. Spine straight, strides long, Dane hit the exit door bar with startling force, a high-pitched alarm sounding his escape. Outside, his hair gleamed like fire for a few short seconds before being snuffed out, Dane ducking into a cab that peeled away.

Alex shot back around the corner, nearly running into Bas and Ryan who were hustling out of the press room.

"What just happened?" Bas said, as the exit door slammed closed.

"He left," Alex gasped in shock.

Dane had made a different choice, gotten into a different car.

"Where'd he go?" Ryan asked.

Alex blinked rapidly and gave his head a hard shake, confirming this was in fact reality. When the scene didn't evaporate like his nightmares always did, he turned his gaze to his teammates. Then over their shoulders, down the hallway, to Dane's parents making their way out of the press room and through the gathering crowd.

"I've gotta go," he said, words forming before his brain consciously made the decision.

Was there any other decision to make? Maybe this was the start of Dane standing up for himself, for the real Dane Ellis, the one Alex used to know and love. In which case, Alex wanted to be there to see and encourage that man's return. And if it was the start of a breakdown, one Alex had contributed to over the past week, ostracizing and taking his anger out on Dane? Well then, Alex needed to be there to clean up that mess too. He owed it to his team. They couldn't afford to lose another teammate because of his poor decisions.

He yanked off his coat and tie, tossing them on the floor with Dane's. "Can you hold them off?" he asked Bas, side-eying the approaching Ellis army. "Give me a ten-minute head start?"

Wallet in hand, Bas dug out a wad of cash and slapped it into Alex's palm. "Fare money. Go. I'll do what I can here. Call me."

"Thanks." He folded his fingers over the bills and ran full tilt for the door, Coach's booming "What the hell is going on?" clashing with Mrs. Ellis's "Where's my son?" behind him.

He dove into the first cab in line. "Did you see the tall redheaded guy who just left?"

"Yeah, left in a hurry," the driver said.

"Can you get that cab's driver on the horn and find out where they're headed?" He shoved the wad of cash at the driver. "Please, it's important."

"You ain't gonna attack him or anything, are you?"

"No," Alex said. "I'm going to thank him."

THE CAB STOPPED at the curb to the River Walk's main entrance, and Alex cursed under his breath. Either this was the one San Antonio tourist trap Dane knew off the top of his head, or he'd told the cabbie to take him somewhere crowded where he could get lost. Alex was betting on the latter.

Then again, Alex also bet it was easier for him to get lost in the crowd here than Dane. Wrinkled dress sleeves rolled up, tan forearms bared, and hair mussed from running his hands through it the entire cab ride here, Alex looked like any other local out for a weekend drink. Except for his height, which put him noticeably above most. He stopped into a tourist shop for sunglasses and a ball cap, regretfully a Spurs one, feeling like a traitor to his Nuggets the instant he put it on his head. But it did the trick. No one gave him a second look as he reentered the stream of people and let it usher him along the winding stone path by the river. As his eyes scanned for his wayward teammate, Alex thought back over the disastrous week, comparing this Olympics to the last.

Four years ago, he'd garnered attention for being a minority athlete on a predominately white team. This go-round, there was more diversity, but everything else was magnified. Whether it was the captaincy or the solar flares thrown off by Dane's celebrity, the crush of responsibility, the unrelenting media, and the poisonous team tension had overwhelmed him.

How much of that poison had he injected himself?

He groaned in acknowledgment. He'd fueled the tension from day one. He'd convinced Coach to keep Dane off his relay team, had lobbied hard against Dane when Mo had gone down, and once overruled, hadn't let up punishing Dane. He'd hounded him in practice and, by his chill toward him out of the pool, recruited others to his cause. Not to say Dane, with his stunts at Trials, then in Colorado, and folding to his parents at the airport here, had done himself any favors. But Alex was just as guilty of poisoning the waters drowning their team. If he'd pushed too far and sunk their chances for more medals, he'd never forgive himself.

He had to find Dane. He couldn't change the past, but he could try to control the present and maybe change the future. He was the captain. It was his responsibility.

Alex pulled out his phone, opened the list of team contacts, and scrolled down to Dane's number, typing out a text.

Let's talk. I want to call a truce.

Thumb hovering over Send, Alex hesitated, the vestiges of past betrayals lingering, but then the image of Dane storming out the exit door, turning his back on his parents today, rooted Alex firmly in the present. He pressed Send.

A ding sounded behind him.

Spinning the direction of the ringtone, he lifted his sunglasses and peered into the late-day shadows blanketing the stairs behind him. There, leaning against the stone wall, poorly disguised in an "I LOVE SAN ANTONIO" hoodie he must have bought on the fly, stood a tall familiar form with bright white teeth peeking out of glowing red scruff.

Dane was unmistakable.

As was the transaction he was about to partake in.

Fuck.

Cash in hand, Dane was about to exchange it for a baggie of joints. The teenage dealer looked like he hadn't showered in a week, eyes red-rimmed and glazed over.

Alex didn't think twice, just acted. He crossed ten feet in five and stepped between them, facing the dealer. "He doesn't want any."

"That's not what he said."

"Alex, don't," Dane whispered low behind him.

"He's changed his mind," Alex said, ignoring his teammate, focused on the dealer. "He doesn't want any," he repeated.

"*What are you, his bitch?*" the dealer sneered in Spanish, likely thinking Dane wouldn't understand. Stupid assumption, seeing as the kid was pastier white than Dane. Then again, he was also stoned out of his gourd.

Alex glanced around, making sure they weren't drawing unwanted attention, then stepped forward, looming over the boy. "*So what if I am?*" he growled, continuing the Spanish charade. "*Or maybe he's mine. Either way, I said he doesn't want any.*" He switched back to English. "Get the fuck out of here."

The kid erupted into stoned laughter. "Whatever, bitch. I'll smoke it myself." Pocketing the weed, he rolled his bloodshot eyes and stumbled back to the main drag.

Alex waited for the crowd to carry him off before rounding on Dane. His earlier intention to make peace once again took a back seat to rage. "What the fuck, Ellis? You know we have drug testing Monday."

"It's not doping."

"It's still against the rules, and Coach will bench your ass. I haven't spent the last week training and running us into the ground, getting you integrated in the relay lineup, only for you to go and blow it for a fucking high."

Dane slouched back against the stone wall. "You don't want me on your team anyway. I'm not worth it."

"Yeah, I said that last week when I was pissed at you for

compromising the team," he admitted. "And even though I came after you tonight to call a truce, I'm wondering now whether I should, because what you almost did, *that* would compromise the team worse."

"You what?"

"Check your texts." Hooking the sunglasses in his collar, Alex waited as Dane read his message.

Stormy eyes shot from the screen to his. "For real?"

"For real, when I sent that message two minutes ago, but smoking up, Dane..." Alex inhaled, recharging to rant, then reconsidered and checked his temper. That Dane had been willing to sacrifice his career for a time-out from reality meant he was farther off the rails than Alex feared. And haranguing him more wasn't going to help.

Sighing, Alex leaned a shoulder against the wall beside Dane's. "Look. I—*we*—fucked up. We let all the shit between us boil over, and we sidelined Mo. We can't keep going at each other like this, or it's going to cost too much. Teammates, medals, careers, reputations. And after what happened at the press conference today, and what I overheard—"

"What you overhead?"

"You standing up to your parents."

Teeth sinking into his lower lip, Dane hung his head, and Alex couldn't tell if he was hiding a smile or an impending breakdown.

Alex reached a hand out, clasping Dane's shoulder. "You've got enough battles without me leading another against you." Alex squeezed, then dropped his hand. "Not a good trait in a team captain."

Dane's conflicted eyes flickered up to him, then away again. "I started it, years ago."

"Yeah, you did." Alex fell the rest of the way back against the wall, matching Dane's slouched posture. He breathed deep and let the bottled-up hurt and indignation go on a giant exhale. "But we're grown-ups now. Fucking Olympians. And you're the best freestyler in the world. I was a fool for not putting you on medley relay to begin with, when you're our best shot at gold. This is about more than you and me and what happened when we were kids."

"Kids." The resignation belying Dane's single word tore at Alex's chest. "I'm sorry."

Alex lolled his head to the side, staring at Dane's beleaguered profile. "Were you really to blame?"

"I didn't stand up to them when I should have, so yes."

"Then thank you, for the apology and for standing up to them today."

"What you said yesterday about pretending . . ." Dane's gulp was audible. "I couldn't just sit there, *pretending*, at the press conference while you and Bas were so real."

"We're not perfect."

"No, but you're you, *real*. Sitting next to you, how could anyone not see right through me?"

"Because you're a damn good actor. You're just off the script now."

Dane chuckled, the sound kind of sad, also kind of relieved. "Shitty first act, almost destroying everything for a high." He glanced up, obviously chastened but seeming to climb out of his funk. "Thank you, for saving me just now. I know that was stupid."

"You had a bad day."

The swirling gray in Dane's eyes parted, making way for clear bright blue. "*We've* had a bad day."

Alex contemplated asking Dane more about the argument with his parents, but he didn't want the storm clouds to converge again. His gaze drifted past Dane to the colorful umbrellas on the other side of the river. A little color in their evening, in Dane's cheeks, would be a good thing. "Pot might not be allowed, but you know what is?" He brought his eyes back to Dane's. "A drink. We do have the day off tomorrow."

With minimal arm twisting, Dane followed him over the bridge to the restaurant. The outside tables were full, but two stools were open at the end of the bar. They were nearing the bottom of a tequila-laced pitcher, Dane relaxed and talking animatedly now from under his hoodie about their prospects and competition in Madrid, when Alex's phone vibrated on the bar top for the umpteenth time.

"Probably Coach," Dane said. "Wondering where we are."

Alex was loath to interrupt their reprieve, but Dane was right. They needed to check in. He flipped the phone over, a picture of Bas staring up at him. "Not Coach, but close."

"Go," Dane said. "I'll settle the tab."

Alex slid off his stool and out the glass entry doors, phone vibrating in his hand again. "Bas," he answered. "I'm sorry, I was—"

"Just tell me you're all right."

"I'm all right."

"And Dane?"

"He's okay too, better even."

"His parents are hella angry. They were ready to send out the National Guard, but Coach and Roger talked them down."

"He just needed some air. We both did."

"I hear that." Bas's words were nearly drowned out by a familiar buzzing in the background.

"Are you in a tattoo parlor?"

"I needed some air too."

Ink-stained air.

Fuck, if it wasn't one of his teammates, it was another. Escape seemed to be on everyone's agenda this evening, whether or not it was smart. And Alex had thought Bas past making ill-timed decisions, having learned his lesson at the last Olympics. "Do you think now's the best time for new ink?"

"I'm the one doing the inking."

Alex covered his face with his hand, as if the futile motion could block out the answer he already knew. "On who?"

"The pup."

Yep, reality-hand-block did not work. He groaned into his palm, cursing adulthood and being the responsible one. "Same question. Do you really think now's the time?"

"Jacob'll be fine," Bas said. "His head'll hurt worse from the liquor."

Alex dropped his arm, letting it flop at his side. "You do

know he's underage, right?"

"He's over eighteen."

"Not for the tattoo, Stewart. The booze."

"He showed me an ID that said he was twenty-one."

Because like many a student at schools with decent party scenes, the rising junior Longhorn had a fake ID. Alex rolled his eyes even though Bas wasn't there to see it. "I thought you couldn't swim with a new tattoo."

"I've got some watertight bandages. I'll touch it up, if needed."

Well, that was one problem solved, kind of. The other, though . . . "You're explaining the hangover to Coach."

"If he's even around tomorrow."

"Bas, after—"

"Not gonna fuck up this time, Cap."

Before Alex could reply, a commotion broke out behind him. Dane's hoodie had fallen back as he exited the restaurant and the fans were swarming.

"Shit!"

"What's wrong?" Bas asked.

"Big Red's drawing a crowd."

"If I were you, I'd grab a bit more air before coming back here. Wait until his parents and publicist are gone for the night."

"Roger that," Alex said. "Take care of the pup."

"Take care of you and Big Red." Alex could hear the smile in his best friend's voice and promptly hung up on him. Eyes on Dane, Alex watched as his teammate graciously signed autographs but declined to be in any selfies. He still had some wits about him. "Time to roll?" he asked once Dane fought his way free and over to him.

"Back to the hotel?" Dane sounded as thrilled with that prospect as Alex.

Alex shook his head. Bas's advice to stay away had sparked an idea that, once formed, couldn't be put out. More air would do them both good, would stoke that spark to life. "Do you really want to go back there?"

"No, but this hoodie is too damn hot." Dane yanked at the collar. "And this hair—" he waved at his bright mop "—is too damn red."

Alex grinned. "I can fix that."

CHAPTER NINE

FUCK THE SCRIPT.

At least Dane had accomplished that goal today.

Press conference, botched.

Parents, pitchfork angry.

Backbone, found, sort of.

First Olympics, almost jeopardized.

Only to be saved by the guy who'd made the past ten days a living hell.

The guy he still desired.

The guy whose sexy grin ensured Dane would follow him anywhere.

Including to the outside of a darkened Goodwill store. Dane guessed he was about to veer even further off the script. "It's closed," he said.

Alex slid his sunglasses back on and adjusted his cap, tucking under the ends of his dark curls. "That's what I was counting on."

"I don't get it."

"Make sure that hoodie's up good." He skulked down the side alley between buildings, and Dane, after zipping up the stifling hoodie and yanking it down over his forehead, shadowing his face, followed cautiously.

They cleared the back corner, and Alex pumped his fist. "Score!" He dashed over to the mound of bags by the rear exit door.

"What're you doing?"

"They're not supposed to, but people leave donation bags after hours." Kneeling, he rifled through a grocery bag brimming over with clothes, tossing items aside at Dane's feet. "This is how we got the best stuff as kids."

The remembered fondness in Alex's voice chilled Dane's blood. Had those five outfits he'd worn at camp been donation finds like this? The "best stuff" in Alex's wardrobe? Dane had realized quickly that summer—by Alex's single beat-up duffle, his lack of electronics, and the way he'd counted every penny—that Alex came from a different world than him. Dane had been too focused on living in the moment, too caught up in the attraction like no other, that he hadn't scratched beneath the surface. Hadn't wanted to because then it would have been real. And reality was the last thing he'd wanted that summer.

Things had just gotten very real.

Mo had been right. Life had been more unfair to Alex, and Dane had been the one whining. Like a privileged ass. Alex hadn't made his life a living hell—Dane had done that just fine on his own. And he'd made Alex's life hell too, if he were being honest. He hung his head, a more sincere apology than the one earlier on his lips.

Alex cut it off with a slap to his shin. "Don't just stand

there."

"Is this legal?"

"Probably not, but we always left behind what we could, be it our clothes or money. We didn't steal anything. We just wanted first dibs."

Dane hid his self-reproach behind a cough and knelt, digging out his wallet and withdrawing a fifty. "This cover it?"

"More than." Alex smiled wide, and Dane's fingers itched to touch its corners, to trace and part those full curved lips. That smile made his stomach flip now as much as it had when he'd spotted it across the pool the first day of camp.

That smile was his ruin and his salvation.

An elbow jostled him out of his daze. "Dig in," Alex said.

Dane patted the sides of a black trash bag—felt like clothes—and pulled it toward him, untying the orange plastic strings. "What am I looking for?"

"The last thing anyone would expect you to wear."

"To where?"

"A club."

Dane froze. "We're going dancing?"

Alex's eyes cut to his, mischief kicked up a notch, along with one corner of his mouth in a devastating smirk. "I know you can."

"Barely."

"Don't worry, I'll lead."

Countless nights they'd danced together in the dark, in the narrow space between their dorm room beds. Bodies close, lips brushing, hearts beating as one. "But we never went out?"

"You never told your parents 'no' before today either." Alex held his gaze, challenging him to take that next step. Would he risk being seen, risk the pointy end of his parents' pitchforks, for a chance to have Alex's body close again? A chance to maybe touch, to maybe taste those lips again . . .

Fuck yeah.

He ripped open the first bag to Alex's deep, throaty laughter. Another gift on this strange day. After pawing through a layer of baby clothes, he unearthed a pair of dark jeans and a navy button-down. "How's this?" he said, holding it up for Alex's inspection.

"*Ay dios*, you're hopeless." Alex swatted the clothes out of his hand and shoved a different bundle at him. "More like this."

Dane unfurled the fabric—a stretchy black top that might as well have been mesh for how see-through it was and jeans that looked like they'd had a run-in with an angry lawn mower. "I'm not wearing this."

"I know. I am."

Dane muffled a strangled gasp, imagining Alex in that top. Before his body ran away with his mind, a gray cowboy hat landed in his lap.

"You're wearing that for sure. It'll cover up the red."

Dane trailed his fingers along the wide felt brim. When in Rome, or rather Texas . . . He searched deeper in his bag, finding another button-down. This one chambray, with Western-style stitching and scuffed pearl snap buttons.

"Now you've got it," Alex said, grinning. "This'll go

with." He tossed him a white ribbed tank top and retied his bag. "Grab the dark jeans and we're set."

Bags repositioned, Dane slipped the fifty into the donation box while Alex tapped at his phone. "We gonna change at the club?" he asked.

"Nope, at the next stop."

Which turned out to be a Walgreens down the street. Dane spotted the Restrooms sign in the back-right corner and made it two steps that direction before Alex bumped his hip with a plastic shopping basket. "Supplies first."

In the hair aisle, Alex grabbed a bottle of styling gel, then one row over, a foundation compact and tube of eyeliner. Dane balked. "I'm not wearing makeup."

"One, you're already wearing makeup from the presser, because I know you're sunburned. Two, do you want a night out where no one bothers you?" Dane couldn't argue either, and Alex dropped the items into the basket. "That's what I thought." He disappeared around the row-end, then returned with a bottle of Febreze. "Here," he said, handing Dane the freshener and clothes. "Go to the bathroom, spray down the clothes, and get changed. I need to grab a few other things and pay."

Dane brandished the bottle of Febreze. "Don't you need to pay for this?"

"I'll tell the cashier. Go." Alex hustled away, and Dane, afraid of what "a few other things" might include, opted for ignorant bliss a while longer.

In the restroom, he tossed his cowboy hat on the purse hanger in the one toilet stall and hung the clothes over the metal stall sides, going to town on them with the spray, thinking the entire time that this night out plan was increasingly insane. The prospect of dancing with Alex again sent heat purling through his belly, but doubts and anxiety worked on his nerves and weakened his legs. How was he supposed to handle any of this?

"It's just a dance club." He yanked his outfit down, held each piece under the dryer a few seconds, and continued to coach himself as he changed. "Find a girl who isn't too drunk, dance a safe distance apart, keep your hat on and head down." He could do that... *If* he ignored Alex dancing.

Not likely.

The memories he'd brushed aside earlier came roaring back.

Music had coursed through Alex's then-rangy body, his long legs, narrow hips, and firm ass moving perfectly in time with whatever tune they'd played or whatever song Dane had hummed in his ear. Smooth and seductive, dancing as natural as swimming for Alex.

Not for Dane. White boy head-bob, that was about all he could manage on his own. Years of cotillion classes were wasted on him. He'd been awkward, offbeat, and murderous on his partner's toes. Until Alex moved behind him, pressed his front to Dane's back, and splayed his fingers across his hip bones. Leading. Something Dane had been expected to do when dancing with girls. With Alex, though, Dane hadn't had to worry about that. All he'd had to do was lean back and give his body over to the hard one behind him. Following. Something he'd been as eager to do horizontally.

His first taste of freedom.

His last.

It'd take an act of God, or a very firm grip on the nearest piece of furniture, to keep Dane from reaching for that freedom again tonight. From reaching for Alex. He'd already gone too far today. Maybe he should buy some rope and tie himself in place. "Because that wouldn't look weird or anything," he muttered.

"What wouldn't look weird?"

The door whooshed closed at the end of Alex's question, and the flip of the lock ramped up Dane's nerves. "Nothing," he said, fumbling the buttons of the shirt.

"How's it going in there?"

Dane opened the stall door, eyes downcast as he tried to straighten out his shirt. "There are a lot of snaps."

Alex inhaled sharply, and before Dane could wrap his head around that sound, around the blush streaking those high cheekbones, Alex had already moved on. To standing right in front of him. "You're supposed to leave the shirt open."

Dane lifted his hands, and Alex batted them away. He grabbed the uneven shirttails and ripped the buttons apart, the staccato snaps mirroring Dane's stuttering heartbeat. Alex's grip on the chambray lingered, as did his presence in Dane's space, and with each heaving breath, each whiff of cologne tinged with chlorine, a pore-deep scent no swimmer could shake, Dane's paper-thin resolve shredded.

He started to reach for what—*who*—he wanted, then

Alex stepped away, rotating and digging into the plastic shopping bag in the sink. He returned with a pair of scissors and a razor, shoving them into Dane's hand. "Cut off the sleeves, then shave. There's gel in the bag."

Dane rubbed his other hand over his jaw. Hipster cut notwithstanding, he kind of liked his scruff. His parents never tolerated it at home.

"Coach is gonna make you lose it before Madrid," Alex said, as if reading his thoughts. "And it's a fucking beacon."

No denying that. Between his beard or his smile, Dane couldn't say which would attract more attention in his current state.

"My outfit?" Alex said.

"In the stall."

"Thanks." Alex brushed past, shoulders grazing, and Dane fought back an excited shiver, stopping his curling fist just before the razor sliced his palm. Moving to the sink, he shrugged out of the shirt and took the scissors to the sleeves. "What did Bas say on the phone?"

"Just checking in. He suggested we stay out a while longer to let the dust settle." Alex's dress pants appeared over the door. "He couldn't talk long. He was too busy inking the pup."

"Jacob?" Dane tossed his newly sleeveless shirt over the hand dryer, dug the shaving gel out of the bag, then sat the bag on top of the shirt so he could run water in the sink. "Is that the best thing right now, with training and all?"

"The hangover will be a bigger problem."

He scrubbed down his face and lathered on the foaming

gel. "He got the pup drunk?"

"Jacob's a student athlete at UT with a fake ID. I'm sure it's not his first run-in with tequila." Alex's dress shirt flopped over the pants as Dane swiped one cheek clean.

"What's going on with those two?"

"What do you mean?"

"Mentor-mentee or something else?"

"I don't know which way the pup swings."

A final swipe of the other cheek. "But we both know Bas will fuck anything that moves."

The door swung open behind him. "Do we?"

Dane's gaze shot to Alex's reflection in the mirror, and he dropped the razor. He was sure it clattered against the sink, but he couldn't hear it for the blood whooshing in his ears. Blood that beelined south as his gaze made a similar journey down Alex's body. The mesh top showed off his broad chest better than Dane had imagined, and those ratty jeans fit just shy of decent. It wasn't like he hadn't seen Alex shirtless and in jammers daily, but that was Alex the swimmer.

Unreachable. A safe distance away.

This was Alex the man. Standing five feet behind him.

Looking like everything Dane had ever wanted.

His gaze swept back up and met Alex's in the mirror. He held the heated stare until it burned, then cast his eyes aside with a muttered "Fuck."

"Finish up so I can put on the final touches," Alex said, voice low.

Dane wiped down his face and the sink, as he wrangled

his body and hormones in line. Talk about something else, someone else. What had they been saying right before Alex stepped out of that stall looking like sin? Oh, right . . .

"Before, I didn't mean . . . Bas and I haven't—"

"I know. He'd have told me." Alex tossed the compact at him. "Doctor the pale bottom half of your face."

Dane glanced in the mirror over his shoulder. Sure enough, postshave, his jaw was a lighter shade than the rest of his pinked face. He dotted and patted, unhappily reminded of his mother, until Alex took his mind off it with more talk of Bas and Jacob.

"He'll tell me about the pup too. If something develops there. At best, it'll be a summer fling. Bas doesn't do commitment, not since the last Olympics."

But did Alex do commitment? Dane couldn't give him that, no matter how much he wanted to. He hadn't been lying at the press conference when he'd said he was terrible boyfriend material. His life was twenty-four-seven swimming and posing, with a freelance coding gig snuck in for his sanity's sake. He didn't have room for anything—anyone—else. And why the hell was he thinking about a future he couldn't have? He could have tonight, though. Where only he and Alex existed, dancing in a crowd, in disguise and unknown. He could take a night off and get lost, pretending he and Alex were sixteen again. As close to real as he could get. He could make pretending work for, not against, them.

Alex skirted around Dane, leaning closer to the mirror to doctor his eyes and run styling gel into his hair. Dane, careful not to touch, tossed the razor in the bag, gathered their clothes, and shoved them in there too. He grabbed his overshirt and shrugged back into it, leaving it unbuttoned this time.

"All right, your turn," Alex said.

Dane turned back around and lost his breath, again. The charcoal around Alex's wide, expressive eyes made the dark brown irises pop, all the warm earthy shades swirling together, utterly captivating. Dane couldn't have torn his gaze away if a gold medal depended on it.

Those eyes got closer, Alex in his space, as he ran gelled hands through Dane's hair, slicking it back. Only those captivating eyes kept Dane's from rolling back in pleasure. He clenched his jaw, fighting a moan, and when he spoke, it came out rough and gravelly. "I thought I had the hat for this."

"In case you lose it," Alex said, his own voice a timbre or two lower. "The gel makes it look darker, less noticeable."

"You're good at this disguise thing."

"More like good at the club thing." He stepped back, observing his work, and Dane inhaled through his clenched teeth, hoping it wasn't too audible. "When Bas and I were at SC, we went out a lot. I miss it."

"Didn't get a lot of practice with that in Chapel Hill."

Dane reared back at the threat of eyeliner, only stopping when Alex's thumb and index finger captured his chin. Alex flicked his finger against the sensitive spot beneath Dane's chin, an erogenous zone neither of them was likely to forget, and Dane froze. "Not fair."

Alex shrugged. "Close your eyes," he smirked, and Dane

caved. "You didn't stray far. Charlotte to Chapel Hill. It's what, two hours?"

"You met my parents, right?"

Pressure on his chin was all the answer Dane needed. "Look up," Alex clipped.

"They're both alumni, Dad's family for generations. There was no getting out of that one, being a double legacy and all."

"You didn't have to go back to Charlotte, to SwimMAC, afterward. Mo's at Nation's Capital. DC, LA, I'm sure any club would be happy to have you."

Alex's hand dropped from his face, and Dane felt the loss acutely. He reached for the trailing hand and wrapped his own around Alex's forearm, keeping him close. "Not everyone's as brave as you, Alejandro."

It would have been so easy to pull Alex forward, against his body, against his lips. But as unfair as life had been to Alex already, he deserved someone better than Dane. He deserved a future Dane couldn't give him. All he could give Alex were the next few weeks, his efforts in the pool and at being a real teammate, including blowing off a little steam tonight.

As teammates.

That was all.

CHAPTER TEN

TWENTY YARDS OUTSIDE the club's main entrance, Alex's forward momentum halted, reversed on a dime by Dane's death grip around his arm.

"This is a gay club," Dane exclaimed under his breath.

"Round of applause for the rocket scientist." The same-sex couples necking in line, and the two groups of bachelorette parties, if Alex read those pink boas and plastic tiaras right, were dead giveaways.

"I didn't think we were going to a gay club."

"You thought we were going to a regular club dressed like this?" He gestured at their attire and made-up faces.

Dane blanched ten shades paler and his icy eyes, haunting lined in black, grew huge. This was clearly more of a plunge than Dane had anticipated.

"I texted Jacob and got the name of this place," Alex said, trying to distract Dane. "He said it's the best club in town, gay or not."

Silence descended again, only the thumping beat of music from inside the club and Dane's quick, short breaths filling the void between them. After the press conference today, and the hungry look Dane had given him in the bathroom, Alex was determined to help Dane off that cliff. But as much as Alex wanted to push—to give Dane a taste of the life he could be, *should be*, living, so he'd accept who he really was—this had to be Dane's choice. Alex wasn't going to force him out of his cushy closet. Sure, he'd open the door, but Dane had to take the step out.

"We can find a different place," he offered.

Dane's answer was immediate. "No!"

That was enough of a step for Alex. Before Dane could retreat, or yack all over his shoes, Alex grabbed his hand and dragged him past the velvet rope toward the front of the line. "Give me your ID."

"Then they'll know who we are."

"Bruiser there—" he tilted his head at the over-muscled, chrome-domed bouncer "—is going to take one look at the dates and hand them back." A bluff Alex was counting on, since there hadn't been time for fake IDs. Given their height and build, they looked plenty old enough. He was also counting on their height and build for distraction.

Dane slapped his ID into Alex's palm, and, hand in hand, Alex skipped the line and marched them right to the bouncer.

"You're going to let us in," Alex said, holding the licenses out to him. Despite being loath to flaunt his body, Alex made sure to stand so his and Dane's front sides were in Chrome-Dome's view and their backsides, both encased in painted-on jeans, his own with strategic rips beneath each ass cheek, were in view of the security camera.

Bas had taught him this trick in college, when they *were* underage and trying to get into clubs with fake IDs. Guys like him and Bas, like Dane, were the sort other guys noticed, bought drinks for, hung around the club longer for. The kind of eye candy the bachelorette crowd liked to dance with, without fear of being groped. All generating money behind the bar and at the door.

As expected, the big bruiser spent more time checking them out than their IDs. Dane's hand tightened around his, probably thinking they'd been found out, rather than checked out. Chrome-Dome's head canted toward his ear with the Bluetooth headset, then a lecherous grin stretched across his gnarly face.

They were in.

He reached into his pocket, drew out a card, and, along with their IDs, handed it to Alex. Plain white, *BURKE SECURITY* printed in bold, black letters over a local phone number. "Call me sometime, if you want to ride a different cowboy."

Dane made a strangled sound, and Alex had to stifle his own laugh long enough to haul Dane inside. Around the corner, in the main entry hall, he doubled over, clutching his sides and wiping his eyes, laughing harder than he had in ages.

"Did he just say that?" Dane gasped, dumbstruck.

Alex unfolded and clapped Dane's shoulder. "Prepare for worse, Cowboy."

Dane's eyes rounded again, nearly sending Alex into another fit of hysterics, but then a gaggle of women staggered down the hallway, propelling them forward. Taking Dane's hand, he led them the rest of the way inside the club.

It was like most of the others Alex had visited in LA. Bar at one end, three deep with people trying to order drinks. Pub tables around the support poles for half the space, then open the rest of the way up to the raised platform at the other end where a DJ and dancers worked their magic. A handful of reserved booths lined one long wall, and on the opposite wall, shadowed nooks and crannies for those seeking privacy. The only major differences he could discern between this club and the ones in SoCal were more macro-brew signs and cowboy hats.

Making their way to the bar, their height caught the bartender's attention, and that of nearly everyone around them, clearing a narrow path through the crowd.

"Well, this is a treat," the bartender said, and for the first time that night, Alex worried they were caught. Dane had shot way past worried, if his death grip on Alex's hand was any indication.

Alex played it cool. "Yeah, how's that?"

"Two new faces and the both of you gorgeous," the bartender said with a wink. Dane's circulation-killing grip loosened, and blood rushed back into Alex's fingers, the tingling almost painful. "What'll it be?" the bartender asked. "First round's on me."

"And the second's on me," came a voice behind Alex.

Glancing over his shoulder, Alex favored the attractive blond standing behind him with a smile. "Mighty nice of you."

"Not as nice as that ass."

And thus began the line of suitors to approach them over the next half hour. Alex kept one hand in Dane's, anchoring him and making sure he didn't bolt, but their disguises held, as did every man's interest in them. After his second drink, Alex slid the third toward Dane, and with each sip of liquid courage, Dane's hand in his loosened a little more, the Dane Alex remembered from camp slowly surfacing.

Genuine smile full of innocence and gleaming teeth, not the fake for-the-cameras one that had become Dane's default.

Bright, alive eyes, not worn down by conflict, not deadened by Dane's fight against his parents and against himself.

Flushed freckled cheeks, not brought on by sunburn, exertion or anger, but by flirtatious attention.

This Dane was beautiful. *This* Dane was the one Alex had fallen in love with.

Now, if he would just take a couple more steps . . .

Alex slipped free his barely tangled fingers, and Dane didn't flinch. Smiling, Alex whispered in Dane's ear, "Come find me when you're ready."

Without a backward glance, Alex wound his way into the mass of writhing bodies on the dance floor. The crowd engulfed him, men dancing on either side of him. He closed his eyes and let the light buzz and music overtake him, let it wash away the tension that had dogged him for . . . he couldn't remember how long. As much as Dane had needed a night out, so had Alex. An escape from the captaincy, from the press, from the weighty responsibilities and nagging guilt.

Other than Dane, no one here knew him. No one cared that he was gay or Hispanic. No one would blame him for injuries, lost medals, or a dent in farm profits. He was just another body in the sea of dancers, a nameless guy out for the night, looking for a temporary break from reality. Dancing, he felt free, more like himself than he had in far too long.

Bodies swapped in and out around him, and Alex, in his own world, didn't distinguish one from another until the mix of sweat and cologne was pierced by a waft of chlorine and Tropicana. Long tapered fingers settled on his hips, and a cowboy hat landed on his head. An arrow of heat shot straight to his dick when warm breath and the brush of chapped lips tickled his ear.

Dane had usually been the one in front when they'd danced, but Alex could lead from this position just as well. He covered Dane's hands and pressed his body back, leaving Dane's no choice but to move with him. Dane caught on fast, dipping and swaying with him, each movement teasing them both.

Yeah, he could still lead, and Dane could still follow like a pro.

"Do you have any idea how hot you are?" Dane rumbled in his ear.

"Do you have any idea what it means in Texas to give your hat to someone?" Alex countered.

"Not until about ten minutes ago. Some guy at the bar wanted mine."

"You didn't take him up on it?"

"Told him it was already spoken for."

Heart ramming against his rib cage, Alex tipped his head forward to hide his face behind the hat's rim. *Fuck*, he wanted this to be real. Wanted Dane as much as he had when they were kids, and judging by the rock-hard cock nestled against his ass and the hot mouth doing wicked things to his neck, Dane still wanted him too. But just for tonight? Was that enough for Alex?

God knew, it'd been more than a single-season drought for him in the sex department. Between USOC and teaching, plus the farm, there'd been no time for dating. A random hookup, maybe, but that assumed he wouldn't rather pass out in the four spare hours a day he had to himself.

Now, in a rare moment when he did have a night off, here was Dane, all but offering to end that drought. It'd be simpler to take Blondie from the bar into the bathroom and jerk off together, but that's not what—not *who*—Alex really wanted. Who he wanted was dancing behind him, so very close, but for all the steps Dane had taken forward tonight, history predicted he'd walk them back. How much did Alex care? He should. If Dane sobered up tomorrow and regretted tonight, it could royally screw things up with the team, even more so than they had been. He'd chided Bas earlier, yet here he was, on the cusp of creating more drama, more distraction than Bas ever had. As captain, responsibility lay with Alex, and he'd already fucked up once, inciting Dane to a fight that had cost them their senior member. He couldn't afford another misstep.

But Christ, that hard, hot body writhing behind him . . .

He lifted his head, twisting it to ask Dane, "How drunk are you?"

Dane snaked an arm around his waist, yanking him back from the man dancing in front of them. "Sober enough to know you're the only one here I want."

Alex's heart abandoned its assault on his ribs and lodged itself in his throat.

As if he knew, Dane licked a path up the side of his neck, soothing, and also making Alex's head spin. "You're all I've ever wanted."

Fuck reality.

Alex reached a hand back and grabbed Dane's ass, holding him close, as if he could somehow push Dane's dick through two layers of denim. But that's not what Dane liked, and that thought alone had Alex's erection warring with his zipper. Lifting an arm, he tangled his fingers in Dane's gelled locks and held that hot mouth against the crook of his neck, the nips and kisses revving all the right motors. Their bodies continued to move together, more rocking than swaying, one of Dane's hands drifting lower to tease the crease where hip met leg, then dragging up the side of his dick straining behind his fly. Arm going limp, Alex lowered his hand out of Dane's hair and down his smooth cheek. Dane angled his face so he could catch two of Alex's trailing fingers in his mouth, sucking.

Alex burned alive, the sensory overload too much and not enough. He bucked back hard, chasing more, and buried his face in Dane's neck, groaning, tasting, wanting to crawl inside.

Dane released his fingers with a pop. "Fuck, Alejandro, please."

Now *that* was the way Alex liked to hear his name roll off Dane's tongue. Gravelly, wrecked, with a ragged curse and needy plea on either side. That voice, combined with the other signals Dane was sending . . . If they weren't in a room full of other people, Alex would have dropped to his knees right then and given them both what they so desperately wanted. Needed. But they weren't alone, and there was something else Alex wanted more. Needed more. He lifted his face, and hidden behind the brim of the cap, Dane gave it to him, bringing their mouths together after ten long years apart.

And it was even better than Alex remembered. Dane kissed like every meeting of their lips was the last, full of desperation and longing. He'd never been allowed to have this, to be who he was, and Alex just as desperately wanted him to understand it didn't have to be that way. Hand to his face, he gentled the kiss as he turned in Dane's arms. Chest to chest, Alex coaxed a needy moan out of Dane, the contented sound settling deep in Alex's soul, beginning to stitch together the tears left behind a decade ago. Alex slid his tongue between Dane's lips, and Dane met him with eager caresses, against his tongue and over his body. Chest, shoulders, back, ass, hauling him closer as their bodies rocked together.

While their kiss was all about savoring, about renewing a lost connection, even if only for tonight, their lower bodies were all about release, keeping time with the up-tempo music, moving with increasing speed and desire. All too aware this could only be for tonight. Alex's orgasm barreled toward him, and when Dane slipped a hand between them, cupping Alex through his jeans again, his desire nearly jumped the tracks. Alex tried to scoot back, to put a little separation between them, but Dane lowered his other hand, sneaking the tips of his fingers into the slit of Alex's jeans and teasing the curve of his ass. Alex moaned, and Dane's lips against his curved into a smile. Alex hauled him back in, trapping Dane's other hand between them as Dane rubbed him off in earnest now. There were dark corners and bathrooms for this, but those seemed miles away and the bodies were packed so tightly on the dance floor, Alex doubted they were the only ones engaging in such public displays of affection. Or rather, indecency. And Dane seemed just as intent on reliving their past teenage glories, sticky jeans and all.

They were fast approaching the point of no return, maybe past it already, but a last thread of responsibility wove through the haze of desire. Alex had to give Dane one more out. "You sure you won't regret this in the morning?"

Club glitter sparkled on Dane's face, bringing out the lively sparkle in the thin ring of blue around his dark pupils. "The only thing I'd regret is walking away from you. Again."

The thread snapped, restraint vanished, and Alex arched into Dane's hand. Alex offered Dane his finger again, and Dane curled a tongue around the tip, then sucked it down, as if it were Alex's cock. The move had its intended effect.

Alex's cock swelled, on the edge of bursting, and Alex wanted nothing more than to get Dane there with him. Fast. And he remembered just how to do it.

Withdrawing his finger, he pulled Dane into another kiss and snuck his damp finger under his shirttails, plunging beneath Dane's waistbands and down his crack. Dane hissed, his hand around Alex's cock squeezing. Both of them moved with renewed urgency, Dane's upstroke matching each teasing swipe Alex made around his rim. At the edge, panting more than kissing, when Dane had stroked him to within a second of release, Alex whispered against his lips, "Say it."

"Fuck me," Dane groaned, ravaged and tilting his ass back. "Please."

Alex pressed the tip of his finger past the tight rim, thrusting inside, and Dane jerked in his arms, ramming his cock so hard against Alex's that Alex came with him, hips pumping as they spent together.

Panting returned to breathing returned to languid kisses, and Dane smiled against his mouth once more. Alex knew if he pulled back, they'd both look somewhere between drugged and dopey, ridiculously in lo—

He cut off the thought, dragging his mouth along Dane's smooth jaw to his ear. "We're a mess."

"I want to get messier."

Bad idea. But post-orgasm, post-incredible make-out with his first love improbably returned, against all better judgment, Alex's brain played third chair to his dick and his heart. "Go hail us a cab out front. I'll settle the tab."

"Aye, aye, Captain." Dane captured his lips in another

kiss, halfway between searing and sloppy, then stumbled toward the exit.

Alex glanced around and found no one paying them the slightest bit of attention, thankfully. He readjusted the askew hat on his head and made his way to the bar, trying to prevent anyone brushing up against him and worsening the sticky, uncomfortable mess in his jeans. He paid the bartender, who slipped him a card like the bouncer's, and contemplated a stop by the bathroom to clean up, but worry crept in at what trouble Dane could get up to out front, especially without his hat as a disguise.

Hustling outside, Alex eyed the cab line, worry escalating to panic when he didn't see Dane's tall, broad frame or red hair anywhere near it.

"Hey, Cowboy!"

Alex turned toward the bouncer's voice. "Horse done gave out on you," Chrome-Dome said with a chuckle and jut of his chin over Alex's shoulder. Alex whipped around, gaze landing on the side-exit stairs where Dane was sitting with his arms curled around the metal railing, dozing off. "Looks like you rode him too hard."

Alex laughed out loud. A perfectly ridiculous ending to a wildly ridiculous night, in the best possible way. "Time to put him to bed, I guess."

The bouncer, Burke, helped him get a deadweight Dane to his feet and into a waiting cab. Alex tipped him with a smile and handshake, then slid in next to Dane, giving the driver the address for their hotel in Northside.

As soon as they were on their way, Dane scooted over

like a heat-seeking missile, snaking his arms around Alex. "I missed you."

Alex caught the driver's curious gaze in the rearview mirror. With Dane's gel-darkened hair drying out and getting brighter by the minute, it was possible the driver recognized them, or at least Dane. Reality came screaming back, stifling the already suspect air in the cab. Alex took off the cowboy hat, placed it back on Dane's head, and wrapped an arm around his shoulders, curling him in toward his body to block the driver's view.

"Giving me your hat," Dane mumbled. "You know what that means."

"It's your hat." Alex kissed the nape of his neck and inhaled deep, taking in the intoxicating mixture of sweat, sex, and swimmer while he still could.

Dane, in turn, dropped a kiss at the hollow of his throat. "I know," he said. "I gave my hat to the man I love."

Dane snuggled down, a snore rumbling out of him, before Alex could find his words, before he could decide whether that was the alcohol or Dane talking, and thankfully, before he could give his heart to the man he knew better than to love again.

CHAPTER ELEVEN

IT WAS LATE morning by the time Alex dragged himself out of bed and to the training facility. While they technically had the day off, his body demanded at least a couple of hours' work, be it in the pool or gym. He'd put on jammers under his track pants, favoring the pool over weights, not wanting to smell the alcohol he'd sweat out. And either option was better than sitting in his room, worrying over whether he'd done the right or wrong thing with Dane last night.

Calling a truce was unquestionably the right thing. The team couldn't handle another round of divisive drama, not when they needed to focus and come together. Whether that truce still held after he and Dane had come together in an entirely different sense was another question. But worry aside, it'd been a good thing for Alex, the relaxation and release sorely needed. He hadn't slept a morning away in he couldn't remember how long. But he'd have to wait to find out whether last night was a good or bad thing for Dane and the team, for better or worse.

Following the sounds of *SportsCenter* to the athletes' kitchen, he trudged inside and was met with a snapshot of *worse,* not related to him or Dane. At the counter, side by side, stood Jacob, bent half over, head pillowed on his folded arms, and Bas, dreadlocks loose, dressed in a tee and ink-stained jeans. Bas bobbled a hunk of ginger, saved it from hitting the floor like he would a hacky-sack, then added it to greens, blueberries, and bananas already in the blender. He topped the fruits and vegetables with a cup of almond milk, a container of yogurt, and a generous squirt of honey. The ingredients varied by availability, but Alex would recognize the "Bas Special" anywhere—an unholy concoction guaranteed to detox the most hungover of athletes. Like, say, Jacob.

Or Dane, who staggered in with his USA Swimming tee on inside out and his untied sweatpants sagging so low Alex glimpsed an auburn trail leading down below. Dane cleared his throat, and Alex forced his gaze up. Face scrubbed clean of yesterday's makeup and club-glitter, Dane's skin was red too, sunburn glowing, and his washed hair was drying in a million different directions. Taken altogether, he looked like a tired, grumpy rooster.

Thank fuck the facility was closed to visitors today.

Bas glanced over his shoulder, caught sight of Dane, and mumbled an "Aw, hell," no doubt seeing the same train wreck Alex did. He pulled more ingredients from the fridge and nudged Jacob, who slowly came to life, unfolding and retrieving another glass from the overhead cabinet. As Bas revved the blender, Dane scrunched his eyes closed, forehead wrinkling as if in pain. The whirring, grinding noise was enough to drown out the TV and revive Alex's own headache. He could only imagine the trolls chipping away inside Dane's head. Taking pity, Alex grasped him by the elbow and led him over to a table.

Splaying out in a chair, Dane laid a hand over his stomach and hung his head back, groaning.

"Feeling that good, huh?" Alex said.

Dane cracked open one eye and squinted up at him. "Ugh."

Chuckling, Alex lowered himself into the adjacent chair. "About what I figured." What he couldn't figure, though, was how Dane felt about *him* this morning. If Dane even remembered last night, which, by the looks of him, was a fifty-fifty shot.

Before Alex could ask, or chicken out, behind them on the television, the coverage cut to yesterday's press conference with Dane storming out, then to his father behind a pulpit this morning, preaching about forgiveness and self-acceptance through God.

"Fucking hypocrite," Dane groused, and Alex whipped his gaze back around. Dane carried on like he hadn't just cursed, or just read Alex's mind. "He was rehearsing in my room yesterday—preaching to himself in the mirror like he always does—about pride and team unity. Changed his tune pretty fast."

Perceptive despite his hangover, Jacob, bordering on sickly green from what must have been rapid movement, already had the remote in hand, changing the channel as he dropped into the seat across from them. A bandage peeked out from under the sleeve of his Shelby Cobra vanity tee.

Alex grabbed onto the change of topic like a life preserver. "Show us the ink, Pup."

"Nuh-uh," Jacob replied. "I spent an hour wrapping this." He held out his arm and pushed up his sleeve, showing off the waterproof bandage and wrap above his biceps.

"*I* spent ten minutes wrapping it." Bas joined them, passing out the glasses of green goop. "Unwind it," he said to Jacob. "I've got more watertights in the room."

Jacob, midswallow, inhaled sharply and choked. Rookie mistake. The key to a Bas Special was not to smell it, because again, unholy. Just guzzle. Alex gulped down two swallows while Jacob, still sputtering, unwound the wrap.

Uncovered, the tattoo on his outside left shoulder was oily from lotion and red, but that did nothing to detract from Bas's distinctive artwork—an abstract piece with intricate lines and curves, in the unmistakable shape of a Longhorn, the tip of its horns and its muzzle accented in burnt orange. It was the perfect design for the rising UT junior and Texas native.

Sullen mood forgotten, Dane leaned forward for a closer look, his expression adorably awestruck. "This is amazing."

Alex agreed, shooting Bas an approving nod.

"Think I could get one?" Dane asked, and Bas's blond brows raced north. Alex laughed into his glass. "What, I'm serious!" Dane insisted.

Bas reined in his surprise, grinning. "I usually design ones for my teams." He walked Dane and Jacob through the various team tats on his colorful upper body.

"I recognize that one." Dane pointed to the memorial tat

for the last Olympics.

"That's right," Bas said. "Mo's got it, on the back of his right shoulder. Did that one and his newborn's initials on the other. Guessing I'm going to have to add two more for him."

"And me?" Dane asked, hopeful.

Bas nodded. "We win, I'll ink you."

Dane held up his glass, and Bas clicked his against it, sealing the deal. Alex's heart soared much higher than it should. It was a small gesture, a promise he wasn't sure Dane would even keep, since it'd mar that perfect skin, but the fact he showed interest, the fact Bas was including him, meant maybe Dane had turned a corner with the team. Maybe last night was for the better, in more than just the sticky-jeans kind of way.

Of course, having Dane as part of the team meant he could join the gang-up on Alex as well. "Why don't you have any ink, from USC or the last Games?" he asked.

Alex floundered, surprised Dane had been paying that close attention to his body, and also not wanting to divulge his silly phobia.

Bas covered for him. "He's holding out for relay gold."

Smiling, Dane slouched back in his chair. "Get ready, then."

Alex shoved his shoulder. "Drink your shake, Ellis." He *was* holding out for relay gold, but he was also terrified of needles, which was why Carla was on chemo duty with their mom instead of him. He could only make it as far as the hallway outside the treatment room. Carla could sit inside and keep her company, offering more than Alex could.

Forcing back the influx of guilt and worry, Alex finished his shake while Bas, Jacob, and Dane talked animatedly over designs. As other teammates wandered in, there was a hilarious string of almost stumbles when the first few laid eyes on Dane at their table, but there were just as many tempered smiles and nods, Ryan's the biggest of all.

Alex didn't think it was only the fact that Dane was sitting at their table. He'd made a stand yesterday at the press conference, cutting at least a few of his parents' strings, and their teammates respected him for it. Perhaps for the first time respecting more than Dane's sheer talent. But how was Dane feeling about that press conference a day later? Did he regret making that stand? Did he regret what it had led to between them?

There was a hard slap on the door behind them, and Alex twisted in his chair. Coach's eyes narrowed. "Boy, y'all are a motley crew today."

Bas held up his shake without turning around. "On it, Coach."

Hartl's upper lip curled, and Alex laughed at his obvious disgust. "What part of day off didn't you fools understand?"

"Had to swim first, Coach," Ryan said, voicing the dilemma most of them faced. They were all addicted to the water.

"Then had to eat," Kevin added from a table over, where he stood assembling sandwiches with Sean and Mike. "What are you doing here?"

"It's hot as hell out there," Coach replied.

"Welcome to Texas," Jacob drawled to a room full of laughs.

"All right then, I'm gonna go watch film. Any takers?"

The scurry that followed was comical. Ryan didn't bother making an excuse, just bolted with what was left of Bas's shake mix, a "Bye, Coach" thrown over his shoulder.

Kevin picked his sandwich up in a napkin and darted out. "Braving the heat for the Alamo."

Sean shoved the rest of the sandwich stuff back in the fridge, grabbed Mike by the sleeve, and followed Kevin. "We're with him." Not likely, but any excuse to avoid film.

"What about you fools?" Coach said, glaring at Alex's table.

"We still have to hit the pool," Alex said.

Coach pointed at Jacob. "He's not getting in the water with a fresh tattoo."

"Bas will rewrap it," Jacob countered.

"Not risking infection. You're with me, Pup."

Jacob pushed out of his chair, the picture of abject misery. Bas rolled his eyes and rose beside him. "I got you into this mess. Can't let you suffer alone." Jacob brightened a little, though both men looked like they were facing execution as they followed Coach out.

When it was just him and Dane left, Alex asked, "You going to be okay in the pool?"

Dane tossed back the rest of his shake like a champ and slammed the glass down. "This shit's disgusting but works like a charm."

"Had something like it before?"

"Pretty sure Mo stole the recipe. Only thing I could keep down over spring break in Tahoe."

"Partied a little too hard?"

Dane shook his head. "Altitude sickness."

"So that wasn't your first bout of it in Colorado Springs?"

"'Fraid not."

Alex felt a twinge of guilt at how smug he'd been that first day of practice, seeing Dane struggle. Then another sort of guilt walloped him when his phone vibrated with an incoming call from Carla.

"Excuse me." He pushed back from the table and moved to the other side of the room, phone to his ear. "What's up, sis?"

"You got a couple minutes? It's been a rough few days for Mom."

He put a hand out, steadying himself on the counter. "Is she okay?"

A chair scraped back, and Dane was at his side the next instant, hand sliding over his hip. Alex nearly dropped the phone, only Carla's voice outweighing the shockingly casual, affectionate touch. "She's fine, just tired after the week of treatments. I think a quick chat with you would perk her right up. Get her eating again."

"Mom's not eating?"

"Her last treatment was Friday, *hermano*. You know it takes her a few days to recover. I'm hoping by tonight. Now, can I put her on?"

"Yeah, yeah, yeah," Alex rushed to say.

Dane squeezed his hip, and Alex glanced up, meeting concerned, alert eyes. "Everything okay?" Dane mouthed.

Alex swallowed the lump in his throat and nodded. Dane gave his hip another squeeze, then moved off, gathering their glasses and taking them to the sink, leaving Alex to his conversation but not leaving him alone. It was a surprising comfort, having someone near as he dealt with the most troubling part of his life, the fear that welled up anytime he had to face his mom's mortality. She sounded winded, tired at first, but midway through the conversation, her knitting needles started to click and her voice perked up, both good signs. After he finished telling her about the week ahead, and they said their goodbyes, Carla came back on the line.

"You did the right thing," Alex told her. "You call me anytime."

"How're things there?" she asked.

His gaze drifted again to Dane. "Getting better."

"You get Big Red in line?"

The start of an impossible smile. "Working on it."

"I'm sure he'll want to hit that before the Olympics are over."

For Dane's sake, he resisted replying, *Been there, hit that*, and moved on to setting up a time to talk in a couple days, finishing the call with another round of *goodbye*s and *love you*s.

He pocketed the phone, eyeing Dane, who placed the last glass in the drip rack and pulled out the sink stopper, letting the water drain. "Your mom's sick?"

Alex grabbed a dish towel and started drying. "Breast

cancer, second time in three years."

"That's why you haven't been at the meets lately?"

He nodded. "I did enough to remain active and competitive but otherwise stayed close to home. Spent more hours training at USOTC. I didn't want to go far, in case . . ."

"Crap, man, I'm sorry to hear that. I remember seeing her on TV during the last Games. She seemed cool. Real excited for you."

"Still is, just running low on energy these days, after everything."

Dane dried off his hands and leaned a hip against the counter, angling toward him. "That's why your sister called?"

"Mom just finished a chemo week, which tires her out. Can't eat, can't do much of anything but knit. I wish I could be there more."

"I'm sure they understand. They must be proud of you."

"They are. It's just hard being a man down at the farm. I feel guilty, being here, doing what I love. I've had more of a life these past couple weeks, hell, the past couple days . . ."

Dane cast his gaze aside, blush hitting his cheeks, as he ran a hand through his hair, making an even worse mess of the tangles. "Listen, about last night . . ."

Alex bobbled the glass in his hands, almost dropping it. He didn't want to hear this—the regret, the retraction, the rejection. He'd rather suffer in awkward silence and tuck last night away with the rest of his good Dane memories. "You don't—"

Dane's hand landed on his hip again, and Alex's eyes darted up, meeting Dane's sincere blue ones. "I'm sorry I passed out on you. It'd been a long day ending with a lot of shots." He smiled shyly, attractive as hell. "I don't even remember them all."

"What do you remember?" Alex ventured, setting the glass and dishrag aside.

"Us getting hit on," Dane said. "A lot. You wandering off to the dance floor. Please tell me I didn't pass out facedown on the bar."

Alex stared into those eyes, searching for any sign Dane was playing him. And saw none. Dane was genuinely worried, maybe a little embarrassed, and more than a tad apprehensive. And Alex didn't see regret either. In fact, Dane's thumb caressing his hip bone gave the exact opposite impression. His mind might not recall all of last's night details, but some part of his body did.

A different sort of sadness settled in Alex's gut. As much as he wanted to close the space between them and remind Dane of all they'd shared on the dance floor, a teammate could walk in at any second. And the last thing he wanted to do was spook Dane after things had gone so well with the team this morning. He had to let him off the hook, for now.

"Nah," Alex said, and Dane blew out a giant breath. Alex couldn't resist needling him a little, though. "You passed out on the steps outside, clutching the stair rail."

Dane covered his face with a hand, groaning behind it.

"Our bouncer friend was rather amused," Alex added.

Dane groaned louder, mortified eyes peeking through his fingers.

Alex laughed, jostling Dane's shoulder. "Come on. Let's

get in the water. It'll drown out how stupid you feel right now." He stepped past Dane, only for the other man's hand to clasp his arm and turn him back around.

"Thank you," Dane said, eyes and voice soft. "I would never have done that last night on my own, and I needed it. More than I knew."

It was getting harder and harder not to close that distance between them, not to jog Dane's memory with words or actions. Alex bit his tongue and nodded.

"And thanks for being the bigger man and calling a truce." Dane dropped his hold and swept his arm around the area. "Here, this morning with the team, that was a nice change."

Alex could tell Dane his actions at the press conference had done more for him than Alex, but that's not what Dane needed to hear right now. Dane needed that pride and team unity his father had planned to preach about. Dane needed to do what Dane did best. *Swim.* As captain, Alex could give him that, with the whole team standing to benefit now. "Well then, get in the pool," he said, a playful challenge belying his smile. "And earn it."

CHAPTER TWELVE

EARNING IT, DANE knew, wasn't only about swimming hard. He also threw himself into being a teammate. Alex opened the door with his truce Saturday night. His teammates opened it wider Sunday morning. And Dane stepped through it, coming out on the completely foreign—and welcome—other side.

They spent the day off having fun, a word Dane had to be reminded the meaning of. Lazy laps in the pool, a whale-turn competition judged by Jacob, once he and Bas escaped from film hell, then marathon-watching *The X-Files* in the hotel lounge with the rest of his teammates. The fact that his hidden geek could guess any episode by name and number from only a few seconds viewing probably earned him more cred than anything he'd ever done in the pool.

And when practice resumed the next day, and Jacob faltered, the first time Dane had seen the remarkably mature kid off his game, he shouldered mentor duties with Alex and Bas, offering encouragement and staying within Jacob's orbit at all times. Every swimmer had off days, but the rook was putting so much pressure on himself to keep up with the vets that one missed mark turned into two, and compounded until he was spiraling, cursing the weekend off and suggesting his backup should swim the relay instead of him. More like he probably needed another day off, the grueling training catching up to him. If Dane had thought training was tough, he couldn't imagine what Jacob was going through. Texas was a top collegiate team—sure, Jacob trained hard there—but this was another ten or so levels more intense.

Dane listened, observed, and told Jacob a few of his own worst-day stories, which usually ended with Mo whacking him upside the head. Dane didn't follow his mentor's lead there, but he did let the pup know he wasn't alone in his struggles. Dane hadn't been oblivious to Jacob in his periphery last week when no one else would approach him. Knowing he hadn't been totally alone had kept Dane treading water. The least he could do was act as the pup's nearby life raft now. Which he thankfully only needed for a day. Passing out early that night, Jacob was back to his usual self the next day, pirate quips and all, the wonky day before a blip on the radar.

After that, everything, and everyone, in and out of the pool, clicked. Dane was grateful, and more than that, relieved, to be a part of the solution and not the problem. Press, visitors, and sponsors excluded from practices, he could focus on pleasing his coach, captain, and teammates, taking and, when asked, giving advice, contributing to the overall increased productivity. Coaching Ryan on the freestyle leg of his IM runs. Coordinating the free relays so

Alex had one less thing on his plate. Shuffling along the pool deck timing his captain's backstroke laps, the sight and speed too captivating to miss. And at the end of each day, he declined his parents' and sponsors' dinner invitations, not wanting to hear the lectures about Saturday and preferring to finish his day with his team instead. They ate, discussed the next days' practices, then downshifted in the lounge watching more TV, Dane with his computer on his lap, coding or hacking. He'd even helped Kevin, a crypto master's student at Michigan, with a summer coding project.

Dane did everything he could to earn his spot on the relay team, the acceptance of his teammates, and the attention of his captain. His and everyone's efforts paid off. They became a team, Dane included. More so than he'd ever felt at SwimMAC, or even at Carolina under Mo's wing. He'd always been separate and apart somehow. This was a different, better experience. Knowing that this experience was what Alex loved most about the Olympics, seeing the light in his eyes and upturned corners of his mouth, made earning it even more worthwhile. Dane wasn't just giving the team his all; he was giving his all to Alex. Having failed to do so in the past, he was making up for it now.

Alex's regard, his appreciation, were a handsome reward. Warm brown eyes staring across the pool or hotel lounge at him. Hips and shoulders brushing whenever they stood close in the kitchen or sat side by side on the bleachers. Lingering handholds when one pulled the other out of the water. Longing gazes aside, he could explain away the others as teammates and two six-and-a-half footers in tight spaces, but for Dane, the casual touches were more. A past and a future coming into focus.

And with each touch, another memory from Saturday flashed behind Dane's eyes.

Hands threaded together on Alex's hips.

Glitter, music, and hot, sweaty bodies.

The ends of Alex's curls tickling his nose.

His face buried in Alex's chest, lulled to sleep by the comforting smell.

A kiss dropped softly on the back of his neck.

Most of the night was still a blur, but together with the mess he'd found in his jeans the next morning, Dane was increasingly certain more than a truce had been struck.

He hated that he couldn't remember every detail and was too embarrassed to admit his memory lapse to Alex.

"What do you think, Ellis?" Ryan asked from halfway down the hall ahead of him.

Snapping out of the fuzzy outtake reel, Dane moved from where he stood, still holding open the locker room door, and caught up with his teammates.

"We challenge the girls to a swim off," Ryan said.

"Why?"

"Because I'm fucking tired of early morning practices," Bas griped.

"Maybe if you slept at night," Alex replied. "Where were you last night anyways?"

Bas waved him off, and Alex slapped down the hand, laughing. The sound warmed Dane's insides, pooling low in his belly.

His belly...

"Let's totally blow their minds," Dane said, an idea forming. "How about a challenge out of the pool? A cook-off."

Ryan shook his head. "Mo was our best cook, and he's gone. Now, we're stuck with Disgusting Smoothie King over here," he said with a jut of his thumb at Bas.

Dane grinned. "Mo was my mentor, in more than just swimming."

"Motherfucker!" Bas punched his shoulder. "You've been holding out on us."

Us.

Said like he was one of them.

Included.

He shared a smile with Alex, those dark eyes molten, and Dane recalled seeing them like that on Saturday. Up close, *so close*, swirling with heat under the club lights. If they'd been that close...

Ryan's teasing tone interrupted once more. "Well, you've been shoving appetite-killing shakes under our noses every morning. What'd you expect?"

"All right, then." Bas slung an arm around Dane's shoulders, a laughable impossibility two weeks ago. Now, it felt right, like maybe Dane had found a place with this team. With Alex and his friends. "Kitchen's all yours, Big Red. Prove yourself and we'll challenge the girls."

"My son does not have to prove himself to you. And he will not be reduced to team cook."

Dane stumbled at the sight of his father sitting in the

team kitchen, one knee crossed over the other, nose in the air like he owned the place. Bas was the only thing that kept him upright, tattooed arm clasping his shoulder tight. The fly specialist also found his words faster, as irreverent as ever. "Your boy offered."

"Bas," Alex mumbled low, but loud enough to draw his father's glare.

Ice-cold. Unnatural. Dangerous.

From the same eyes Dane had inherited. Did his shoot icy daggers like that when he was angry? Had he leveled Alex with those imperious glares? Regret formed a knot in his gut, but the one in his chest, growing out of fear for the reason behind his father's appearance, his obvious wrath, was magnitudes larger.

Fear for Alex more than himself.

Dane stepped forward, into his father's line of sight, shielding Alex. "What do you want?"

"The car's waiting outside." His father stood, buttoned his suit coat over his vest, and adjusted his tie. "You're coming with me."

"We need to eat," Ryan said, rallying to his side. "Then we have a team meeting."

His father ignored him, addressing Dane. "I've cleared your absence with Coach Hartl."

Translation: He'd gone over Dane's head like he was a child who couldn't run his own life. Like he and his mother always had. Pulling his strings.

Indignation dissolved the knot of fear in Dane's chest. "But you didn't clear it with *me*."

Bas stepped to his other side, mirroring Ryan's defensive stance, while a more familiar heat hit Dane's back, Alex's body close.

"Dane," Alex whispered behind him, wary.

If there was a warning there, Dane didn't heed it. "Unless it's an emergency," he told his father, "I'm not going with you."

"You've ignored our invitations every night this week."

"Because I had more important things to do, with my team."

"It's no longer an invitation. Roger would like a word about your sponsorships."

Dane flung out his arms, branded jammers and track jacket on display. "I'm not wearing enough flair for him?"

A hand pressed lightly against his lower back. "Dane, let's go," Alex said, tight and with caution. "You can call Roger from your room."

"This is serious, son," his father chided. "Your actions Saturday could jeopardize your sponsorships and the team's."

The hand on Dane's back shook, as did Dane's insides, fear slamming back into him, heart beating triple time. On the outside, though, he forced himself calm. Did his father mean the press conference or the night out with Alex? "What actions?"

His dad cut another dangerous, icy glare at Alex, before his gaze drifted back to Dane. "I'll discuss those with you in private."

"Anything you have to say to him, you can say in front of us," Ryan fronted. "We're a team."

"You stay out of this," his father snapped, the icy exterior cracking, revealing white-hot anger underneath.

Alex must have seen it too, because his hand curled in the fabric of Dane's shirt, tugging him slightly back.

Dane glanced over his shoulder, meeting his captain's wary gaze.

"He knows something," Alex said. "Stay here and call Roger. See if there's really a problem."

The fear in Alex's eyes was Dane's tipping point. "No," he said. "I'm gonna go see what they *think* they know."

Bas stepped closer. "You sure about that, Ellis?"

Dane nodded, and the wariness in Alex's gaze gave way to pride, making Dane's heart trip for an entirely different reason. Ryan and Bas nodded as well, the both of them puffed up, bodies hard, defensive on his behalf. So this was what it was like to have friends, teammates, who had his back. No matter what his father said, he'd do anything to keep this.

"You'll fill me in on what I miss at the meeting?" he said to Ryan.

"You got it."

"And I'll be sure to make that bet on your behalf," Bas said, rubbing his stomach. "Look forward to judging that contest."

His father made a disgusted grunt and stalked out, barreling down the hall toward the exit.

Alex thumped Bas's shoulder where they stood. "Don't poke the angry troll."

Dane chuckled, the joke just what he needed before

facing said troll. His laugh died, though, when he met Alex's concerned stare. "I'm getting in that car *for you* this time," Dane said.

"I get that," Alex said, seeming to struggle for the words. "I'm worried about him, not you."

Meaning Alex understood he would return. That he wasn't turning his back on him.

"I'll be fine," Dane said. "And I'll be back. An hour, two tops."

Alex smiled, small but sure. "We'll see you then."

DANE SAT ACROSS from his father in the limo, tight-lipped and arms crossed, keeping up a defensive front as much as holding his insides together. Retribution for the press conference was long overdue. Closed practice and his phone's Ignore button had allowed Dane to put it off a few days, but that reprieve was over. Judging by his father's stern expression and the heavy silence during the car ride, he was in for more than the usual scolding. If his mother and Roger were here, as his father had claimed, she'd have filled the car with idle surface chatter until she could rip him in private. She was a master at filling dead air. His father, however, was a master of creating the void. Whether it was a preacher thing, or an asshole thing, Dane couldn't say.

Roger wasn't at the house either, once they reached it. Walking into what had to be the most expensive rental in

San Antonio, Dane peered through the gleaming foyer to the family-of-twenty dining room with its massive oak table and crystal chandelier. Only his mother was standing there, on the other side of the table, in front of a wall of windows overlooking a lush, green golf course. Dressed all in black, hair teased out to there, she looked like a harbinger of the devil.

Get on with it, Mo's voice coached in Dane's head. He'd made a stand once today already, and while scary, it had felt good. Right. Alex and his team had had his back. Now he had to go it alone, make a stand for himself and them.

Not waiting for his father, Dane marched across the marble foyer and into the dining room. "What's going on?"

"Sit down, dear." His mother gestured at the end of the table closest to her, set for three. "Shannon has brunch ready for us."

"Shannon?"

"The private chef we hired." She said it like it was a matter of course. Then again, why would she do any differently here than at home, where they also had a personal chef? Dane had only learned to cook for himself in college, at Mo's insistence. He'd kept up the practice by giving their home cook the night off whenever his parents were out of town, but she still made sure the fridge was stocked for his particular diet. This Shannon person... "I can't just eat anything. I'm in training mode. My diet's regulated."

His mother rattled off the list, and Shannon appeared on cue, setting out plates with his usual midmorning fruit and protein blast.

"Sit, darling," his mother said again.

He took the seat closest to the foyer, closest to the exit. "Where's Roger?"

His father held out the chair across from him for his mother, pushed it under as she sat, then claimed the seat at the head of the table, his briefcase on the floor next to the chair. "We thought it best to discuss this amongst ourselves first."

Dane fidgeted against the uncomfortable, ornately carved chair back. "Discuss what?"

His mother held up a hand, gesturing silence, as Shannon entered with the coffee tray. She sat it on the table, then asked, "Anything else, Mrs. Ellis?"

"Leave us," his father barked in reply.

Dane dropped his fork, the clatter of sterling silver on china ringing in his ears, but not nearly loud enough to drown out the roar of rushing blood his father's increasingly foul mood set off. Shannon started back to help him, and Dane waved her off. "I'm good, thank you, Shannon." Once she'd left, he pushed his plate aside and rested his forearms on the table. "Is someone going to tell me what the fuck is going on?"

"Dane, language," his mother scolded.

His father leaned to the side, rooted around in his briefcase, and righted himself holding three red file folders. Dane clenched his hands in front of him, to stop them from shaking and to prevent himself from cracking his knuckles. He had a feeling he wasn't going to like what was in those folders.

"We know what you were up to the other night," his mother said.

"Swimming? That's all I've been up to since I got here."

His father tossed the first of the folders in front of him. "That's not all."

The roar in Dane's ears grew louder. When he was sure his hand wouldn't shake, he reached for it. Inside were a couple snapshots of him with the drug dealer at the River Walk. "I didn't buy it. Alex—" He cut himself off. If they had pictures of this, what was in those other two folders?

"Is Alex also the reason you can't buy your own clothes anymore?" His father tossed down the second folder, and Dane didn't have to look to know what was in it. His father opened it for him, using his index finger to push pictures under his nose. Half a dozen photos of him and Alex digging through the bags behind the Goodwill.

"We'd had a bad day," Dane said. "We decided to go out and blow off some steam, but we needed disguises."

"You should have done a better job." His father threw down the last folder, open. The pictures were dark, lit by dim club lights, but even grainy and shadowed, disguised in clothes that were not their usual, he and Alex were unmistakable on the crowded dance floor. Their figures taller, more defined than those around them, and fitting oh so perfectly together.

Memories rushed in with each picture he flipped over.

Hands all over each other—dancing, touching, teasing.

In this picture, Alex dancing in front of him, hand in Dane's hair while Dane's hand was somewhere low the camera couldn't see. But Alex's slack jaw, visible under the lip of the cowboy hat, made it pretty clear where Dane's hand had wandered.

Palming the length of Alex's erection. Stroking the curve of his ass through the rips in those secondhand jeans.

In the next photo, his face buried in Alex's neck.

Alex's curls tickling his nose. Dane begging for more. The wish granted, Alex turning in his arms, giving him an out, and Dane refusing to take it, sealing their mouths together.

Their make-out caught on another dozen pictures. A particularly erotic one with Alex's finger in his mouth.

Sucking, wishing it was Alex's dick in his mouth, and in his ass as Alex pushed a finger inside him, throwing them both into orgasm. Coming together.

Their blissed-out faces after, nuzzling.

Even on dim celluloid, their connection was as unmistakable as their bodies. As their identities. Dane's cheeks burned.

"Don't bother denying it," his mother said. "Your face says it all."

Dane skated his fingers over the picture of Alex smiling wide, happy. He'd done that; he wanted to do it again. But that look was only for him, not to be captured by some stranger on film. "Where did you get these?"

"We paid the pap from the press conference to follow you," his father said.

Dane swallowed hard, closing the folder. He thought they'd been careful. Disguised. Not well enough. Because his parents were always watching.

"If any of this got out," his mother said, "you'd be done. You'd lose your sponsorships."

"Drug test me. I've been clean since before Trials. And Saturday night, Alex put a stop to it before I did anything stupid."

"That boy," she muttered, and Dane shot a murderous glare across the table, forceful enough she actually looked quelled, until his father broke the stare down.

"What do you want, Dane?" he asked.

Alex.

But that was the last thing his parents wanted to hear, and that answer, which had so readily come to mind, scared Dane more than a little too. He'd never put another person, much less a guy, at the top of his priorities—ahead of swimming, ahead of his sponsorships, ahead of himself. He'd been infatuated with Alex ten years ago, just acknowledging his attraction to men, but if someone had asked him then what he wanted, it would have been to go back to the life he knew, not the one he was afraid to live. He was still afraid of it, but he was beginning to think he was more afraid of walking away from it again.

He'd protect that truth, just like he'd protect Alex. He fell back on the old answer, hoping to divert his parents. "To swim and be the best. To win the gold."

"And to please your sponsors," his mother added.

"Of course."

"If that's what you want, then now is not the time to fall back into bad habits."

Alex, a bad habit? The notion caused Dane to rage. If

anything, Alex had been good for him. Helping Dane shave time off his laps, thawing the ice between him and his teammates, saving him from near career-ending stupidity. But his parents didn't want to hear any of those things.

"Do you understand what's at stake here?" his mother asked. "Don't throw away twenty-six years of hard work over a passing phase."

A passing phase that had lasted his entire life to date and would continue to last the rest of it. Rage boiling over, he shot to his feet, hands slamming the table. "This—" he sent the folder full of club pictures careening across the table at his mother "—is not a passing phase. When are you going to get that? Do I have to call a press conference and officially announce it for it to sink in?" Even as he bellowed, the thought scared the hell out of him. Announcing to the world something he hadn't even admitted to . . . But he had . . . Words from the cab the other night filtered back to him, words he'd spoken to Alex, *the man he loved*. He'd fight for him, for them, and for his team that needed them. He split a glare between his parents. "If that's what it takes, I'll do it."

"You'll do no such thing," his mother snapped.

"We won't let you, son," his father added.

"What do you mean, you won't let me?"

"Keep your head down and get in line." Translation: stay in the closet. "If you don't, we'll make sure you won't veer from it."

"Threats, threats, and more threats. What are you gonna do? Tell the sponsors? They'll probably love it. A new angle to play. Tell the world? No, because that only hurts your image. God forbid you two have a son who is—"

"You've handed us leverage," his father cut him off, voice as cold as the ice in his eyes. He spread his hands at the pictures strewn across the table. "More than a little."

Apprehension shot up Dane's spine, immediately recognizing the trap they'd laid. The trap he'd stepped right into.

A trap his mother confirmed. "We have no intention of ruining you, but him . . ."

Alex was no longer a pretty face his mother wanted to recruit or a soul his father was encouraging him to save. He was the enemy, confirmed as much by Dane himself, by the fact he wanted Alex enough to risk it all. Dane's rage burst under a groundswell of fear. "If you do something to Alex—"

"You'll do what?" his mother said, sweet as honey. Deadly as a copperhead hiding in the weeds. "Stay focused, Dane. Don't force our hand, and you'll have nothing to worry about."

Fuck. He'd given them all the leverage and kept none for himself. They still held all the strings, including, until he was thirty, control of his trust fund, which was the named party on all his sponsorship contracts. They still held all his power and money, everything he'd need to fight them, or leave them behind and live on his own with Alex. Tax benefits, his parents had said. Control, he now realized. And because he was their golden goose, they'd never do anything to burn *him* or jeopardize *his* sponsorships or income. Or the family's reputation. But Alex, he was fair game. As much as Dane wanted him, he didn't want to be the reason Alex lost everything he'd worked so hard and sacrificed for.

That would be even more unfair than turning his back again.

"Do you understand, son?" his father asked.

For Alex's safety, Dane needed to get back in the car. Again.

He sank into his chair, defeated. He'd been an idiot to think he could ever beat his parents at their own game. But at least he knew the game now—saw the whole board—and could protect his king, his captain. "I understand. I'll stay in line."

"Excellent, that's done then," his mother said brightly, brushing off the entire conversation like they hadn't just blackmailed their own son. "Now, let's eat."

It was the same meal Dane ate every day.

It'd never tasted worse.

CHAPTER THIRTEEN

SITTING IN DANE'S spot at the top of the bleachers, needing the sun's heat to chase away the chill that had blown in with Reverend Ellis, Alex waited for the rest of the team to clear out after the meeting before checking his phone again. Still no response to the text he'd sent Dane before the meeting. He didn't much expect one, but he'd wanted Dane to know he and the team had his back with whatever he was walking into.

Alex's chest had expanded with pride and something else at the stand Dane had made against his father. He was getting there. Growing that backbone that had been missing ten years ago. Missing just a few days ago even. Alex had seen it, had felt confidence surge through Dane, vibrating under his palm earlier. But in the time since, had Dane been able to hold firm without the rest of them at his side? Alex wanted him back in the safety of the training facility, with his team, and if he had his way, Alex would have Dane in his arms tonight too. Their escapades on the dance floor were still seared into his brain, had left him wanting more, and that desire had only grown this past week with each touch, each lingering gaze. Dane might not remember all of it, but he remembered the underlying feelings, the underlying want.

"What's that weird look on your face, Cantu?"

Head whipping up, Alex spied Coach at the foot of the bleachers, stopwatch he must have come back for dangling from his hand.

"What look is that?" Alex asked.

"I think it's called a smile."

Alex grinned wider, proving Coach's point. "You've seen me smile before."

"Not like you have the past few days. Things are better?"

He nodded. "You must see it too. The team's gelling, hitting their marks, shaving off time. Jacob had that one bad day, but since then, we're looking good."

"I meant with you." Coach leaned a hip against the stair post. "You seem better, like you've got your energy back."

Alex pocketed his phone, grabbed his goggles and cap off the bleacher, and pushed to his feet, heading down the side stairs. "The day off helped." In more ways than he could mention, but suffice it to say . . . "That was the first time off I've taken in a while. I needed it, more than I realized. Things are better at home too. Mom's doing okay, and the farm's fine without me."

"Good to hear. And things between you and Ellis, that's resolved? I was worried after the presser Saturday, but he's been a real team player this week."

Things were far from resolved, but in the way Coach meant, yes. "We buried the hatchet. He's got enough issues with his parents." He met Coach's eyes, owing him an apology as well. "I'm sorry for fighting you about his spot on the relay team. He's an asset. I had no business vetoing him."

"He's an asset now because you got him, and yourself, in line. Good job, Captain."

"Thanks for trusting me."

"Always." Coach slapped his back, then headed out.

After checking his phone once more, Alex moved to do the same, but Bas appeared on deck, graphics tablet in one hand, their gear bags in the other, saving Alex the trip to the locker room. "To the hotel for break?" Alex said.

Bas dropped their stuff in the aisle, blocking Alex's exit. "Not until you fess up."

"About what?" Alex asked, playing dumb. He knew about what. He was surprised Bas had let it go this long without an interrogation. He'd have to thank Jacob for distracting his best friend. "I'm just glad things are coming together finally," he deflected.

"And what about you and Dane?" Bas said with a leer. "You two coming together?"

Alex threw his goggles at Bas, who caught them swinging around one finger.

"Don't think the rest of us haven't noticed the way you two are acting around each other."

"How's that?"

Bas threw the goggles back at him with a knowing smirk.

Alex caught them against his chest. "You've all welcomed him into the fold too."

"Because I told everyone to follow your lead."

Alex hung his head, humbled to have such a loyal best

friend and co-captain who worked to get the team in line behind them, no matter the dramatic shifts of the past few days. It hadn't just been Alex working hard to get everyone in sync. Bas had been too, silently, behind the scenes. Taking an immeasurable load off his shoulders. A long, long way from four years ago. "Thank you."

"I owed you, for last time." Bas threw a leg over the bottom bleacher, straddling it and sitting in the shade, leaving enough room on the end for Alex to do the same. "But you can still thank me by giving me the *whole* story."

"I followed him to the River Walk. Like you said, we all needed some air after that disaster of a press conference." He left out the bit about the almost drug deal, picking up with their visit to the bar, Dane getting mobbed by fans, then going someplace a little less noticeable.

"Someplace you came back from smelling like booze, sweat, and sex."

"How the hell have you held your tongue this long?"

"Not gonna look a gift horse in the mouth. Following your lead, we've been swimming the best we have all training. I don't want to see that go sideways, especially after the Reverend's appearance this morning. I want gold for us—for you—this time."

"Nothing happened."

"Bullshit, Cantu."

Yeah, there was no getting out of this, given Bas's determined look. "Okay, fine," Alex said, cracking. "We made out and got off on the dance floor, but he doesn't remember it."

"More bullshit."

"He was hammered, Bas. I believe him that it's blurry."

"He remembers well enough to keep things flirty."

Alex glanced out at the pool, squinting as sunlight reflected off the water. "Since that night, he's been the Dane from ten years ago. The real Dane."

"Or has *that* Dane, *your* Dane, always been an illusion? Daddy snapped his fingers this morning and he went running."

Alex's gaze shot back, defiant. "He didn't go running; he went searching. You were there. You saw it go down. He made a stand."

"But how long will that stand last? When will your Dane disappear again?"

"You say that like it's bound to happen."

Bas hung his head, attempting, and failing, to hide how fast his face had fallen. "None of us want to see you get hurt."

"I'm a big boy," Alex gritted out, moving to stand, furious that Bas wasn't on his side. And furious at himself for thinking, with each passing minute of Dane's absence, that Bas would be proven right. "I can take care of myself."

Bas grabbed his wrist, halting his retreat. "But will you?"

Alex wrenched free but respected Bas enough to sit and listen. He owed him that much, after years of friendship and for his efforts this past week. "What's that supposed to mean?"

"You spend so much time taking care of everyone else, Alex. Your family, this team, Dane. But someone has to look out for you too."

"And that someone's you?"

Bas made a sweeping motion with his arm toward the pool and locker room. "That someone's *all* of us. You're our captain."

Overwhelming humility swamped him again. "Thank you," he said. "And my eyes are wide open. I'm not going to dive into shallow water with Dane."

Bas laughed, though it didn't sound very amused. "I'm more worried about you diving into the deep end without a life preserver."

"Hopefully, I'm a good enough swimmer to manage."

"I hope so too. In the meantime . . ." Bas laid his tablet on the bleacher between them, the SC-branded cover folded back so the screen was visible. "What do you think of this?"

Alex didn't have to ask what it was—the intricate, breathtaking design spoke for itself. Olympic rings dangling from the mouth of a stylized war eagle. A testament to his Mexican heritage. Alex swallowed hard around the lump in his throat. "Bas, this is—"

Bas tapped the stylus against the metal bleacher. "It's just a rough sketch."

"I don't know if I deserve—"

"You deserve it, Alex. Now, if we win relay gold, will you let me ink you finally?"

Even his fear of needles wouldn't stop him. "If we win the relay gold, I'd be honored."

DANE STOOD OUTSIDE the locker room, hating with every fiber of his being what he was about to do. Throw days of team bonding down the drain. Turn his back on Alex. Rip his own heart out. Because that's what it felt like. He'd been so close to having everything, privileged in the way he longed to be, with love and acceptance, only to have his past privilege trample the dream.

Better to trample his dream, though, than let his parents trample all of Alex's. Would they destroy his swim career? Or make it difficult for him to get a teaching job? Or God forbid, make life harder on the Cantu family than it already had been? Dane couldn't let any of that happen. Not until he found some leverage on his parents and turned the tables. Until then, he had to do what he could to protect Alex and minimize collateral damage. He prayed it wouldn't ruin their chances for gold—surely, they could be professional, if nothing else.

Inhaling deep, he shouldered his bag and pushed into the locker room. Head down, he could hear mumbled whispers and feel eyes on him, tracking him past the showers and sinks to the rows of lockers. He'd missed lunch, missed the team meeting, and no doubt word of his father's surprise visit had made the rounds. All of them speculating what he would do. And dammit if he wasn't about to prove their worst expectations true.

He should have called Coach and told him he wasn't feeling well so he could avoid this whole mess. He wanted to go to his room, get on his computer, and start searching for any way to get the upper hand on his parents. But even that was impossible. His parents' driver had dropped him outside the Natatorium and would wait for him there until after practice, with orders to take him directly back to the house for a dinner party with the sponsors.

Caged, with no escape.

"Need help with that?"

Dane's head whipped up at the sound of Alex's voice. He didn't think he could find his words, even if his life depended on it.

He luckily didn't have to—the question had been directed at the pup, the two of them handling wraps for Jacob's tattoo—but Dane's stuttering steps had drawn Alex's attention. And the look he gave him almost made Dane cave. Caring, concerned, comforting. The same one from outside Mo's triage room in Colorado, the same one Alex had given him their last night of camp, when he'd already begun to mourn the love he was about to lose. No one had ever looked at him like that before or since, had ever loved or cared about him like that before or since Alex. And Dane was about to lose both, again.

Turning his body and watery eyes away, he shuffled into the opposite row and dropped his bag on the floor. He sank onto the bench, head hung, elbows on his knees, cracking his knuckles.

Across the aisle, Alex shooed Bas and Jacob out, and

unlike outside Mo's room, when he'd approached with caution, he wasted no time crossing the aisle and throwing a leg over the bench, sitting close. Trembling, Dane fought every instinct that screamed for him to tilt sideways and nestle into the warm, strong body beside him. When Alex's hand moved in his periphery, lifting and nearing his face, Dane shot up his own, blocking the advance. That touch would be the end of him, the end of the tiny bit of resolve he clung to for Alex's safety.

"Don't," he said, voice rough from his strangled sobs in the back of the limo.

Alex lowered his hand, fingertips lightly touching the outside of Dane's thigh. "What happened?" he asked in a shaky whisper.

Dane lifted his face, angled toward him, and lost his words again at the worry and fear swirling in Alex's dark brown eyes. So much concern for him. Alex had no idea he should be more concerned about himself.

Unaware of the danger, Alex inched closer and curled a hand over Dane's thigh. "Talk to me, please. Tell me what's going on."

"I have to leave after practice. Dinner with the sponsors tonight."

"Okay," Alex said with a relieved sigh and a squeeze of his thigh. "We knew you couldn't avoid them all week. Put on the poster boy smile, do your Southern charm thing, then come back and tell us how awful it was."

Oh, how he wished it was that simple. He covered Alex's hand, thumb caressing the back of Alex's palm, stealing a final touch. "I'm sorry," he whispered, entranced by the sight of their hands together.

Alex flipped his over, lacing their fingers. "Sorry for what?"

"I remember what happened Saturday night. All of it."

As quickly as Alex had taken his hand, he snatched his away. "And you're sorry?"

"It can't happen again."

"Dane, look at me."

"It's too big a risk," he told his shoes instead.

"Dane, look at me." When he still didn't lift his face, Alex grabbed him by the chin, forcing his gaze. Dane gasped at the betrayal blacking out the concern. Those were the eyes that had stared back at him each time he'd gotten in the car. "Tell me this is a joke."

"I can't."

Alex's fingers dug into his jaw. "So we're back to that, then. To 'I can't.'"

"I'm sorry," he repeated, pitifully.

Alex's touch slid away, for good, and Dane felt it like the tears that wanted to fall, like his heart that was already on the floor. "No, I'm sorry," Alex said. "For thinking you'd left the privileged ass behind. For thinking you and me . . ."

Dane hung his head, unable to withstand the sadness and fury rolling off Alex. "I think I should skip practice this afternoon."

"Yeah, I think that's a good idea." Alex stood, looming over him. "We can manage without you."

"Alex! Alex!"

"Shh. Not so loud. You'll startle him awake."

"Isn't that the point?"

"Just shake him lightly."

"Or don't," Alex grumbled, eking one eye open. He slammed it shut when Bas knelt beside him and sun streamed over his shoulder from the window at the end of the hotel hallway. A shadow fell a moment later, light muted behind his eyelids, and Alex cautiously opened both eyes this time. Jacob had moved behind Bas, blocking the morning light. "Thanks, Pup."

He nodded as Bas put a hand to the wall beside Alex's head. "You sleep out here?"

"Obviously." Alex stretched out his legs, flexing his feet, and glanced right, to where his bag still sat against Dane's door. Untouched and unmoved. The door hadn't opened since he'd drifted off just before sunrise. "He didn't come back last night."

"What would you have done if he had?"

"Tell him to get back in the fucking pool." Hand to Bas's shoulder, Alex pushed himself to standing, muscles protesting—legs, back, heart. The last most of all. They'd just begun again, only the barest flicker of hope, and yet the rejection stung, sharp and fierce. But not enough to blind him to everything. While there was no hope for him and

Dane, there was still hope for Dane and the team. As captain, Alex wasn't going to make the same mistake again, ostracizing Dane at their expense. The team, especially their relay squad, needed Dane if they wanted medals, if they wanted gold. "That's what I was waiting here to tell him."

"He's already back in the pool," Jacob said.

Swaying, Alex was glad he still had Bas by the shoulder to hold himself up. "He's what?"

"Limo dropped him off a half hour ago," Bas replied. "He stayed at his parents' rental last night."

"So not even the hotel's good enough for him anymore?" Bitterness crept in, belying his good intentions, but if he couldn't be honest with Bas and Jacob, who could he gripe to?

Jacob shrugged one shoulder. "I think he was trying to give you space."

"Or hide," Bas added.

Letting go of Bas, Alex leaned back against the wall and scrubbed his hands over his face and into his hair. "Fuck, this is such a mess."

"You want me to beat his ass for you?" Bas offered.

Some part of him did. Did that make him a bad person? Some part wanted Dane to hurt as much as he did, but another part suspected Dane already did. He dropped his arms and gave Bas a small, sad smile. "I appreciate the offer, but we still need him in one piece."

"What do you need?" Jacob asked.

"To swim." Alex stretched down and grabbed his bag. The water would help him forget, at least for a while, as would shifting into captain mode.

When he righted himself, it was to Ryan careening around the opposite corner. "Cap, your phone off?"

Alex pulled it out of his pocket and pressed the home key. Nothing. "Charge ran out."

Ryan came to a stop beside them. "Coach wants to see you. Some sort of emergency."

A knot lodged in his throat. Dead phone. Emergency. Was it his family? His mom? Everything else slid away as panic took hold.

Bas, recognizing the signs, shoved his shoulder. "Go. We'll run interference at the pool."

"Thanks," he threw over his shoulder, already sprinting down the hallway.

He bypassed the elevator, slamming through the stairwell door, then out of the hotel and across the street to the training facility. He barreled through the lobby, past the pool and locker room, to Coach's temporary office. He skidded to a halt just inside the doorway, rearing slightly back at the scowl on Hartl's face. Something was wrong, in a big way.

"My family?"

"Fine, as far as I know."

Alex let out a huge breath and braced his hands on his knees, fighting to steady himself. If not his family, then what? He'd venture a guess it involved Dane. Had his sponsors pulled out? The team's sponsors? Had his parents made threats? Found out about Saturday night? What the hell kind of shit-storm had he just walked into?

He swallowed hard, forcing himself steady, and rose, thanking all that was holy his shaking legs held him up. "What's this about, then?"

Hartl was situating himself behind the desk, closing a red file folder in the middle of it. "Have a seat," he said, sounding as grim as he looked.

Alex lowered himself into the visitor chair. "Coach, what's going on?"

The desk chair squeaked as Hartl leaned back, folding his hands on his stomach. "Something you want to tell me?"

"About what exactly?"

"You've been under a lot of pressure lately. With your family, the captaincy, and your feud with Ellis."

"Which have all been resolved." Not the latter, anymore, but he wasn't going to let it stand in the way. "Didn't we just have this conversation? You said I'm doing better." In a decidedly different, more positive tone.

"Maybe there's another reason for that."

Another reason? What was he implying? "What's this about?"

Leaning forward again, Hartl pushed the file folder toward Alex. *Cantu, Alejandro* was typed on the label, along with a barcode and his birthdate. An official USOC file, and whatever was in it was not good. He could ask Coach to tell him, or he could suck it up and see for himself. He snagged the folder by the corner, slid it into his lap and opened it up, revealing what he instantly recognized as drug screen results, having seen and filed more than a few as a USOC admin. In the upper right-hand corner were his name, date of birth, and medical record number. Above the results, the date of the blood draw, this past Monday. He scanned the results, heart stopping when he read the *POS* next to a performance-enhancing drug they regularly tested for.

Coach must have heard his breath catch. "Again, Cantu, something you want to tell me?"

Alex cleared his throat, laying the folder back on the desk, open. "I haven't taken anything."

Coach pointed at the tests results. "Those say differently."

"I don't know how that's possible. I swear, Coach, I'm clean." Hell, he could barely stand the needles necessary for the blood draw and had passed up numerous meaningful team tattoos because of the same fear. He certainly wasn't daily injecting with 'roids.

"The tests tell a different story. You know what I have to do."

Alex rocketed to his feet, voice rising. "It's a lie. Someone wants me off the team. I don't know—"

Or did he? Would Dane's parents go this far? Jeopardize their son's shot at more medals to protect their conservative image? Why was Alex dumb enough to even ask the question? Of course they would. And of course Bas had been right. The real Dane had caved, the illusion of *his Dane* shattering once more when push came to shove, bowing to his parents. Only this time, he was taking more than just Alex's heart with him. His career was also going down in flames. He'd been lulled into a false sense of security, only to have the rug pulled out from under him.

Just like Dane had done at the end of developmental training camp.

"Cantu," Coach said. "Did you hear me?"

He shook off the cresting wave of fury. "No, I'm sorry."

"You're suspended. You need to go home."

"What about a retest?" He ran a hand through his hair, grasping at the ends like he was grasping at straws.

Coach shook his head. "You know how this works, Alex. You do get a retest, but there's no guarantee USOC will let you back on the team. This—" he nudged the folder with a finger "—is in the record. The Committee's all over our asses now."

"And will stay that way, if I'm on the team."

Coach nodded. "I'll let you know their decision."

"We both know what it'll be."

Coach stood and rounded the desk, resting back on its front edge. "Alex, I'm disappointed, but the pressure you put yourself under was immense."

"You don't believe me?" Shock wearing off, stinging betrayal surged to the forefront. This was his coach and boss, the man who'd been his mentor for more than half his life, as good as a second father. Someone who should know him better than a computer test readout. Who should believe he'd never do something like this.

"The turnaround this week is hard to ignore."

"We've turned it around because Dane and I called a truce," Alex argued, arms flailing. "No one's fighting anymore."

"Or because you're doping."

"I can't believe this."

Coach pushed off the desk and rubbed his shoulder. "Go home, Cantu."

Alex shrugged off the condescending gesture, leveling Hartl with a withering glare. "What happened to trusting me? Always?"

"I have to look out for the team."

"Then look out for them." He flung out an arm toward the locker room. "Get to the bottom of who did this."

"And who do you think that is?"

Red. That's all he saw. Red.

"One guess."

CHAPTER FOURTEEN

ALEX SHOVED THE last of his belongings into his beat-up suitcase just as a commotion erupted in the hallway outside.

A scuffle, a solid mass hitting the wall on the other side of his door, and a jumble of voices, Dane's ragged Southern drawl the loudest. "Let me in to see him."

"I want to talk to him first," Bas said, then to someone else, "Hold him."

"Got him," Ryan said, and Jacob echoed the confirmation.

Alex cursed under his breath. He hadn't escaped fast enough.

After the meeting with Coach, he'd returned to the cleared-out locker room, everyone already in the pool. He'd emptied his locker, stuffed all his gear in his duffel, and raced back to the hotel, hoping he'd make it out before practice finished.

He checked the time on his phone. It hadn't been more than twenty minutes. Coach must have interrupted practice with the news, and the group now outside in the hotel hallway had predictably deserted.

Alex rushed to finish packing, preparing to bolt as soon as this inevitable confrontation was over. Yanking his phone charger from the wall, he stuffed it in his suitcase and zipped it up just as the electronic card reader beeped and the door lock disengaged.

The door swung open, and over Bas's shoulder, Alex glimpsed Dane struggling against Ryan and Jacob, who held him pinned against the opposite wall.

Planting his feet shoulder width apart, Alex stood tall, hands on his hips. "Go ahead, let him in," he said. "I have a thing or two to say to him."

"Alex," Dane pleaded, fighting the other swimmers' hold. "It's not what you think." His blue eyes were bright with fear and desperation, the torture Alex had seen in them yesterday ratcheted up tenfold. "I tried to prevent this."

Standing over the threshold, Bas held his arm out behind him. "No, let me talk to him first."

Fuck that. Alex was ready to have this out and get it over with. He'd shoved aside his anger and resentment this weekend, and again this morning, for the sake of the team, and for Dane, but it'd rallied back with a vengeance, his good deed having been royally punished. "What's left to say? You were right, Bas. I was fooled by the illusion. Learned my lesson the hard way. Again." He turned his back on them, striding into the bathroom to give it a final check, and when he returned, everyone was inside his and Bas's room, Dane front and center.

"My parents did this."

"No shit." Alex hauled his duffel and suitcase off the bed,

dropping them at his feet. "They found out?" he said to Dane.

"Found out what exactly?" Jacob asked.

But Alex only had eyes for Dane, whose icy blues were suddenly interested in the carpet. "They had someone following us, taking pictures," he said, red slashes coloring his freckled cheeks.

Those pictures wouldn't mean a damn thing if Dane hadn't been living a lie his entire life. And getting away with it. "But you're not the one getting punished, are you, Ellis? It's never you who pays for your actions. First Mo, now me."

"They made threats, so I promised to stay in line, to stay away from you."

"And you believed them?" If he weren't so angry, Alex's cold, bitter laugh would have broken into a sob. Instead, he choked it off in a hoarse growl. "You fucking turned your back on me, again. I thought this time would be different. But it's not, is it? Ten years later, and it's the same shit, just a different day. Except this time, it's not only my heart that's ruined. My career's shot too."

"I was trying to protect you."

"I don't need your fucking protection." He yanked up the handle of his suitcase, wrapped his duffle around it, and started for the door.

Dane scurried between him and the door, blocking his path. "Let me talk to them again."

"And do what? Admit the truth to them, to the team, to yourself? Or are you going to keep hiding, making more excuses and striking more deals they'll never keep?"

"They control everything."

"Including my future, which they just ruined."

Jacob approached, a cautious hand raised and slowly coming down on his shoulder, giving Alex enough warning so as not to be taken by surprise. "We'll find a way to prove the tests were false."

Ryan leaned against the AC unit under the window. "You don't know how this works, Pup."

"What's that supposed to mean?" Jacob looked to each of them, big green eyes confused and beseeching, landing last on Bas.

"It's too late," Bas answered. "Alex can get retested, but by the time the Committee rules, the Games will probably be over."

"*Probably*," Jacob urged.

The kid's dogged determination on his behalf was the only bright spot in this mess. Alex hated to dash his hopes, but he'd been around USOC all his life. He'd seen enough doping scandals to know how this rolled.

"I'm sorry, Jacob," he said. "Without evidence I didn't dope in the first place, it's not likely to go my way in time."

"Of course you didn't dope."

"He can't prove that, without proof the test was rigged," Ryan explained.

"What about innocent until proven guilty?"

Bas threw an arm over Jacob's shoulders. "You're naive, Pup, but not *that* naive. You know that's not the way it works in competitive sports."

Jacob shrugged him off, bottom lip between his crooked

teeth. "I'm not naive. Just hopeful."

"Stay that way," Alex said, grabbing his suitcase handle again. "It'll help hold this team together. I'm headed home."

Bas yanked him into a hug, slapping his back. "We will clear your name, if nothing else."

Alex coughed, failing to dislodge the lump that made his words come out hoarse and scratchy. "Come home with the gold. That's all that matters now. And I'm sorry for being so stupid and making that harder on you. Of all people, I knew better. I've been a shitty captain."

"You aren't stupid or a shitty captain," Dane said, close behind him. "And the gold isn't all that matters."

Alex half turned, eyes on the man who'd crushed his heart, twice, and now his career too. "Oh, but I was, because I forgot it's your image that matters most to you and your family. Pleasing your parents and sponsors, being the Dane Ellis they want you to be. I was in the way of all that. Are you happy now? I'm out of the way. You can go back to living your lie."

"I never wanted this, Alejandro." He raised a hand, as if to cup his cheek.

Alex batted it away. "You never wanted me either. Not enough."

THE DOOR SLAMMED closed behind Alex, and three pairs of eyes swung to Dane.

Angry, accusing, hurt.

He deserved all of their judgment. And none of it was as harsh as what he was aiming at himself.

A useless apology was on the tip of his tongue when a fist banged at the door. Dane charged across the room, hoping that Alex had come back, and nearly pulled the door off its hinges to reach him. His gaze landed on Kevin instead.

Hope died where he stood.

"Coach wants you back in the pool," Kevin said. "Now." Pale, wide-eyed, and bouncing on the balls of his feet, Kevin was the picture of frightened impatience. Dane guessed Coach hadn't been so diplomatic in handing down that order.

Ryan pushed off the windowsill, headed for the door. "Wait," Dane said to him, then to Kevin, "Give us a minute."

"Coach said *now*."

"A minute," he bit out, harsher than intended. "Please," he added, softening the demand.

Kevin hesitated, but after a second, leaned against the opposite wall, waiting.

Dane let the door close and turned back to Bas, Jacob, and Ryan. Not a one of their expressions had softened either. *I'm sorry* wasn't going to cut it. "I'll fix this," he said instead. He had no idea how yet, but he would.

He had to.

Bas pushed past him, shouldering him hard. "I'll believe it when I see it."

Could Dane blame his skepticism? Or Ryan's, who followed him out the door without a glance? Jacob, however, stopped at his side. "Let me know if I can help," he said softly.

"You believe me?"

He tilted his head, smiling shyly. "I see the way you look at him."

Dane's heart leapt into his throat. "Is it that obvious?"

"No," Jacob said. "I just see . . . more."

"What's your story, Pup?"

Jacob ran a hand over his shaved head; the blond mop was growing back fast. It was only a matter of days before awkward Chia Pet tufts would necessitate another buzz cut or styling gel. "I've spent most of my life on guard," he said quietly.

All thoughts of Chia Pets fled. As quickly as Dane's heart had risen, it sank at the notion anyone had ever raised a hand to someone so gentle. "Jacob . . ."

He shook his head. "It's not what you think. I'm just more used to seeing beneath the surly than others."

"That why you sat next to me on that top bleacher?"

"No one should be alone." This kid was far older than his nineteen years. Not naive, just hopeful, and willing to see *more* in people.

Dane pulled him into a hug. "Thank you."

"Fix it, like you said." Jacob drew back, smiling. "That'll be thanks enough."

Fix it.

Dane pondered how all through morning and afternoon practice, and his distraction showed. As did the rest of the team's. They were off their marks, slow, none of them eager to be in the pool without their captain. Dane least of all.

He called his parents as soon as he got out of the pool and back to his room. He wanted to know exactly what the heck was going on. No answer.

Next, he dialed Mo.

"Get on a fucking plane to Colorado," his mentor interrupted halfway through Dane's catch-up.

"You gonna let me finish?"

"At the risk of breaking my leg again by kicking something out of frustration at your goddamn stupidity, yes, carry on with your come-to-Jesus moment."

"My what?"

Mo growled. "Keep going."

Dane laid the rest out for him, and when he finally reached the end, Mo lit into him.

"You have the fucking skills to fix this, Ellis. And if you don't get on a fucking plane by the fucking morning, I'm never fucking speaking to you again."

Dane didn't think he'd ever heard Mo curse that much. But he was hung up on a different word than the f-one. "Skills?" he asked.

"You're a hacker. You have the skills with a computer to fix this. Do it."

Mo hung up, and Dane stared down at the phone in his hand, taken aback by the gift Mo had just given him.

His skills.

The same skills he'd used to protect his memories of that special summer a decade ago. Skills that could save Alex's summer now. Could save Alex's dreams, and maybe also make his own possible.

Dane shot out of his seat, a plan forming, but how the heck was he going to get out of here? Coach had them on lockdown, strict curfew with bed checks and all, in order to keep news of Alex's suspension from leaking. Was he really going to let that stop him? From going after Alex, after the man he loved?

"The man I love," Dane said aloud, getting used to the words. Practicing for what was about to come. Because he needed to go to Colorado—to tell Alex the truth and to fix this—and he needed help to make that happen. Texting Jacob, he asked him to corral the rest of the team and bring them to his room in an hour.

That done, he rang Roger.

"Dane," his publicist answered on the second ring. "How are you?"

"It's been a tough couple days," he admitted.

"I thought as much. You didn't seem yourself last night."

Dane slumped on the end of the bed, phone to his ear. Was he really going to do this? Make the irrevocable step forward.

Out.

Glancing up, his gaze snagged on the open laptop on the desk, pictures of him and Alex from the *Knights* folder displayed on-screen. That was his real self. That's who he wanted to be. And he needed Roger's help getting there, if he was going to make this work for him and against his parents. Leverage. He just hoped and prayed Roger was on his side.

"I haven't been myself in a long time. That's what I wanted to talk to you about."

An hour later, he had a new PR plan. And access to a private jet that would take him to and from Colorado.

Five minutes after that, there was a knock on his door. Bas, who hadn't said a word to him beyond what was necessary at practice, was the first through the door, followed by Jacob, then Ryan, who was worn out after practicing in Alex's relay spot that afternoon. The rest of the guys showed shortly thereafter, all of them piling into his single room.

He dialed Mo as they settled. "Wanted you to hear this," he told his mentor.

For all the years Mo had never tried to set him up with girls, had run interference with other teammates who had, and had never once hesitated to take him to task and tell him the truth, and most of all for the spot on the relay team Dane had cost him, he deserved to be a part of this.

"Get on with it, then."

Dane pushed off the dresser, moving to stand in the middle of the room. "There's something I need to tell y'all." The conjunction came naturally, part of being honest, but it felt odd rolling off his tongue. He'd been trained out of saying it as a kid, but this was who he really was, and if he'd learned anything from his mother, it was not to do anything halfway. Except this wasn't a sale. This was his life, his future, and more importantly, the life and future of the man he loved.

"You were saying," Ryan prompted from where he was leaning against the door.

"Right, something I've only just started saying aloud. Some of you may suspect." He eyed Jacob on the end of the bed. "Some of you may know." He glanced at Bas, who'd taken up the AC windowsill spot. "But I need to say it, to you. And there's someone else I should have said it to first, but I can't do that, so I'm doing this for him."

"Spit it out, Ellis," Mo grumbled from the speaker, and Bas's lips twitched.

Out with it then. "I'm gay."

Ryan's eyes grew wide, maybe not expecting him to actually say it, but his shock gave way to a smile, as a smattering of whispers spread across the room.

"Keep going," Bas said, the twitching corner of his mouth hitching higher. He'd known, and it seemed he was happy about it, or at least happy Dane was admitting it, which was the confidence boost he needed to say the rest.

"I'm gay, and I've been in love with Alex Cantu since we were sixteen."

More than mere whispers greeted that announcement. Gasps, whistles, and a few *What the fuck*s.

"So what, you're gay for Alex?" Kevin said.

Bas shot him a murderous glare. "That's not how it works."

Kevin lifted his hands, placating. "Hey, you and Alex are my frame of reference, and you were both out when I met you. I don't *know* how this works; that's why I'm asking."

"He's attracted to men, though probably none of you fools," Bas replied, adopting Coach's favorite word.

Dane chuckled, improbably. "Bas is right. I'm attracted

to men, generally, though Alex is the only one I've ever been in love with. We went to training camp together," he explained. "We were roommates . . . and more."

"Is that why Alex was kicked off the team?" Sean asked.

"If I was there, I'd hit you," Mo shouted from the phone. "Coach and the Committee don't care."

"Well, we all know he wasn't doping," Sean replied.

"How do we know that?" Mike said.

"He checks our lockers every night for drugs," Jacob chimed in.

"Maybe he was replenishing his supply," Mike countered.

Dane shook his head. "He stopped me from smoking up Saturday, after the press conference, and he sure as hell didn't keep any for himself."

"He wouldn't jeopardize his team's chances," Bas said. "He already felt guilty enough about losing Mo. He wasn't doping. He didn't need to. We were already under record time in practice."

"And he's terrified of needles, isn't he?" Dane asked. "That's why he's never gotten a team tattoo."

"Scared to death of 'em," Bas confirmed. "Dreads every blood draw."

"So what gives?" Sean said, looking back and forth between them.

Dane shrugged. "Me. I'm the reason he was suspended. My parents found out about us."

"From when you were kids?" Kevin asked. "Because until this past weekend, you two hated each other as adults."

"After the press conference, Alex called a truce. We went out together, to a club, to drink and dance and blow off some steam. My parents had someone tail us, taking pictures."

"Of you dancing?"

"Don't be an idiot." Ryan pushed off the door. "I'm guessing you did more than dancing?"

Dane nodded. "My parents are worried. About my image, sponsorships, and their image. They don't approve."

"You're twenty-six," Kevin said.

"I've never acted like my own man before. I didn't give them a reason to think I would now. They made threats, including against Alex, so I backed down. They carried through with them anyways."

"Your parents have the juice to do that?" Ryan asked.

"Unfortunately." He cut his eyes to his computer and back, smiling. "But I've got some juice too. Thing is, I need you to cover for me."

Bas moved from his perch, stopping right in front of him. "Cover for you?"

"While I'm gone tomorrow."

"Where are you going?"

"Colorado Springs."

Bas's stare was hard, assessing. "To get Alex?"

He answered with all the love-fueled confidence he felt, amazed at what that kind of juice could do. "To get Alex, and to help clear him."

Bas's serious face transformed into a huge smile. He lifted a hand between them, palm open for a clasp. Dane slapped a hand in his and Bas yanked him forward, into a backslapping bro hug.

"Aww yeah," Ryan drawled, piling on.

Jacob practically jumped from the end of the bed, joining the group hug. "Whatever you need, man."

"Thanks, Pup."

Bas pulled back, hand still clutched in his. "Bring our boy back, Ellis."

"My boy," Dane said with a smirk.

Bas laughed. "Yeah, he's yours."

Dane breathed easy—free—for maybe the first time in his life.

CHAPTER FIFTEEN

KITCHEN TABLE AND counters cleaned, Alex slung the dish towel over his shoulder, leaned against the cool stainless steel fridge, and closed his eyes, the past twelve hours finally catching up to him. Weary from a restless night and a dream destroyed, he almost dozed, lulled by his dad's snores from the adjacent family room, but on the edge of standing sleep, Dane's face came to mind, followed by those damning test results, and rest slipped from his grasp.

Getting home late yesterday, he'd thought half a bottle of tequila would do the trick, but then he'd spent the dark hours of the morning puking it back up, stomach soured on alcohol and despair. At sunrise, he'd crawled off the bathroom floor, forced down two pieces of toast and a bottle of water, and driven out to the farm, hoping a hard morning's work would knock him out and blank his mind. But it wasn't enough, nor were the hours spent in the kitchen, preparing his family's lunch, then cleaning the kitchen top to bottom after. Alex continued to walk the zombie edge, a dark cloud looming over him.

In forty-eight hours, he'd gone from having everything

he wanted within reach—an unbeatable team, multiple gold medals, and Dane—to grasping at empty air, all hope of medals, his career, and Dane gone. Not only had he been suspended from the team, he'd probably also lose his job at USOC, maybe his side coaching gigs, maybe also his teaching position. And lost jobs meant lost money. No bigger apartment with a second bedroom for Carla, no funds to contribute to the farm, no rainy-day savings, and no way out for himself.

All gone because of something he'd never even consider doing. He'd made it clear to his teammates that drugs of any sort—performance, recreational, or otherwise—were strictly off-limits. And now *he* was being punished for using a banned substance. Only the banned substance that had gotten him into trouble wasn't drugs; it was Dane Ellis.

He'd foolishly hoped for a second chance with a man he could never have, a man who would never own up to himself or his feelings, his parents and his image always standing in the way.

Outside of what it'd cost Alex, his stupidity had also cost the team two medley relay swimmers. First Mo, taken out in the crossfire, and now himself. Dane and Ryan were excellent swimmers, but after two weeks of drama and shifting lineups, Alex wasn't sure they could bring home the gold that had eluded the team four years ago. If they fell short of gold again, it'd be because Alex had been weak and had forgotten to act like the captain his team needed. He'd set his responsibilities aside instead, his dick and heart overruling his head. What bothered Alex most, though, was the shred of sympathy he still felt for Dane. Dane had loosened up at the club. He'd had fun and been free, and maybe even a little in love, if his words could be believed. It hurt Alex deep to know that Dane—*his* Dane—was doomed to the poster boy's cage, unless he made a different choice, unless he accepted himself and stood up to his parents once and for all. He'd tried, they'd hit back, and he'd caved. Alex couldn't hold fear of coming out against him—only Dane would know when he was ready for that—but he could hold letting others take the fall against him. He'd flown back to his gilded cage, and Alex had paid the steep price for his flight out.

"Careful, *mijo*, you're going to shred that dish towel."

Eyes snapping open, he spied his mom clutching the doorframe leading to the back porch, to which she'd retired with Carla after lunch.

She shuffled forward, and Alex jolted into motion, stepping toward her. "Let me help."

She shooed him off with her knitting needles. "I can walk five feet to the table."

He knew better than to argue. It was a wobbly five feet, and he stayed at the ready the entire time until she collapsed into a chair with a huff. "You can breathe now," she said with a wink, knowing exactly what he'd been thinking.

He let the held breath out slowly. "Carla still outside?"

"Cursing Excel. Hurts my heart." Before getting sick, his mom had managed the farm's books, her days filled with invoices, order forms, and spreadsheets. Carla was training to take the reins, a little sooner than expected. "And it's too hot out there for me." She wiped sweat from under the edge of her brightly colored headscarf. "Even in the shade."

Snagging a glass out of the dry rack, Alex filled it with cold water from the fridge door and slid it in front of her. "How are you feeling?"

She took small sips, easier on her stomach. "Better than last week."

"Which I wasn't here for." He worried a nick in the table with his nail, until she stopped him, hand over his. He couldn't help but notice how flaky dry and pale her skin was in comparison to his, lacking its usual golden brown tone.

"You had more important things to take care of than a sick old woman."

Turning his hand over, he squeezed hers. More than could be said for the words failing to squeeze past the lump in his throat. "Mom," he croaked.

She kissed the back of his hand, then dropped it, taking up her knitting again. "What happened to those things?" she pressed, undeterred.

He should have made a break for it when he'd had the chance. His dark mood had scared away questions when he'd shown up unannounced this morning, but his mom braved the storm now, no matter her own battle.

"I got kicked off the team," he answered.

"Not the first time. Soccer, first grade."

The surprising response, and the amusing memory it invoked, made him laugh, his first since everything had gone to shit yesterday. "Two practices and I was done," he said, recalling his bumbling display of ineptitude on the grass pitch. "You took me to the pool the next day."

"You do great things in the water, *mijo*, but on dry land . . ."

"I was a mess. All limbs and zero coordination."

She smiled, tapping his arm with a needle. "You grew into them."

"Still hate soccer." Before he or she could say more, his phone rang, trilling ringtone piercing the quiet afternoon and causing his dad's snores to stutter. He dug it out quickly, silencing the third incoming call from Bas today, the sixth since last night.

"Don't want to talk to your best friend either?" his mom asked.

He laid the device facedown on the table, waiting for his dad's sleep to resume, then answered quietly, "He's calling to check up on me."

"Tell me what happened."

"I'm accused of doping."

"Like the East Germans?"

He nodded. At her age, that's exactly where her mind would go.

"Did another team fix the results?"

Stinging tears pricked the backs of his eyes, and his shoulders sagged with relief. He hadn't realized until just now how much he needed her to believe, without question, that he wasn't guilty. Bas, Ryan, and Jacob had rallied behind him yesterday, but after Coach's betrayal, he needed his family's backing too. He needed the people who knew him best to believe he fought fair and worked hard for everything he earned. And they did. He folded over, resting his head on his forearms on the table, gathering himself as his mom's hand soothed over his back.

"Thank you," he said between gulping breaths, straightening after another minute. "I needed you to believe."

"I may be sick, but I'm not stupid. I know my son." After another sip of water, she relaxed back in her chair, needles clicking, blue thread looping in and out as she added to the blanket she knitted. "Now, really tell me what's going on."

"I pissed off the wrong people. Fell in love with their son."

"The redhead next to you at the press conference?"

Chin, meet floor. "How'd you know?"

She winked. "A mother always knows, and he couldn't take his eyes off you either. His parents don't want you together?"

"To say the least."

"What about this boy? What does he want?"

"Honestly, I don't know."

She pressed her lips together, dark eyes flaring with more life than he'd seen in weeks. Mama Bear protecting her cubs. She'd always been fierce when it came to her kids. He'd been heckled at a swim meet once, shortly after coming out, and her verbal takedown of the heckler, and his parents who didn't think their son had done anything wrong, had been epic, earning a standing ovation from the other spectators. He was lucky as hell she had his back, always.

That shred of sympathy for Dane made itself known

again.

"He's not out, Mom, and I can't force him to be."

She simmered down, a little. "What do *you* want?"

Dane, but that was a pipe dream best forgotten. "I want to swim."

"Then swim. Since when have you ever given up?"

"You need me here."

Simmer heated to a boil again. "Do not use us as an excuse to give up on your dreams. Not when you've given up so much already."

"What have I given up? I went away to school, I teach and work at USOC instead of here full-time, and I'm always gone when you need me most."

"You've not been to as many meets the past few years."

"You've been counting?"

"Of course I have, so don't tell me you haven't given anything up."

"Mom . . ."

"If not for the responsibility you feel toward us, would you be here still? In Colorado? Or would you be in California with Bas?"

She'd watched the press conference, had heard Bas's comment. He'd be lying if he said he hadn't thought about it before she'd gotten sick. But then she had, and all thoughts of leaving had been shifted to the back burner. She'd put the pieces together, though, just like she had about Dane.

She clasped his hand. "What we need—me and your father, your brothers, your sister—is a son to be proud of, a brother to look up to, and a good man to admire. Doesn't matter where you are to do any of those things. Here, Colorado Springs, or California, just do what you do best. And that means not giving up. You have to fight for your dream. That's how you'll fight for us."

His hand flattened on the table beneath hers, surrendering. "There's not enough time, and it's out of my hands."

"Was it out of your hands when USOC turned you down the first two times you applied to the program? Or when you decided to swim only backstroke and became the best in the world? Each of those times, someone told you 'no' and you said 'no' back. Why are you saying 'yes' this time?"

Because this time his heart was broken too.

She must have read it on his face. She lifted a hand, cupping his cheek. "Oh, *mi querido*."

He turned his face into her palm, fighting back tears again. She was right, he should fight, but hopelessness seemed too great a foe when he was so damn tired, mind, body, and soul, and so damn sick to his heart.

The dogs barked outside, startling him, but not half as much as his brother, Javi's "What kind of fancy-pants shit is this?"

Alex and his mom glanced toward the front door, to where his brother's long shadow stretched across the front porch, and that's when Alex heard it over the dogs' racket. A car bumping down the gravel road toward the house. His gaze whipped back to his mom, who looked as confused as he felt.

"You expecting any visitors?" he asked.

She shook her head.

He stood, helping her up, and they crept down the hallway. By the time they reached the front porch, a black town car was pulling to a stop in the gravel circle in front of the house.

Alex's stomach hit the wooden planks beneath his feet. There were only two possibilities as to who was in that car. A representative from USOC or Dane's parents. Neither outcome would be good.

"What's going on?" his dad said behind them.

"They're here for me." Alex shifted his mom's weight to his dad and stepped to the edge of the porch, praying no one noticed his shaking legs as he prepared to meet his fate.

The car door opened, and it was not a fate Alex had expected.

Dane climbed out of the car, squinting against the bright midday sun. Dressed in jeans and a wrinkled tee, hair a red rat's nest, auburn scruff matted along one side of his jaw, and the rest of his face somewhere between flaming red and sickly green, Dane looked a sleep-deprived mess, worse even than Alex.

Alex stepped back, not forward.

And met his mom's hand, pressed lightly against his spine. "I think you know what he wants now." Alex could hear the smile in her knowing voice.

"Isn't that Big Red?" Carla asked, drawn from the back porch by the commotion.

Alex nodded, still speechless.

His mom gave him a firmer push, and he stumbled down

the first porch step. No going back now. Putting one foot in front of the other, he descended the steps and came to a stop in front of Dane.

"What are you doing here?" he asked, voicing the only question that mattered in this present world gone mad.

Clear blue eyes stared back at him, full of the same affection he'd seen there Saturday night, had seen for the first time ten years ago across a pool. Together with Dane's shy, self-deprecating smile, the real one, it was a beautiful and dangerous combination.

And beautiful, dangerous words followed. "I came here for you."

CHAPTER SIXTEEN

ALEX STOOD THERE, wide-eyed and slack-jawed, and Dane gave serious consideration to putting that open mouth to good use. Since seeing the pictures from the club and experiencing the flood of memories that came with them, kissing Alex again had shot to the top of Dane's to-do list. Second only to helping him get his spot back on the team. But seeing Alex dressed down in worn jeans and a threadbare Broncos tee had kissing vying for first place. The ravaging would have to wait, though, until Alex's family wasn't looking on.

A jingle of metal off to their sides snapped the scene back into action. Two leashed cattle dogs fought the leather straps held by one of Alex's brothers, Dane guessed, given the striking resemblance.

"Didn't know we were having visitors," the brother said.

"Manners, Rafe." The younger of the two women on the porch descended the steps. "I'm Carla," she said, hand outstretched.

"Dane Ellis," he replied, shaking it. "Pleasure to meet you."

"Why don't you come inside, Dane," the older woman said. Alex's mother, standing between his father and other brother, was worryingly frail, but the smile on her face was as bright as the colorful scarf around her head. "You'll fry out here in the sun."

Dane pushed his rolled shirtsleeve up his arm, flashing his sunburn. "A week in the Texas sun, ma'am. Afraid I'm a lobster already."

She smiled wider. "All the same, come inside." She turned into the house, calling over her shoulder. "Alex, help your guest with his bags."

Your guest.

Alex must have told her at least some of what was going on. Carla didn't let him dwell long, looping an arm through his. A warm hand brushed his other shoulder, Alex slipping his computer bag off, leaving little shocks in his wake. Dane bit back a whimper as Alex's touch lingered. He wanted to reach up, cover that hand with his own, or bend his head and drop a kiss on his knuckles, taste his skin again, but they'd put on enough of a scene as it was.

Carla led him up the front porch steps, Alex on their heels. The farmhouse's yellow paint was faded and peeling in some places, but everything had its place on the porch, and all of it was colorful. Vases of fresh sunflowers, pink and green throw pillows in the giant white rocking chairs, and stained-glass wind chimes dangling in the space between each porch column.

The color came into Alex's mother's cheeks too when, inside, Dane kissed the back of her hand, deploying his full

Southern charm as he introduced himself properly. He didn't know what Alex had told them about him, but in any event, he needed to be on his best behavior. Alex's father, Manny, was more reserved, assessing the situation. Noticing the orange knitted blanket on the back of the couch, and the framed Bronco's poster and tickets on the wall, Dane asked questions about the team's upcoming season, and the big imposing man was talking animatedly within minutes.

Rafael and Javier also introduced themselves, before disappearing back outside, claiming work. Manny followed, once he settled Maria at the kitchen table. Alex hung back, dropping Dane's bags on the floor by the door. Dane tried not to read too much into it, telling himself Alex had set them there out of the way and not as an indication he wasn't welcome.

He followed Carla down the hallway, taking time to survey the pictures lining the walls. Alex had a big family that worked hard and loved hard, if these photos were any indication. Pictures like this didn't exist in Dane's house. Every family portrait, school photo, and publicity still were cold posed affairs. None of them genuine. Never candids of mother and father kissing by the barn door. No blurry shots of brothers wrestling in the cornfields. No pictures of brothers looming over what appeared to be their little sister's prom date.

Carla sighed dramatically beside him. "Worst day of my life."

Dane laughed as they continued into the kitchen.

"When's the last time you ate, Dane?" Maria asked from

her chair at the table.

"You don't need to feed him," Alex said, shoulder leaned against the doorjamb. "He can fend for himself."

"He cooks too?" Carla said, brow raised.

"He claims. But he also gets altitude sick. Go easy until he adjusts."

"In that case..." Maria reached behind her into a cabinet. She righted herself and tossed Dane a long, narrow pack of crackers. "Saltines. Good for an upset stomach." She would know, as both a mother and chemo patient.

"Gracias," he said, palming the crackers. "*These always do the trick*," he continued in Spanish, earning another smile as he popped one in his mouth.

"Have you ever made empanadas?" Maria asked.

He shook his head and swallowed before answering. "No, ma'am."

She shifted her gaze to Alex. "Why don't you show Dane around, and when you're done, bring him back here." Her dark brown eyes, the same as Alex's, swung back to him, sparkling with mischief. She was giving them privacy, on purpose. He might like Mrs. Cantu, and it seemed she might like him too. "We'll see about those cooking skills then." She switched back to Spanish. "*Have to know you can take care of my Alex.*"

"*I want to*," he answered. "*He takes care of all of us*," he added, then startled when the screen door banged shut behind him, Alex gone.

"Go," Maria said. "And don't go easy on him," she added with a wink.

He snagged two more crackers, shoved them in his mouth to settle his stomach, and tossed the package on the counter on his way out.

Rounding the corner of the house, he saw Alex disappear into one of the big white barns. Dane hurried inside after him, stumbling when the sudden dim lighting and bales of hay conspired to take him down.

Alex wrapped a hand around his biceps, steadying him. "Careful."

That gravelly voice, the heat of Alex's body close, the smell of his sweat that triggered another rush of weekend memories, moved kissing Alex to the top of Dane's to-do list.

Leaning in, he rested his forehead against Alex's and brushed his lips over the corner of his mouth. After all he'd cost him, this had to be Alex's choice, his move. Didn't mean Dane wouldn't beg. "Please, Alejandro," he whispered. "This has been the worst two days of our lives, and I just need to kiss you, to rewind to Saturday, to ten years ago. Just, please."

Alex groaned, the sound going straight to Dane's dick. He canted forward, his grip loosening and becoming more of a caress, lips brushing.

Then gone. Nothing but air.

Hitting the brakes, Alex tore out of his arms and reeled back. "What are you doing here? You should be in the pool."

Dane started forward, like a magnet inside him had been switched on and he couldn't stand to be apart from his paired end, even a few inches too far. "The team's covering for me."

Alex held up a hand, forestalling his advance. "While you do what?"

"Help clear your name."

Alex's eyes grew wide, before he ducked his head, shaking it. He sat heavily on a stack of bales, hands braced on his knees. "This is my fight, Dane. One I'm not sure I can even win."

Determined, Dane ignored Alex's caution and stepped between his spread legs. He skirted a hand under Alex's chin, senses firing at the midday scruff tickling his palm. He ignored the shot of desire and lifted Alex's face, forcing his gaze. "I brought this fight to you. It's *our* fight. You don't have to do everything on your own." He glided his hand up to cradle Alex's face. "You shouldn't have to. Please let me help you. I think we can win this."

Alex nuzzled into his palm, sending a surge of warmth racing to Dane's heart, expanding his chest, and making the collapse that came with his next words almost unbearable. "How do I know you're not going to leave?" Alex said, barely a whisper, eyes downcast. "That you won't change your mind again tomorrow?"

Hand lowering to curl around Alex's neck, Dane lowered himself too, kneeling between Alex's legs. He wasn't sure his legs would hold him after that last deserved blow, but more than his own potential humiliation, he didn't want to stand over Alex. He didn't have the right to, not when he was the one begging for forgiveness and another chance he didn't deserve.

"You don't know," Dane said. "And that's my fault. I've

never given you a reason to think otherwise. But I'm here now."

He squeezed Alex's neck, drawing his gaze. Eyes locked, Dane stretched up slowly, lifting his other hand to Alex's cheek, thumb skating over his bottom lip, making his intention clear, and giving Alex the out he'd given him on the dance floor. He didn't take it, and Dane brought their lips together, gently, despite the blinding desire bubbling just below the surface. Instead, he gave Alex a slow, thorough kiss, full of all the promises he'd only just found the courage to make, delivered in the sincerest gesture of his life.

He pulled back and waited for Alex to open his eyes, pleased to see them darkened. "Let me prove it to you. Please."

Alex held his stare, and Dane held his breath, praying he'd done enough to make his case. He needed to do this for Alex, who'd never compromised himself, who'd shown him what it was like to live honestly. Dane would be damned if he allowed his parents' lies to bring this good man low, not when he could do something about it.

Alex blinked. "How can we win?"

Dane blew out a huge, relieved breath, and Alex laughed, the sound music to Dane's ears. "Hard part's done." He shifted back on his haunches and dropped his hands, landing atop Alex's on his knees, squeezing. "There's this thing I can do with computers."

"What sort of thing?"

"I can find things."

Alex tilted his head, a grin playing at the corners of his

mouth. "You're a hacker?"

"A passably good one."

"Like your cooking?"

Dane smiled, eager to show Alex another of his secret skills. "Better."

Alex's grin widened, but only for a second, before it dimmed. "You can't just change the results. That's no better than what was done to me."

He patted his knee. "I wasn't going to. I need to get into USOC's system, here at headquarters so I'm behind their air gap firewall. Once I'm in, I can search for a ghost of the original record."

"A ghost?"

"A lingering copy. If I can find that, it'll establish a record of the original test results, before the negative was changed to positive. I may also be able find the user who made the change."

"Then what?"

Dane pushed to his feet and held out a hand to Alex, hauling him up. "Then we confront the culprit and convince them to tell the Committee my parents paid for the switch."

Alex's hand spasmed in his. "You'll be implicating your parents."

"It's no worse than they deserve. And maybe it'll be enough to get their hands off my trust fund and contracts so I can live my life the way I want to." Using Alex's hand in his, Dane pulled him closer, chest to chest. He ran his other hand up Alex's arm, entranced by the motion, across his collarbone, pinpricks rising in its wake, and down over Alex's chest, landing on his pounding heart. Alex shivered, and Dane lifted his eyes, meeting warm dark brown around blown-wide pupils. The slide into his future was so very sweet. "With you."

"I don't want to be the one who turns your life upside down."

"Too late. You did that ten years ago." Dane closed the scant distance between them, skimming his lips along Alex's strong jaw, tasting the lingering tang of sweat. Desire roared back to life. "For the better, even if I'm just now figuring that out." He traced a path up to Alex's ear, those dark curls, that smell he couldn't get enough of, tickling his nose as they stood cheek to cheek. "Now I've turned yours upside down, and not for the better. I need to do right by you, Alejandro. Let me, please."

Alex's warm breath painted the side of his face, then lips brushed the corner of his, returning the earlier tease. "Yes."

Dane didn't have to ask if Alex's answer was to more than just his question. Alex angled his face in and captured his mouth in a kiss filled with so much need, mirroring Dane's own, that Dane staggered backward. A stall door broke their fall, providing the surface they needed to stay upright while devouring each other.

Mouths connected, tongues tangling, Dane reached for the other parts of Alex he craved. Fingers creeping under the rough cotton tee, he clawed at the smooth, hot skin beneath. Abs, ribs, pecs, all of it defined, hard, undeniably masculine. Undeniably Alex.

What—*who*—Dane wanted.

Groaning into his mouth, Alex clutched his ass and jerked Dane's lower body flush against his, rocking their hips together. Cocks hardening as fast as they had on the dance floor, friction and release were the only imperative.

Dane wanted, plain and simple, and everything he wanted was in his arms.

"Alex! Dane!" Maria's shout jolted them apart. "Come inside now and help me with these empanadas." She was calling from a slight distance away, the porch likely, but still too close for the comfort they'd been about to engage in.

"Fuck." Alex threw out a hand, bracing it next to Dane's head against the stall door. "I can't believe she can still do that."

Dane lifted a brow.

"Four kids," Alex explained. "She knows exactly how long to leave one in the barn with a boy or girl before the good stuff starts to happen. Which is when she always hollers and interrupts. It's like fucking ESP or some shit."

Dane reached down, palming Alex's erection through his jeans. "Right on time."

Alex's arm gave way, and he sagged back against Dane, the weight on top of him heavy, wonderful and perfect. And relaxed, which Dane counted as a win. If nothing else went as planned today—if they didn't get the evidence they needed to clear Alex, or if Dane didn't get what he needed to break free of his parents—at least he'd given Alex this moment of peace.

He nipped and pecked at Alex's lips, knowing they had to wind this down, for now.

Alex pushed back with his arm, trailing hand lingering on Dane's face. "Thank you," he said, smiling softly and caressing Dane's cheek.

Dane turned into the touch, kissing his palm. "For what?"

"For also being right on time."

Another win. Dane was racking up the medals.

Now, he just had to make sure Alex got his too.

CHAPTER SEVENTEEN

ALEX PARKED HIS truck at the shadowed end of the sparsely populated USOC lot. Early evening, with half the staff already on their way to Madrid, it was a ghost town compared to usual.

Glancing right, Alex stared at his unexpected passenger and partner-in-almost-crime. Dane was typing furiously on his laptop, a crease between his brows and his too-white teeth digging into his bottom lip. Ginger nerd masquerading as poster boy jock. Alex still couldn't wrap his brain around it.

"When did this start?" he asked.

"This?" Dane replied, not looking up.

"The hacking. I remember you gaming a lot at camp." Almost every morning, Alex would wake up in his bed or Dane's, and there'd be a laptop open on Dane's chest. Alex had written it off as a rich kid with too many toys and too much free time. But this wasn't idle time and idle games anymore. "This is more than *World of Warcraft*, isn't it?"

Dane paused briefly, seemed to consider his answer, then resumed typing. "After I got home from camp. There were certain things I wanted to protect."

"You mean a porn stash?"

"Not exactly." Before Alex could ask what exactly had turned those freckled cheeks so red, Dane went on. "Then it continued as a sort of rebellion. It was one thing I could keep to myself. And I had to major in something in college."

"CompSci?"

Dane nodded. "I'm glad I can put it to use, for you."

For him. Because Dane had come to Colorado, for him.

Colossal mind-fuck, right there.

Dane had come up with this plan to clear him, convinced the team to cover for him while he snuck out, and hadn't told his parents about any of it, if his incessantly vibrating phone was any indication. Dane had silenced it earlier, before getting to work on empanadas with his mom. The rest of Alex's family had wandered in and out of the kitchen through the afternoon, making small talk, and Dane had followed the Spanglish exchanges with ease, deploying the genuine charisma that lay beneath the act. He'd been polite, gracious, and even a bit self-deprecating, making fun of his sunburn and his accent, which Alex noticed he wasn't holding back as much. By the time they had finished cleaning up, he'd won them all over and promised a return visit.

Which they might be making sooner rather than later. Because as they sat in the USOC parking lot, Alex realized Dane's plan had made a critical, possibly fatal, assumption.

"I'm not sure we can get in," he said.

"What do you mean?"

"I'm suspended and also probably fired." He lifted a hip, pulled out his wallet, and withdrew the key card from the outer pocket where it'd left an impression in the worn leather. "This thing may not work anymore."

"Good thing I have one too."

"Yours doesn't get us into the admin offices."

A couple more keystrokes and the flash drive lit up, whirring to life. "I didn't mean mine. Here, hold this," Dane said, extending the computer to Alex.

Alex took the laptop from him, and Dane retrieved his bag from behind the seats. He dug around inside and yanked out a card on a lanyard.

"Trade ya." He took back the computer and tossed the card in Alex's lap.

Alex flipped it over and gasped at the picture staring up at him. "How the hell did you get Coach's card?"

"Pup's got all kinds of skills. Filched it from Coach's things last night."

"No shit?"

"No shit." Ejecting and palming the flash drive, Dane powered down the computer and shoved it in his bag. "All right, I'm good to go here." He looked back up at Alex, blue eyes bright and eager.

Alex's stomach flipped, and not in the good way. Was he really going to risk both their futures? The team's? He wanted his spot back on the squad, wanted to be vindicated, but he worried they were skating the edge of breaking and entering, and worried even more so what they might find. Or might not. A wild goose chase with no bird in the end, and so much at risk in the process. "Dane, are you sure? You could get kicked off the team for this too. It's too much to lose, for you and them."

Dane stretched across the console, curled a hand around his neck, and hauled him into another one of those kisses like he'd given Alex in the barn. Not the second one, which was more like their kisses at the club, fueled by desire and a need to rip each other's clothes off. No, this was like the first kiss Dane had given him, on his knees. So full of promise and all the things he hadn't said yet. All the things he was making Alex feel in return, against his better judgment and against everything in their rocky past together.

"I know what I'm doing," Dane said, once they parted, both of them breathing heavy. "Maybe for the first time in my life. I should be the one asking if you want to do this. This could put you in even hotter water, and I've already put you in enough of it. I wanted to see you first, make sure you still wanted this—" he held up the flash drive "—and me, but I can take it from here."

"But it's an easier job with two? I can look out while you do your hacking thing?"

Dane grinned. "Is that a yes?"

Alex nodded, and Dane didn't give him time to take it back. He dropped another quick kiss on his lips and shoved open the truck door. They were really doing this. Excitement and anxiety battled in a race up Alex's spine.

"Come on, Cap," Dane said, smiling face looking out from the hoodie he'd pulled down over his head.

That smile got Alex moving. He wanted more of it, and

more of Dane enthusiastically calling him Cap too. "So, that flash drive is going to do all the work?" he asked, as they crossed the lot to the side entry door.

"You have to get me in front of a computer directly wired to the mainframe, one with the data we need on it, preferably in the lab, but then yeah, the program on the drive will do the work."

Alex palmed his own key card. He had Coach's in his back pocket, just in case, but his card registering here would cause less of a stir. It made sense that he would be here; Coach, not so much. He held his breath and swiped his card over the reader outside the door.

The light turned green, and the lock disengaged.

Dane held the door open for him. "See, worrying for nothing."

Oh, there was plenty to worry about, but at least the first battle was won.

Inside, Alex kept his head down and led them to the lab, careful not to look directly into any security cameras. Dressed as they were, in the track pants and hoodies they'd changed into at the house, they'd appear to the guards watching like any other athletes meandering about the facility. Being after-hours, with limited staff present, they also managed to avoid anyone in the hallways.

Once outside the main lab, Alex peeked through the glass panel in the door. "Clear here," he whispered low.

"Here too," Dane said from two doors down, outside the adjacent offices. "And this is where we need to be."

He slipped inside, and Alex rushed to catch up, quietly

closing the door behind him. He walked down one aisle and Dane the other, both of them checking desks and monitors. "This one's on," Alex said, waving Dane over to the computer with the generic screensaver running. "And it's plugged directly in," he added, jiggling the Ethernet cable running to the wall.

Dane nudged the mouse and the computer woke, displaying a desktop background and password log-in prompt. "Look around," he said. "For any sort of password clues or reminders."

Alex lifted knickknacks on the desk—mug, pen holder, picture frame, inbox—hoping maybe there was a post-it with a password on the back or bottom. He was running his hand along the bottom of the screen when the picture displayed behind the password box caught his eye.

Woman, midthirties, blonde. Robin Meyers, Alex recalled, and at her side was a giant King Shepherd. Dangling from his wide navy-and-orange Broncos collar was a shiny silver tag.

Shepherd Book.

Alex patted Dane's shoulder.

Dane shoved closed a drawer. "What'd you find?"

Alex tapped the dog tag on the screen. "Try *Shepherd Book* as the password."

"Someone's a *Firefly* fan." Smiling, Dane typed in the password.

And it didn't work.

"Dammit," Alex cursed. "I thought we had it."

"Hold on a sec," Dane said. "She's also got a *Firefly*

mug." He flicked a finger against the black-and-white mug with the theme song lyrics on it. "And an eraser in the shape of the Serenity." He toggled the gray spaceship-shaped eraser. "She's a fangirl. Let's try a few other references."

Dane slid into the chair, typing, and on his third try, it worked. His fingers had moved too fast for Alex to register the winning combination.

"What was it?" he asked.

"DerrialHaven2005."

"How did you get that?"

Dane grinned up at him. "Derrial was Shepherd Book's first name. He was killed, at Haven, in the 2005 movie."

Alex couldn't help laughing or ruffling Dane's hair. "Oh my god, you're a total nerd."

Blushing, Dane inserted the flash drive, and a black box appeared on screen. "I'm not nearly as social as the press makes me out to be. I give my Netflix account a workout."

Alex leaned forward and kissed his temple, soothing any insult he might have inadvertently made. "Nerd Dane is kinda hot," he whispered.

Dane turned his face up for a kiss, and Alex gave him one, before moving over to the door to play lookout.

"Can you tell anything yet?" he asked.

"No, I'm just copying encrypted files over. I'm downloading all the test activity from the last week onto here." He tapped the flash drive. "I'll decrypt it on my computer after we're out of here."

"How much longer?"

"Couple of minutes."

Noise outside in the hallway tripped Alex's ears, and he whipped his head back around, peeking out the glass pane. His breath caught. Down the hall, a group was rounding the corner, including Robin Meyers.

"Better make that thirty seconds," Alex said. "Book's owner is on her way back."

"Crap. I thought they were gone."

"Me too." Alex rushed to his side. "Anything I can do?"

"Stop asking me questions." Dane typed faster, and Alex ran back to the door, heart racing, watching as Robin drew closer and closer.

They were going to get caught. The Committee would think they were tampering with the results. He'd be done for. So would Dane. Then what would Dane's parents do? To Dane, to him, maybe even to Alex's family? Dane had said they'd made threats against him. Alex wouldn't put it past the Ellises to exact retribution.

"Dane, we have to go, now!" he exclaimed low.

"Thirty more seconds."

"You've got ten, max." His attention lashed back and forth—to Robin getting closer, to Dane typing faster. She was two doors down, in front of the main lab. He ran back to Dane's side, going for the flash drive. Whatever was on there would have to suffice. Dane grabbed his wrist, stopping him.

Robin laughed right outside the office door. "Babe, we have to go!"

Dane's hand tightened around his wrist. He hit Return with his other, then a half second later, yanked the flash drive out of the computer. He hit another key, and the screen turned black. "That's it. Let's go!"

Alex hauled him up and through the connected doors into the main lab, just as the office door opened. They tiptoed through the dark lab, waited at the door to the hall until the coast was clear, then, hoodies up, slipped out. Trying to walk slow and appear calm was a struggle, Alex feeling anything but. Only Dane's hand in his kept him steady.

They turned the corner, headed for the exit door to the parking lot, only to see a tall form outside the door, flashing his key card to enter. Alex veered left and ran flat out down the hall to his office, dragging Dane behind him, not giving a fuck about how they looked on camera. The chances and consequences of a probably snoozing security guard noticing them on a tiny monitor were far outweighed by the likelihood of the man at the door seeing them in person and the consequences he could bring down on them.

Alex swiped his badge, opened his office door, and shoved Dane inside. He closed the door behind them, leaving the lights off.

"Who was that?" Dane asked, back to the door.

"The Committee chairman."

"Oh, crap!"

Alex slammed a hand over his mouth, whispering harshly, "Quiet."

He listened as the chairman approached, Oxford heels clicking on the linoleum floor. Dane shifted out from under his hand, leaning an ear to the door, listening intently.

The chairman's steps grew louder, then stopped, right outside Alex's door.

They were caught, done for. His gaze locked with Dane's, just visible in the low light. *I'm sorry*, he mouthed.

I'm not, Dane replied without sound, not an ounce of regret in his eyes.

And then the chairman's steps resumed, passing the door and fading as he walked on down the hallway, away from Alex's office.

Eyes fluttering closed, Alex fell back against the door. "Oh, thank fu—"

Dane's tongue down his throat cut off the relieved curse and chased away the rest of Alex's panic, stealing his breath and heart instead.

"Adrenaline junkie," he said against Dane's lips when they came up for air.

"You called me babe." Dane trailed his mouth down Alex's neck, and a shiver worked its way up from Alex's belly.

So good, but so not the time or place.

He pushed Dane back. "Wait to start that somewhere we can finish it." Stepping past him and over to his desk, Alex pulled out a tote bag and started gathering his personal effects.

Dane wandered to his side. "What are you doing?"

"Grabbing a few things, in case I don't get another chance."

"You'll get another—" His words cut off, and Alex followed the direction of his gaze, to the *Knights* swim cap in Alex's hand.

"You kept it," Dane said, voice full of awe and something more.

Alex wanted to give him more, felt confident enough to do that now. "That was the best summer of my life."

A finger slid under his chin, gentle and coaxing, and Dane tipped his face up, just as he'd done in the barn. His eyes were as full of hope as they had been there. No longer ice-cold. More like the clear blue sky of a warm summer day. "*This* will be the best summer of your life," he vowed. "I promise."

Alex believed him.

CHAPTER EIGHTEEN

STANDING OUTSIDE ALEX'S third-floor apartment, Dane looked past the rusted wrought iron railing and older-than-time globe lights, past the pothole-ridden parking lot and faded complex sign, to the moonlit fields across the highway. Beneath the starry sky, they stretched as far as Dane could see, all the way to the shadowy base of mountains in the far-off distance.

"Kind of reminds me of Laurinburg," he said. Since Alex had pulled the *Knights* swim cap out of his desk, Dane hadn't been able to get those hot summer nights, so much like this night, out of his head.

"Except with mountains," Alex said, as he dug keys out of his pocket.

"Granted."

"Town's also bigger here."

"That's not saying much. Most places are bigger than Laurinburg." Their off-campus entertainment that summer had consisted of a run-down strip mall, a run-down movie theater, and a run-down bowling alley.

Alex chuckled. "This is true."

"You're closer to the farm out here?" Dane asked.

"On this side of town, yeah. I can get out to Vineland in fifteen, and Carla can get to Pueblo's campus in about the same."

"But far for you to drive to USOC."

"Plenty of people have longer commutes." He flipped the second deadbolt and opened the door, reaching in to turn on a light. "It's not much, but it's home," he said, holding the door for Dane.

Letting the commute issue go, sensing it was a touchy subject for Alex, Dane stepped inside and surveyed the tiny apartment. Whoever had decorated, more likely Carla than Alex, Dane guessed, seemed to have a similar decorative flair as their mother. Lemon yellow throw pillows on a blue cushioned futon, a brightly striped quilt spread over the top. Matching stitched flowers on the living room curtains and fresh-cut flowers in a vase on the card table in the dining nook. Most of the furniture looked mismatched and roughed up, yard sale finds maybe, but with everything tidy and the bright decorations, the small space felt welcoming.

Like a home.

Made so by Carla and Alex, not by housekeepers or interior designers. Probably at less than a tenth of what a single room of furnishings in his parents' house cost and with at least ten times more warmth.

Dane dropped his duffle on the futon as Alex closed the door behind them, flipping the locks. "What time will Carla get here?" Dane asked.

Alex coasted a hand across his lower back, leaving a trail

of fire in its wake. "She's staying out at the farm tonight."

"She didn't have to." Not that he wasn't grateful for the privacy, especially if Alex was going to tease him like that. He was tired, drained from the past two days of hell, but he desperately wanted to finish what they'd started in the barn, then again in Alex's office. Here, in private, they could kiss, touch, more . . .

"Mom has chemo tomorrow."

And mood killed.

Which was good. Dane needed to stay focused, for at least a few more minutes. He carried his computer bag over to the card table, pulled out his laptop and waited for it to boot up. "She seemed tired but okay this afternoon."

"She's getting better." Alex moved past him into the kitchen, fiddling with the coffee maker. "The post-op chemo isn't as bad. Three months ago, she couldn't get out of bed."

Dane fumbled the flash drive, imagining the weight Alex must be carrying. "I'm sorry" seemed woefully inadequate, but it was all he had.

The coffee maker chugged to life, and Alex stepped back over to him. Dane snagged his hand, tangling their fingers and trying to focus on the positive. "I'm glad she's getting better."

Alex squeezed his fingers, the tight hold just shy of painful. "I hope they got it all this time." Before Dane could find any, much less the right, words, Alex nodded at the screen. "How long will that take?"

Clearing his throat, Dane dropped Alex's hand and got back to work. "A few hours to overnight. It's hard to tell yet."

His brow furrowed. "But you transferred them in less than a minute?"

"Decryption takes time." He entered a few more commands, then slumped in the chair. "All right, that should do it. It'll alert us when it's finished."

Alex laid a hand on his shoulder. "Why don't you go take a shower?"

He ducked his head, sniffed. "Do I smell bad?"

The hand on his shoulder glided up, weaving lightly through his hair. "No, but you're giving the angry farm rooster a run for his money right now."

Eyes slipping shut, Dane leaned into the touch. He hummed, contented, as Alex massaged his scalp, until Alex's stomach, right at his ear, rumbled loudly. "Someone hungry? I didn't see you eat any of those empanadas."

"Was too nervous. But I'm starving, now. First time in a couple days." Dane liked the sound of that, especially if it meant Alex was hopeful about his chances of reinstatement. And about their chances together too. The hand fell out of his hair, and Alex meandered back into the kitchen. "Go, shower, and I'll whip something up. Won't be your level, but it'll be edible."

"I'm sure it'll be good."

"Bathroom's tiny, so use my room to change."

"Thanks."

Dane grabbed his duffel and headed down the short hallway. A closet and bathroom on the right, a single bedroom across the hall on the left. He dropped his bag on the queen-sized bed and looked around. Everything neat and organized in the tight space, but still homey, like the living area. Bed covered in another handmade quilt, the same flowery curtains on the windows, and the same ancient alarm clock on the bedside table. Dane laughed. God, how many times had they knocked that thing into the floor, the two of them trying and so often failing to squeeze into a twin dorm bed. He ran his hand over it, then over the hand-carved medals case hanging on the wall above it. Inside were Alex's two backstroke golds and the relay silver from the last Games. Shining bright, something to aspire to.

If Dane had cost him another three . . .

He shook his head, banishing the thought. They were going to beat this. He continued around the room, to the dresser topped with dozens of framed pictures—of Alex with his family, friends, and teammates. With Bas, Mo, and Ryan from the last Olympic games, and more team pictures from USC. Many were candids, like the photos that lined the walls of the farmhouse. Alex thrown over Bas's shoulder in a fireman's hold. Alex hugging Mo, who was holding up a phone with the picture of his newborn baby. Alex in a tug-of-war over a pool hose with Ryan.

Dane pressed the heel of his hand to his chest, futilely trying to rub away the emptiness there. He wanted to be in those pictures—wished he had friends and teammates like that—but until yesterday, he'd never really been himself to anyone other than Mo, and so he'd never had any other real friends either. Always hidden away, behind the poster boy, for fear of exposure, he'd missed out on all this.

Such a fucking waste.

"I don't hear the water running," Alex hollered from the kitchen.

Dane smiled, melancholy fading. But he was here now, putting his real self out there to his teammates, to Alex's family, and to the man he loved. And he was dying to get back out there and tell him that. He showered quickly, changed into sweats and a tee, and when he returned to the living area, found his computer pushed to the far edge of the table and Alex laying out a training snack. Bacon, lettuce, tomato, avocado, and wheat bread for sandwiches, plus two cups of coffee, Alex's black, Dane's with more cream than coffee, the way he'd always taken it.

"Why are you smiling?" Alex asked.

He gestured at the table. "That you know to do this."

"It's my routine too. At least it used to be."

"Hey." Dane snagged his hand and drew him close. "It will be again." He leaned in for the kiss he'd been craving for the last hour and was stopped short by his phone vibrating on the table.

"That's the third time since you've been in the shower. I don't want to know how many times since the farm."

Dane picked up the device, unsurprised to see ten missed calls and a voice mail from his parents. "Guess the parental units figured out I'm not where I'm supposed to be." He listened to the message from his mother. She'd heard he was sick, from Roger, and they'd tried to stop by to check on him, but Bas had warned them off. He rolled his eyes when she mentioned flying out their private physician to check on him tomorrow. He erased the message, turned the phone off, and tossed it on the futon. "Bas scared them off, for now," he said, taking the chair next to Alex.

"Good." Alex set a sandwich on the plate in front of him. "When did you tell the team you'd be back?"

"I asked them to buy me a day." Dane took a bite, chewed, swallowed. "I told Roger I'd have his plane back tomorrow."

Alex's eyes rounded comically wide, his sandwich splattering on his plate. "Roger, as in your publicist?" The next bit was even higher. "And his plane?"

"Yes, and yes." Dane reassembled Alex's sandwich for him and made sure he had a firm grip on it before explaining the rest. "I couldn't exactly fly commercial if I didn't want my parents to find out."

"I thought Roger was in league with your parents?" Alex said around a mouthful of food.

"They miscalculated." Dane finished off a half, then angled toward Alex in his chair. "You didn't tell me he tried to recruit you."

"As a gay athlete poster boy. I didn't want any part of it."

It'd taken Dane no time to piece together the why of that when Roger had revealed that tidbit to him last night. "Not because you're ashamed, but because you hate the spotlight, right?"

Alex nodded. "Right or wrong, I'm no one's poster boy, for any reason. That's just not me. I'd rather fly under the radar, swim hard, get my medals, and go home. Set an example that way."

Dane could respect that. He could also tease a little too. He jostled Alex's shoulder and whispered close to his ear. "It's a shame. You're kind of hot, Cantu. You on a poster..."

Alex shoved back harder, then crammed another bite of sandwich into his upturned mouth.

"I'm used to the spotlight," Dane said. And Roger had already planned for the shift in image, also revealing that he'd suspected for some time that Dane was gay. "I don't mind being the poster boy, especially for this team and for a good cause, one that's important to me."

Alex bumped his knees, and his voice was soft, a little hesitant, when he spoke again. "If it's important to you, why haven't I heard you admit it yet?"

"Can I show you instead?"

Alex's gaze whipped up, almost as fast as the flush that streaked his cheeks. While he hadn't meant it as innuendo, Dane could see how Alex's mind jumped to a kiss, or more. And Dane wanted things to go there too tonight, but he wanted to show Alex something else first.

He pushed their plates aside and pulled his laptop toward them. He minimized the terminal box that was running the decryption and accessed his personal files, entering the password and opening the *Knights* folder.

The pictures from their summer together filled the screen. The only candids of Dane. The only other time he'd ever been himself, completely.

"This is why I started hacking," he said. "This is what I had to protect."

Alex clicked through the images, pausing a few seconds on each. "Dane..."

"Every day for ten years, Alejandro. Every day I looked at these pictures and remembered you. Remembered that this was the happiest I'd ever been."

Alex fell back in his chair, mouth hanging open, brown eyes swirling with a mixture of surprise, hope, and apprehension. All summed up in a single, croaked word. "Why?"

"Because I'm gay."

It was both easier and harder to say this time. Easier because he'd already admitted it to himself and to others. Had already said the words aloud to his teammates and to Roger. Harder, though, because this was the person whose response mattered most. Scooting to the edge of his chair, he lifted his hands and cupped Alex's face, fingertips tangling in his curls. "Because that summer I met and fell in love with a beautiful boy I wanted to spend the rest of my life with. I'm so sorry I turned my back on you, Alex. I'm sorry I was a coward for so long."

Alex stayed frozen, staring, for the longest five seconds of Dane's life. The suspense was worse than standing crouched on the blocks before a race, waiting for the starting horn to blow. Finally, Alex dipped his face in, kissing one of Dane's palms as he brought his own hands up, covering Dane's. "You're here now."

"*Te amo*, Alejandro," Dane whispered, speaking the words that had been trapped in his chest for a decade. He'd loved Alex from across the pool and across a dorm room, then from across the country and across the years. Across everything that had stood between them. He leaned forward, brushing their lips together. "*Siempre te he amado.*" Always, even apart, that love hadn't wavered.

Alex inhaled sharply, his thumbs halting their caress of Dane's hands, and when he didn't reply after another beat, Dane pulled back. Suspense tore at his insides once more, worse than the altitude ever had. Had he said enough? Had he said too much? "Say something, Alejandro, please."

Eyes darkening, Alex hitched up one corner of his mouth in an attractive, devilish smirk. "Can I show you instead?" he parroted back, and swallowed Dane's relieved, breathless "yes" in a kiss that said everything Dane needed to hear.

Tongue diving between his lips, Alex swept the inside of his mouth, leaving Dane's own tongue no choice but to come out and play, a tangle that sent heat spiraling through him and wrenched a low moan from deep in his throat. Without breaking the kiss, Alex stood and straddled Dane's legs, coming down hard on Dane's lap. Dane thrilled at the contact. Groin on groin, muscular thighs atop muscular thighs, scruff under his palms, and strong, cut arms wrapping around his neck, hauling him close. This was who Dane was, and the man in his arms, Alex, was who he was supposed to love. He'd tried to make it work with girls in high school and college, but the interest, the attraction, had never been there. Because he wanted hard and masculine, and he wanted to surrender, wanted to follow instead of lead. He rolled his hips, rutting their cocks together, and the friction was enough to short-circuit his brain.

Mouth drifting, Alex ran his tongue along the length of

his jaw. "Next time I tell you to shave this, don't."

Dane's head fell back, giving Alex full access to his sensitive neck, and his dick jerked, testing the limits of his sweatpants. "Holy fuck." The curse rolled easily off his tongue, the assault on his senses more than warranting it.

"Eyes forward, Ellis," Alex said.

Dane struggled for the strength to right his head, every bit he had powering his thrusting hips, his other head, but he reached for a reserve, straightening. And was handsomely rewarded for the effort. Alex sat back on his thighs, reached behind his neck, and yanked his tee off over his head. Dane sat frozen for a moment, everything he'd wanted to touch and taste the past two and a half weeks there for the taking. And he couldn't decide where to start.

Reading his dilemma, Alex wove a hand in his hair and drew him forward, bringing Dane's lips to the crevice at the base of his neck. "Start here."

That he could do.

He kissed and lapped, returning the torture, while his hands climbed Alex's body, gliding over ripped abs, tight obliques, and toned delts. The muscled torso was so much harder, more defined, than when they were kids. But God, did it still taste like heaven. Kisses drifting lower, he nuzzled the little patch of dark hair at the V of Alex's sternum, the prickle on his face divine. Alex's answering moan was divine too, rocketing Dane's dick to the edge of pain. He ventured out, the attentions of his hands and mouth converging on Alex's nipples. Dark, rosy circles that shriveled and tensed when he pinched, licked, and took each nub between his teeth.

Alex's hips jerked, slamming down, his cock demanding attention too. Dane grasped the rigid length through Alex's track pants, fisting and stroking. Alex rested his forehead against his, panting as he thrust into Dane's hand, while the back of Dane's knuckles wreaked havoc on his own cock.

It wasn't enough. He needed a better grip, on both of them.

Fighting elastic, he shoved the waistband of Alex's pants and briefs down, then his own, far enough to get their dicks out and in his palm, together. Then he lost his grip on reality as he stroked them as one, his entire world focused on the feel of them together in his hand—hard, hot, and slicker by the second. He buried his face in Alex's neck, sucking hard enough to bruise, but unable to stop himself.

"What do you want, babe?" Alex whispered in his ear, hot and gravelly, the endearment driving Dane wild.

"Want you to fuck me." There'd been no doubt in Dane's mind that that's where this was going. He wanted Alex on him, in him, more than anything. More than medals, more than sponsorships, more than the dollars in his trust fund. He'd give it all up if Alex would just make love to him.

"Then take me to bed," Alex rumbled, and Dane didn't have to be told twice. He ran his hands down Alex's back, inside his pants and briefs, and palmed that perfect ass, boosting Alex into his arms as he stood. Alex wrapped his legs around his waist, and they stumbled down the hall, banging walls along the way as Dane's legs wobbled each time Alex nipped behind his ear or licked the hollow of his throat.

In the bedroom, Dane knocked his duffle off the bed and then, knee to the mattress, laid Alex out, yanking off his pants and briefs in one go. He grabbed Alex's flailing hand with one of his, pinning it to the bed, and took the base of Alex's cock in the other, pumping, while he teased the length of it with a long swipe of his tongue. "I've been thinking about this, about being right here, since the club. I wondered if you'd still taste the same too."

Alex's fingers clenched in his as his hips shot off the bed.

Dane smirked up at him. "That an invitation?"

Alex growled. "Fuck yes."

He circled the tip with his tongue, taking Alex into his mouth, loving the feel of him, the salty, musky taste, the smell that was all his own. Alex's hand spasmed in his again, and Dane placed it on his head, encouraging Alex to pull at the strands, needing that edge of pain to stave off his own mounting pleasure.

Everything about blowing Alex was so heady though, so much a pleasure in itself, that Dane got lost in rhythm, not at first noticing when Alex's tugging became urgent. It wasn't until nails scraped over his scalp, sending a painful arrow of need straight to his dick, propelling him right to the edge, that Dane gasped and Alex's dick slipped from his mouth.

"Get up here," Alex ordered.

"Why'd you stop me?"

"I'm still not sure this is real, and if I only get one chance at this, I want to be inside you when I come."

Dane crawled up the length of his body and rested his elbows on either side of Alex's head, framing his handsome face in his hands before diving in for another long, thorough kiss, reaffirming all those promises he'd made today. "This is real, Alex. It's not a one-time thing. I love you." He rolled his hips, and Alex's softening expression shifted to wanton, a keening moan rumbling out of his throat. "And I want you inside me too."

"Then get the rest of your clothes off, now."

He stripped the rest of the way as Alex reached in the side drawer, tagging a condom and lube. They repositioned so Dane was on his knees, Alex behind him as he rolled on the condom. "I'll go slow," he said. "It may hurt."

Dane looked over his shoulder, praying to God he didn't come from the sight of Alex naked and erect, slicking himself with lube. "It won't," he gritted out.

Alex raised a brow. "Others?"

Dane shook his head. "It's only ever been you there. And toys."

Alex grinned as he squirted more lube into his hand. "How'd you hide those from your parents?"

"In a lockbox. With my swimming medals." Alex laughed, big and full-bodied, and it was the most seductive thing Dane had ever heard. "Fuck, you're beautiful."

Alex's laughter eased into a soft smile, and he leaned over Dane, nuzzling his cheek as his slick fingers teased him open. "You're pretty beautiful too, Big Red."

Dane groaned, riding back on Alex's hand. "I always

imagined it was you. You're all I've ever wanted. Please."

Kissing the nape of his neck, Alex nudged his knees farther apart and pressed the tip of his dick against Dane's opening. But despite how much he wanted it, Dane tensed. It'd been so long, and yes, he'd used toys, but being with Alex was so much more. And Alex was so much bigger.

Alex smoothed a hand over his hip and around, taking his erection in hand. "Easy, babe," he whispered.

The stroke over Dane's cock, as smooth as the voice in his ear, distracted him from the tension, and when Alex pushed a second time, Dane gave himself over. He grunted at the initial pressure, then groaned as the pain gave way to fullness, to a sensation inside him he'd been missing for far too long.

"I need to move now," Alex said, after giving him a few seconds to adjust. His voice was no longer smooth, but as rough and full of need as Dane's.

Pushing back in answer, Dane encouraged the movement Alex promised. It was everything he'd missed and more. Alex all around him—blanketing his back, grunting in his ear, fisting his cock, and filling him full. Over and over, in a race against their bodies, barreling toward the wall, and reaching the finish when Alex panted, "Come for me," in his ear.

Dane had no choice but to follow his captain's orders.

He came, hard, spilling into Alex's tight grip, as Alex's thrusts became erratic, pounding to his own finish. The last thrust was the best, filling Dane full, and Alex stayed buried inside him a long shuddering minute, until they both collapsed on their sides.

Alex's heat disappeared from his back, and Dane heard him yanking open drawers, then the whoosh of tissues pulled from a box. A wad appeared over his shoulder, and Dane cleaned himself up. They ditched the tissues off the side of the bed and rolled chest to chest.

Slinging a leg over Alex's hip, Dane wrapped him up, in his body and the covers. Alex snuggled down, kissing the hollow of his throat again, and Dane was sure his heart would tear through ribs and skin and offer itself to Alex.

"Are you really here?" Alex mumbled, half-asleep already.

Dane hugged him tighter. "Yeah, I'm here, Cap," he said, dropping a kiss on his head, nose buried in the dark curls he loved so much. "And I'm never turning my back on you again."

CHAPTER NINETEEN

THE BLARING ALARM clock jolted Alex awake. He threw out an arm, slapped it silent, and shoved the infernal device off the table to the floor, the least it deserved for being so rude. Groaning, he blinked open his eyes, meeting the shadowy gray light of predawn morning. On a stretch and inhale, consciousness came flooding back. The pleasant ache in his thighs and back, the lingering smell of sex, his morning wood eager but not desperate. Satisfied after a night of multiple rounds. He rolled onto his back, seeking out his bedmate, and met . . . nothing.

Alex shot up, his first instinct to panic and think the worst, chest clenching against an impending wave of familiar heartache. Dane had left again, had set him aside once more. He'd been on the edge of sleep, but Alex swore he'd heard Dane promise to never leave again. And the same promise had been in every kiss they'd shared yesterday. Had Dane broken that promise already? History lent itself to that conclusion, but fuck if Alex hadn't thought they'd changed the course of history last night. His and Dane's future finally headed a different direction, together.

He'd believed him.

Bracing a hand on the empty side of the bed, Alex felt warmth under his palm. Dane hadn't been gone long; maybe he was still in the apartment. Alex inhaled a shaky breath, preparing to call out his name, and swallowed the scent of freshly brewed coffee instead. The ringing in his ears waned, and Dane's deep Southern drawl came through. The words were muffled, Dane speaking low on the phone, but the familiar rumble calmed Alex's racing heart.

But not his racing thoughts. He collapsed back on the bed, staring up at the popcorn ceiling. Dane was here in his apartment, had been here in his bed last night and at his family's farm yesterday. He was really here, but for how long? Was that his parents on the phone? What would they threaten him with this time? Everything about Dane's actions yesterday and his lovemaking last night showed Alex he loved him, but was that love strong enough to withstand the inevitable assault? From Dane's parents, the press, from whatever they faced with USOC.

USOC.

Test results.

Alex shot up again and swung the rest of the way out of bed. He grabbed a pair of clean sweats, hauled them on, and made a beeline for the kitchen table. On it, the computer continued to run commands in the black box. Still not done yet.

A warm breeze wafted around his legs, and Alex followed it to the open patio door. Dane stood outside on the tiny cement balcony, phone to his ear, the other wrapped around the back of his neck. Dressed in his sweats from last night and nothing else, with the first rays of sun peeking over the horizon, his pale skin glowed and his red-gold hair shone like fresh-struck kindling.

Alex was so entranced by the sight he almost missed the words.

"Roger's on board. We might lose a couple sponsors, but we'll gain more." A pause, then a transformation came over Dane similar to the one outside the kitchen earlier this week, when he'd faced down his father. Hand dropping and fisting at his side, he straightened his spine and shoulders, tipped up his chin, and held his head high. But when he spoke, Dane's words carried a certainty Alex had never heard before. "I don't care what the press thinks, and I sure as hell don't care what your congregation or customers think. I love him, and I won't turn my back on him, ever again."

Dane was here. He wasn't leaving. This was real.

Warmth filled Alex's chest, chasing away the chilly tendrils of doubt and propelling him forward. He laid a hand on Dane's lower back so as not to startle him, then glided it around his waist. He circled Dane's chest with the other, hugging him from behind and nuzzling the crevice of his spine.

Dane tangled their fingers together on his chest. "You can keep your money," he said into the phone. "And you can keep your mansion. My home is wherever Alex is." Dane didn't give them the chance to respond. Just hung up and tossed the phone on the little wrought iron patio table, the clatter loud in the otherwise quiet morning. He blew out a shaky breath, and Alex hugged him tighter, happy to shoulder the extra weight, especially after witnessing that stand.

"You might have a new roommate, when this is all said and done." Dane lifted his hand, kissing the palm. "I hope Carla doesn't mind."

Alex turned him in his arms and held his face in his hands, staring into scared but determined blue eyes. "I love you, Dane Ellis."

Heat warmed the cheeks beneath his palms, and Dane cast his eyes aside, suddenly shy. "You didn't say it last night. I didn't know."

Alex wove his fingers into Dane's hair, furthering the charming disarray. "I wasn't sure it was real, that you wouldn't be gone in the morning."

Dane's eyes cut back to his, a spark of mischief there to match the smirk curling his lips. "Even after round three?"

Alex leaned in for a lazy, languid kiss. "I woke up and wasn't in your arms. I panicked, but then I smelled the coffee and heard your voice. Heard what you said to your parents."

"I meant every word." Dane pulled back, hands wrapped around his wrists. "Every word I said to you last night and to them just now."

"I believe you." Alex brushed a kiss along his jaw, the auburn stubble tickling his tongue and stirring blood in other places. Morning wood hardening past merely eager.

Dane was right there with him, capturing his mouth in another kiss that quickly ratcheted up to needy. Flipping them, Alex pressed Dane's back against the glass door while

Dane slipped a hand inside his sweats, palming his ass. Alex groaned and lifted his ass, forcing Dane's fingertips to skim his crease. Dane didn't like to top, but that didn't mean Alex didn't like to be teased too, to be filled too, one way or the other.

Dane took the bait, dipping his hand lower, running a finger around his rim, and Alex ground his erection against Dane's, showing his appreciation. "Round four," he mumbled, and Dane's smile curled against his lips.

Then died when the computer inside pinged. A tiny beep as loud as thunder rolling across the open plains. He tensed in Dane's arms. Would there be anything they could use in the decrypted files? What if they found nothing? His career and future, and now Dane's too, were on the line.

Big hands clasped his shoulders, lightly shaking him out of the rising panic. "We're going to find a way out of this," Dane said.

"What if there is no magic bullet?"

Dane rubbed his thumbs over the sensitive spot at the hollow of Alex's neck, tongue following in its place, obviously trying to distract him. "Then you come to Madrid and cheer on your boyfriend."

Distraction working, Alex looped his arms over Dane's shoulders. "My family needs me here."

"Then we make sure our phones don't have roaming charges, and you watch your boyfriend on TV win the relay gold and dedicate it to you."

Alex nuzzled his temple, chasing away the lingering disappointment with the much better part of that sentence.

"You like that word, don't you? Boyfriend."

"I do." Dane tilted his face in for a kiss, grinning. "And I'll come home and put my gold next to my boyfriend's in that awesome carved case next to his bed."

"No more medals with sex toys," he said in mock scolding.

"I'm never gonna live that down, am I?"

Alex laughed. "Nope, babe, sorry."

Head hung, Dane peeked up through his lashes, smiling wider. "I love it when you laugh." Dane grabbed his hand and pulled him inside. "Let's go, we've got work to do."

At the table, Dane pulled the computer to him and was opening windows and sifting through information faster than Alex could comprehend. It was hard enough to comprehend that Dane, the lost love of his life, had returned, was a hot computer nerd, and was sitting shirtless in his apartment, hacking USOC records.

"This is yours, right?" Dane asked, pointing to the screen.

Alex leaned over his shoulder, examining the test results. His name and medical ID number were in the right spot, and the blood draw date on the left, above the results, was also correct. As was the first drug listed, Verapamil, a medication he took daily for esophageal spasm, a condition he'd been diagnosed with in college. He tapped that line. "That's how I know it's me. Daily medication."

"All right, give me a few minutes, and let me dig for an older version of this file."

"Coffee, then?"

Dane glanced up, lips puckered for a kiss, which Alex gave to him.

"I'll take that as a yes."

"There will never be a no to that question."

Laughing despite his nerves, Alex worked in the kitchen, filling their mugs, Dane's more cream and sugar than coffee.

"Gotcha!" Dane shouted with a smack to the table.

Alex hurried back over. "What'd you find?"

"It was buried deep, but I found a ghost of the first version." He had two test results open on the screen, side by side. "That's it, right?"

Alex checked all the markers again. "Yes, that's the same one."

"Except not." Dane highlighted the differing results for the performance-enhancing drug. *POS* on the later version Alex had been shown. *NEG* on the ghost of the original. "Notice anything else different?" Dane asked.

Alex shook his head.

"Because it's hidden." He made a couple clicks and keystrokes, and another number popped up in the footer. "User ID for the person who entered the data."

"They're different too."

"Exactly." He hovered the cursor over the one on the second set of results. "This is the person who sank you. The person my parents are paying."

"Can you find out who that is?"

Dane nodded, and Alex slid into the chair beside him. Knees bouncing, Alex cracked all the knuckles on his hands. Then his toes.

"That's *my* nervous tic," Dane mumbled.

"See how fucking annoying it is." And see how nervous he was, doing the thing that usually amounted to nails on a chalkboard to him. Unable to sit still, Alex went back to the kitchen for their coffees. "What do we do when we find this person?"

"Tell Coach, tell the Committee. Get the person to sign an affidavit admitting what they did and why."

"Would they really implicate themselves?"

"Maybe it won't be as bad if—" Dane slapped the laptop shut and shoved back from the table, staggering to his feet, the chair tipping over behind him. "No fucking way." He stared at the computer like it'd bitten him.

Setting the mugs on the table, Alex hadn't seen what was on the screen to cause such a reaction. Whatever it was, it couldn't have been good. "Dane?" He glanced back and forth between his boyfriend and the computer. "What'd you find?"

"That's not . . . That's not what I expected."

Stomach in knots, but needing to know the truth, Alex opened the laptop and stared in utter shock at the picture on the screen.

Betrayal ran hot and deep, scorching through his veins and burning away the knot in his gut. Burning right through it. No, that's not what they were expecting at all.

THEIR PLANE TOUCHED down in San Antonio just past noon. They hadn't been able to secure a private hangar, but they had snagged a main concourse gate near the airport exit. They needed to book it, every second one Dane couldn't afford to waste. The clock was ticking down on getting Alex's suspension overturned. The team had one more open practice this afternoon, one Dane was expected to be at, then they were scheduled to fly out to Vienna for international training tomorrow.

"Are you sure about this?" Dane asked as they hustled up the Jetway. "We could have taken this straight to the Committee." That had been Dane's suggestion, clearing Alex his number one priority. After last night's near run-in, they knew the chairman was still at USOC HQ. But Alex had insisted on confronting his betrayer first, anger perhaps eclipsing logic.

That anger held firm, just shy of boiling, judging by Alex's clenched jaw and fiery eyes. "I'm sure," he said. "I need to know why he did this."

"Because my parents paid him a lot of money."

"You sweet-talked the family banker on the way here. No unusual transfers."

"Maybe they haven't paid him yet."

Hand on his arm, Alex halted on the concourse-side of the security gates, other exiting passengers parting around them. "This isn't just about me. I'm the captain. He's our teammate. I have to know why he'd do something like this to me and the rest of the team."

Alex, always bearing responsibility, which, Dane had to

admit, when it was fueling Alex's confidence instead of weighing him down, was one heck of a turn-on. Without thinking, he leaned in for a kiss, but a chorus of "There they are!" stopped him short.

Head whipping to the side, he glanced through the security gates, and sure enough, a herd of reporters were converging, jostling exiting passengers out of their way to get to him and Alex as soon as they stepped on the other side of the security glass.

"Shit!" Alex cursed, and Dane's gaze swung back to him. Worry crept into those brown eyes, but it was kept at bay by anger still. "Who the fuck called them?"

"Someone who wants to stall us so he can cover his tracks."

"How? You have copies of everything already."

"Are the doping rumors true?" one of the reporters shouted. "Are you off the team, Alex? How does it feel to go from captain to cheat?"

Great, just what they needed. An airport full of people, of fans, hearing the false story they'd tried to keep under wraps.

"What's your involvement with this, Dane?" a different reporter called out. "Were you suspended too? Why did you bring Alex back?"

"Dane," Alex snapped, captain-tone demanding his attention. "*Can* he cover his tracks?"

"No, but he may not know that. Or maybe he just wants to cause maximum damage. To both of us."

Alex tilted his head toward the gathering crowd. "Exposing you like this doesn't fit into your parents' plan."

"It does if I disavow you. I threatened the other day to call my own press conference. They're calling my bluff."

They'd set up the last airport ambush, during which Dane had conceded to their demands and backed down. They were betting on *that* Dane to resurface, the old one who turned his back on himself and those he loved. The Dane who cut and run when the going got tough or when the truth hovered too close to the surface.

Alex connected those same dots, a sharp inhale acknowledging the cliff they stood at the edge of. Before yesterday, Alex, resigned to the belief Dane would always leave him, would have made the jump himself. After last night and this morning, though, Dane was beyond pleased, the tightness in his own chest loosening, when Alex held out his hand, offering Dane a chance to prove the declarations he'd made.

Believing he'd stay.

Dane didn't have to think twice, sliding his hand into Alex's. "I said I'm never leaving you again. I meant that. But if you don't want to be thrust into the spotlight, I'll distract them while you find another way out. Or if you want to handle this on your own, I'll leave."

"You'd give up the spotlight?"

"If that's how you want to handle it, yes. This is your call, Cap."

Alex interlaced their fingers. "We stand together."

"Let's do it."

They exited to the gathering crowd of reporters and onlookers, and TSA ushered them out from in front of the security gates into one corner of the check-in area. The press continued to lob questions at them, about the doping rumors, Alex's suspension, and why Dane was there.

"I'd like to make a statement," Alex said, projecting his voice. "On our behalf."

Our echoed through the crowd, and their clasped hands received renewed notice, cameras clicking a mile a minute.

Alex talked over the racket. "Yes, I was accused of using a banned substance. We have evidence, however, that proves the test was falsified. I have never used drugs of any sort."

"We were on our way to tell Coach Hartl that until you lovely people interrupted us," Dane said, laying on the charm, big smile and all. "I have no doubt Alex will be cleared, reinstated, and back to captaining the team at this afternoon's practice, where he'll run my tail into the ground for missing yesterday's practice."

"What substance? What evidence?" several reporters shouted.

"Dane," another called out, "why were you sent to Colorado after Alex?"

He glanced at Alex, who gave him a nod. Moment of truth. Now or never.

Jump.

"I wasn't sent to Colorado. I chose to go there. Snuck there, actually," he said with a smile. "I went there to help my teammate, my captain, my boyfriend." He smiled even wider on that last word. He did like the sound of it. A lot.

Drugs forgotten, the cacophony of clicking cameras, shocked gasps, and shouted questions was thunderous.

"Dane, have you always been gay?"

"Did Alex turn you gay?"

"What do your parents think?"

"I have always been gay," Dane answered, same as he had the night before last to his teammates. "It took me a while to accept and admit that. Twenty-six years, to be exact." He chuckled at himself, and some of the crowd laughed with him. "And this incredible man—" he drew Alex closer, against his side "—who I've been in love with going on a decade, gave me another chance I didn't deserve, and I'm just so happy and grateful to be here with him."

"How will this affect the team?"

"Are the doping and this revelation connected?"

Alex pulled captain's rank and tone again, commanding attention. "My teammates have never had an issue with my sexuality or anyone else's on the team. I don't expect they'll have an issue with Dane's. As for the doping allegations, an official statement will be forthcoming after we speak with Coach Hartl. We appreciate your patience and understanding as we sort this out."

"And on that note, ladies and gents," Dane cajoled, flashing his press-practiced smile and feeling honest about it for a change. "Now, if you'll please excuse us, we've got a name to clear."

"How about a kiss for the cameras?" one reporter shouted, and a round of applause broke out among the onlooking travelers who were standing watching.

Dane directed his answer to them, to the people they swam for, to their fans. "You'll get a kiss when we win the gold."

CHAPTER TWENTY

DESPITE WHAT THEY'D told the reporters, they didn't go to Coach first.

Alex blasted open the locker room door with a two-handed shove and didn't slow when it crashed against the tile wall. It would have flown back in his face but for Dane, totally in sync with him now, reaching out a long arm from behind him and stopping the recoil, clearing his path. Alex ignored the wide-eyed stares of his gasping teammates, his focus solely on the one standing two rows back.

The one whose expression wasn't surprised so much as *Oh shit.*

With good reason.

Alex stalked toward the traitor, Dane's steps thundering in his wake.

"What's going on?" and "What the fuck?" echoed around them. Hands reached for Alex, but he dodged and shook them off, not to be deterred.

He dropped his bags in the aisle, rounded the endcap of the second row, and stood on one side of the bench, Dane on the other, blocking any exit. "Nowhere to run," he said.

Ryan backed into the row, retreating to the corner to make his stand. He straightened his spine, set his feet apart, and crossed his arms. Always trying to play the big man and never quite pulling it off. Even now, the fear in his eyes and the rapid rise and fall of his chest gave him away. "Why would I run?"

"I think the better question is, why'd you do it?"

"What'd he do?" Bas asked from over Alex's shoulder.

"Changed the results on my drug test."

"Tell us, Ryan," Dane said, defensive posture matched, but every bit of his confidence real, even more so now. "How much did my parents pay you?"

"I didn't change your results," Ryan bluffed. "You tested positive."

"No, I didn't." Alex took two steps down the row, and Ryan backed into the lockers, rattling the metal doors. "We have before and after images of the test results, including one with your User ID on it, proving you were the one who changed them."

His guilty eyes darted to Dane.

"That's right," Dane said. "I'm a better hacker than you. Or did the CompSci professors at Florida forget to teach you how to delete your ghosts?"

Jacob entered the fray, shouldering past Dane, his rangy frame so puffed up with anger Alex would have sworn he'd put on twenty pounds and grown a half foot overnight. "You changed Cap's test results?"

"How much did my parents pay you?" Dane repeated.

"Fucking hell, Ryan, really?" Kevin weighed in from

somewhere behind them.

"You were in the room with us the night we found out," Bas said, low and angry. "Why the fuck would you do that? Frame Alex, then let us think you were on our side?"

"Our side," Ryan scoffed, his narrowed-eye gaze cutting to Bas. "You're only ever on his. Always the loyal second."

Bas crowded into the row behind Alex. "What the fuck does that mean?"

Alex appreciated his teammates' support, but he wanted answers, now. From *this* teammate who'd swum in the same circles as him for years, who'd stood on the medal podium with him four years ago. "Why'd you do it, Ryan?" Alex pressed. It had to be more than just Dane's parents and the money that had turned his supposed friend against him. "Because I'm Hispanic? Because I'm gay?" He hated to think Ryan harbored that sort of hate toward him, toward Bas, toward Dane, but he couldn't think of any other reasons.

Ryan threw his arms wide, hands slapping the lockers on either side of the row. "I don't care who you fuck or what color your skin is."

Dane sprung the trap. "So you admit you did it then?"

The traitor's mouth clamped shut.

"What's going on here?" Coach's booming voice bounced off the tile walls. "Ellis, Cantu, you were supposed to come straight to my office."

Alex glanced over his shoulder to reply, and Ryan made a break for it, jumping up on the bench to run out between them.

He didn't make it halfway before Jacob took him down

in a stunt-worthy martial arts move.

Kevin whistled behind them, and Bas choked out an awed "Damn, Pup."

Jacob smiled up at him. "You know you're impressed."

"I repeat," Coach said, interrupting the momentary burst of action. "What the hell is going on here?"

Alex helped Jacob haul Ryan up, each of them holding one of his arms. "Tell Coach why you changed my drug test results," Alex demanded.

Coach's brow furrowed. "*You* changed Alex's results?"

"My parents paid him off," Dane added.

"It had nothing to do with your parents," Ryan said, wrestling out of the hold. "It was about you—" he pointed an accusing finger at Bas, then swung it to Alex "—and you—" then to Dane "—and you and fucking Mo. You guys keep getting older but keep coming back."

"But you're a vet too," Bas said.

"But I'm not a starter, and I'll never get a chance at being a starter, at getting gold for myself, if you're taking spots on the teams and crowding the goddamn podium."

"But you're in our one slot for IM," Coach said. "You're also swimming backstroke, and you're the alternate for medley relay."

Ryan held up that same single finger he'd pointed earlier. "*One* possible gold, one. Then I'm losing the backstroke gold to you," he said, glaring at Alex. "And I'm not even on the relay team, even though I beat both you and Dane in the pool last week. This Olympics was supposed to be my turn to start. My last turn. I wanted my shot, and I took it."

"By making sure I was off the team?" Alex asked, astonished by the team jester's vitriol.

"Yes."

One word, spat with such disdain that it landed like a punch to Alex's gut. Ryan had always been part of the camaraderie he valued most. Always there with a joke, a stopwatch, or a high five, cheering on him and others. How had Alex never seen this resentment and jealousy buried behind his joking facade?

"You called the press on us this morning, didn't you?" Dane said. "You tried to implicate us both."

"He was in Coach's office when Alex called," Bas said, and Ryan hung his head, the final nail in the coffin.

"All right, that's enough," Coach said. "Bas, take Nichols to my office. The rest of you—" his black gaze swung around the locker room full of stunned faces "—get in the pool. We're already ten minutes late starting our last open practice here." When no one moved, he barked, "Move it," and the rest of the team snapped out of their shocked daze, springing back into action. "You two," he said to Alex and Dane, "wait."

Alex collapsed on the bench, adrenaline dwindling and disappointment weighing him down. How had he not seen the festering resentment Ryan carried? Did other teammates feel the same?

Dane moved behind him, and Alex leaned back against his legs, taking what little comfort he could in the knowledge at least something had gone right during the last forty-eight hours.

"You've got proof?" Coach asked once the door swung closed on the last outgoing swimmer. "Something solid I can take to the Committee?"

"It's solid, Coach," Dane said. "I can show you now or after practice."

"Plus you've got a room full of witnesses to that scene just now," Alex added. "And this." He dug his phone out of his pocket, recorder on, taping Ryan's outburst and confession. Alex tagged it off. "I wasn't doping, Coach."

"I'm sorry I doubted you. I should have known better." He glanced up at Dane. "Should have had the same confidence in you that your boyfriend does."

"You don't seem surprised?"

"Caught a little of your impromptu press conference. Bas filled me in on the rest." He ran a hand over his black hair. "Way you two circled each other, it was going to come to one end or the other, love or hate. I thought maybe there was something there, but I didn't want to put either of you in an awkward situation. Glad it worked out this way."

"Thank you," Alex said, "for that." He wasn't ready to forgive the other slight yet.

"Can you get him cleared to swim in time?" Dane asked.

"Come with me, and show me what you've got."

Alex stood to follow, and Coach held up a hand. "No, Cantu, just Ellis."

He nodded in understanding. He was the guilty party, and he wasn't officially cleared, yet. It was technically the right way to handle the matter. Still sucked. Moving back into the aisle, he picked up his duffle from where he'd dropped it and slug it over his shoulder. "I'll just wait in my room," he said, then floundered. "Or I guess mine's gone now."

"Go to mine," Dane said, digging out his key.

"That's not what I meant," Coach said. "I've got to deal with whatever evidence Dane's got and then with Ryan. You get out there on deck and captain."

Alex almost dropped his bag. "You're sure it's okay?"

"Fine by me. I'm sure it will be fine by your team too."

"But what Ryan said, about us repeat performers, maybe other feel that way too."

"Maybe they do, but this is the nature of the sport now. Some, like Ryan, may resent it, but I think, I hope, the bigger portion are happy to learn from your experience." He nodded toward the door, toward the pool beyond where Alex's teammates were waiting. "Go out there, and show them it's worth having repeat performers on the team. Go be a captain, Cantu."

It'd take a while for the hurt caused by Coach's initial doubt to fully heal, but his trust and confidence now went a long way to speeding up the process.

"Yes, Coach," he said, ready to get back in the water, to get back to his dream.

DANE CAUGHT UP to Coach in the hallway outside his office. The older man looked surlier and more wrinkled than his usual, well-pressed self. As hard as the past few days had been on Dane and Alex, it couldn't have been easy on Coach either. Having to sideline his protégé and captain, Dane going AWOL, the Committee and PR likely breathing down his neck.

"I'm guessing I've got you to thank for my missing ID badge," Coach said.

Hedging his bets on Coach's sour mood, Dane skirted the truth. "I didn't take it, if that's what you're asking."

"But you have it." When Dane didn't reply, Coach sighed, tired and frustrated, and held out a hand. "Just give me the damn card, Ellis."

Dane unzipped his computer bag, dug around for the card, and handed it over. "We didn't have to use it."

"Good. Wasn't sure how I was going to explain being in two places at once."

"Speaking of, can I show you what we found?" Dane patted his bag, impatient. "I want to know Alex is clear."

Rather than entering his office, Coach led him into the conference room across the hall. "I want to see what you have before I talk to Nichols."

Nodding, Dane crossed the hall into the room, withdrew his computer, and set it up on the table. Once booted up, he walked Coach through the before and after test results, pointing out the markers that proved this was Alex's sample, the changed *NEG* to *POS*, and Ryan's User ID on the ghost of the changed document.

"Well, that's pretty damn convincing," Coach said, when Dane finished. "And with the recording Alex made, Ryan all but confessed. I'll want to draw blood from both of you after practice today, to further make the case to the Committee, which I'll do this evening. I've already set up a conference call."

Dane barely kept still on the edge of his chair, bouncing as badly as Alex had earlier in the day. "How fast will we know something? We leave for international training tomorrow."

"Alex is here, ready to leave with us, thanks to you. You were right to go after him, and you were right about this." Coach nodded at the computer, then slumped back in his chair. "Not sure I'll ever forgive myself for doubting him and my gut. I knew he didn't dope, but with the test results and how everything had turned around . . ."

"Because he'd gotten through to me," Dane said, pointing at himself. "I was the one holding the team back."

"And now you've brought him and the team back together. Can't thank you enough, Ellis." Sighing, Coach ran both hands over his black hair, slicking it back. Surly had given way to upset, with himself.

"You let Alex go back and swim," Dane said. "Let him go back and captain. That's a good start. And hey, if he could forgive *me* after a decade of turning my back on him, he'll forgive you for doing so this once."

Before Coach could respond, a commotion broke out in the hallway, and the loudest voice of all . . . Patrick Ellis. Demanding to know where his son was. Dane froze. Standing up to them on the phone was one thing, in the airport where they weren't another, but this—face-to-face—

was a whole different battle. He'd known it was coming. He'd just hoped for a moment to breathe first, maybe spend some time in the pool and get a kiss from Alex before he went off to war.

Coach was on his feet already. "I can tell them you're not here."

Dane rose, forcing his legs steady. "No, this is going to happen one way or the other. I'd rather we get it done before we leave."

Coach wrapped his hand around the door handle and paused. "You sure?"

About being with Alex, he'd never been more sure about anything. He had to do this, for Alex, and for himself. "Yes," he answered, and Coach opened the door.

His mother and father charged in like they owned the place. Camera-ready, perfectly pressed, and noses aloft. Cold in their fury, especially his father's eyes.

"Mrs. Ellis, Reverend," Coach said, deflecting their ire.

"What kind of operation are you running here?" his mother snapped. "My son was gone for thirty-six hours, going after that drug user, and you didn't know?"

"Because I asked my team to cover for me," Dane said. "Coach had nothing to do with it. And Alex didn't use any drugs."

"He put that boy on your team."

Always, *that boy*, never *Alex*.

Dane's confidence, his own anger, came screaming back. He'd put a name to the man he loved, even if they wouldn't. "*Alex* earned his spot on *his* team. I'm the one who's lucky to be on it. Just like I'm lucky he still loves me."

"Love," his mother scoffed, rolling her eyes. "You're too young to know what that word means."

"Respectfully, ma'am," Coach said, stepping to Dane's side, "what your son did for Alex is a level of devotion I rarely see from people much older than him."

She waved him off. "It's a phase, Coach Hartl. He hasn't grown out of it yet."

"Respectfully," Coach started again, obviously trying to keep things civil, "I don't think you understand how this works."

Civility wasn't going to work with his parents. "You don't owe them respect," Dane said to Coach. "Not until they show you, me, or Alex some." Then to his mother, "I'm twenty-six. Like I told you the other night, me being gay isn't a phase now, and it wasn't a phase at sixteen. It's who I am."

Painted lips pressed together, she looked stymied. "We can't have a gay son."

"Well, you do." That was the simple truth of it.

His father finally spoke, his voice brooking no argument, full of fire and brimstone, in only two words. "We don't."

A boulder of ice lodged in the pit of Dane's stomach. He'd known it was coming to this, but to be actually disowned by his parents, to be made to feel like he didn't exist in their world because of something he couldn't help, was a regretfully Titanic moment. Only the thought of Alex waiting for him, loving him, kept him from sinking.

"If this is the path you chose, it is not the path to God,

and we cannot join you on it. Nor can you join us on ours."

But it wasn't a choice he made. Being gay was no different than his blue eyes or his red hair. He couldn't change who he was attracted to, who he loved.

"That's a very narrow interpretation," Coach said.

"It's the Word of the Gospel."

"Your narrow interpretation of it. One you're willing to choose over your son?" Coach laid a hand on his shoulder, and Dane swallowed hard, blinking back tears. "A son you should be proud of, for sticking by his friends, standing up for someone he loves, and being one of the best swimmers in the world."

"Dane, please reconsider," his mother said, no real plea in her voice. It was more like a final sales pitch, capped with a threat because that's what she did best. "You'll lose everything."

He held his head high and drew his shoulders back, summoning up that confidence from the airport, the confidence in being himself, in being real. "I've reconsidered all my life, Mom. And if I do it again this time, I'll lose the two things that matter most—myself and Alex."

Another voice entered the fray. "You won't lose everything," Roger said from the doorway, winded but smiling, Bas looking on from over his shoulder. "We were right. After that announcement at the airport, I've had calls from a dozen new companies wanting to sponsor you. Alex too, if you can wrangle him. And all your current sponsors are still onboard."

"Those existing sponsorships are in the Trust's name,"

his mother said.

Bas rapped his knuckles on the doorjamb. "Good thing I know a fantastic lawyer." Dane tilted his head in question, and Bas smiled, wide and more than a little devious. "My mom," he answered. "She's gonna hate you because she's always wanted Alex for a son-in-law, but she'll love you for making him happy."

That block of ice in Dane's stomach began to thaw. Coach chipped away at it some more. "And if you need a job, which doesn't sound like you will, but if you do, I'll make sure you've got one at USOC."

Where he could coach and swim, side by side with Alex, every day. He'd like that, a lot. "I might take you up on that, sponsorships or not."

"Dane, we're your family," his mother urged, changing her tune, a never-heard-before thread of desperation in her voice. With Roger's pronouncement, and Bas and Coach rallying to his side, she was seeing her golden goose take flight.

Fly, babe.

That's what Alex would say, and that's what he did, fighting back, flying high. "Only if I fit into the role that suits you, a role that's not the real me." He looked around, at Coach, at Bas, and thought about Alex and Jacob in the pool, and Mo back in DC. "I've got plenty of family who like me just the way I am."

"Son," his father clipped. "You can't go back from here."

"I don't plan to. I'm going forward, with Alex, with my team, and we're going to bring home the gold."

"And on that note," Coach said, breaking into a smile as he gestured to the door. "Reverend, Mrs. Ellis, I'm going to have to ask you to leave. Respectfully."

CHAPTER TWENTY-ONE

ALEX STOOD BY the window in Dane's room, phone to his ear.

Bas and Jacob were sitting on the end of the bed behind him, Dane against the headboard, inhaling a takeout meal of one of everything from the Hill Country BBQ place they'd eyed since arriving in San Antonio. Last practice done, they'd rewarded themselves with brisket, ribs, mac and cheese, baked beans, and jalapeño corn muffins, a little bit of everything Texan for their last night in Texas.

They'd just started piling their plates high when Alex's mom returned his call from earlier in the day. He filled her in on what was happening, including the possibility he'd be leaving for international training tomorrow.

"You're sure everything's okay there?" he asked. "I'm sorry I was there and gone again."

"Don't apologize, *mijo*. You did what I told you to do. I don't think I've ever enjoyed *SportsCenter* as much as I did tonight, seeing you smiling and happy at the airport and pool."

Needless to say, his and Dane's announcement and the

doping controversy that wasn't had been the lead sports story of the day. Coach had handled the latter well, Roger the former with the glee of a publicist working a whole new angle.

His phone dinged with an incoming text.

"Just sent you a picture," his mom said. "So you'll stop worrying."

He lowered the phone to take a look. On the screen was a picture of his family, holding up the blue blanket she'd been knitting, and in rainbow colors across the middle, the words *Go for the Gold, Alex*, and in what he could tell was a last minute yet heartfelt addition, *And Dane* tacked on beneath his name.

They were behind him, behind *them*, all the way.

"Thanks, Mom," he said. "I don't know what I did to deserve you all." He'd gotten so lucky to have a family that accepted and supported him. They would do the same for Dane too.

"You're a good son, Alejandro. Someone we're all proud of. Though if you boys don't bring home a relay gold this time, I'll repurpose the blanket into mittens and a toboggan for winter." He loved hearing that spark back in her voice, even if it was at his expense.

"We'll see what we can do," he said, grinning.

When he was done saying goodbyes to the rest of his family, they hung up, and he took the phone over to the bed, showing the picture to Dane, then to Bas and Jacob.

"She says she'll be very disappointed if we don't bring home the gold."

"Nuh-uh." Bas waved a rib at him. "I know Mrs. C. That's not what she said."

Alex rolled his eyes and tossed a corn muffin at him. "Fine, she said she'll make mittens and a cap out of it if we lose."

Bas caught the corn muffin and stuffed it in his mouth. "That's more like it," he said around the mouthful of food. "I love that woman."

They all rolled with laugher, even Dane, which Alex was grateful for after what he'd learned of the confrontation with his parents. Dane and Bas had appeared on deck twenty minutes after Alex, and for the rest of practice, the relay teams had run hard. The days off had thankfully not dulled their timing when running as they should. After, as Coach had drawn blood for their retests, Dane had given Alex a recap of the showdown with his parents. Alex could tell it had upset Dane, but they'd both known that's where things were headed, and Dane seemed relieved to have it over with and to have Coach, Roger, the team, and Alex behind him.

"What'd Coach and the Committee say about the evidence?" Jacob asked.

"They wanted to check it themselves, given my personal investment in the matter," Dane answered, bumping Alex's side. "Coach was pretty confident it would get sorted out."

And Dane was confident enough to insist Alex pack his bags for the flight to Europe tomorrow. They sat ready to go next to Dane's, who'd insisted, when leaving Colorado, that Alex bring everything back with him. Alex hoped all his insisting wasn't for naught.

"What's going to happen to Ryan?" Jacob asked.

"He's off the team," Alex answered. "Likely off his club team too."

"I still can't believe he did that," Bas said.

Alex had a hard time wrapping his head around it too. "No one said anything at the practice or after, but how much of a concern is it?" he asked Jacob, the youngest member on their team. "Us returners hogging spots and medals."

"It's out there," Jacob replied. "You can either resent it or learn from it. Most of us choose the latter."

Alex reached over and ruffled the short mop of hair growing back on his head. "Thank you, guys, for sticking by me. I know I don't make it easy."

"You take on too much," Bas said. "But that's why you're the captain. And we're behind you. Especially that one." He held a hand out to Dane, who shook it. "You proved me wrong, Ellis. Couldn't be happier about that."

As they finished eating, talk moved to lap times, seedings, and likely competitors, time passing unnoticed until the knocking of nightly bed checks sounded down the hallway.

"That's our sign to go, Pup," Bas said. "Let's leave the lovebirds to it."

They gathered up the takeout boxes to toss in the hall trashcan, and Alex and Dane unfolded from where they were nestled together against the headboard.

"Thanks for helping with the takedown, Pup," Alex said, following them to the door. "Those were some impressive moves."

"I'm just glad you two are back and happy," Jacob said,

pulling first him, then Dane, into bear hugs.

Bas approached next with a backslapping bro hug. "Glad I was wrong."

Before he stepped away, Alex asked, "We're not the only lovebirds here, are we?" He hadn't missed how Jacob and Bas were even more connected at the hip than when he'd left and how they gravitated toward each other in any situation.

The pup picked up his pace to the door, confirming Alex's suspicions, and Alex clasped Bas's arm, holding him back. "Do you know what you're doing there?"

"Not doing anything," Bas said, playing dumb.

If this threatened the team. If it cost them the relay gold like another of Bas's mistakes had four years ago . . .

"I won't fuck up again," Bas said, reading his mind. "Now, turn off that captain brain for a night," Bas added, knowing him too well. "Enjoy your last night off with your boyfriend before the chaos starts tomorrow."

"*If* it starts tomorrow, for me at least."

Dane slung an arm around his waist, hauling him close and kissing his temple. "It will."

"He's right," Bas said. "And if this afternoon was any indication, heaven help us all with you back as captain."

He skirted out of the room before either he or Dane could lob a comeback.

The door clicked shut behind them, and Alex turned in Dane's arms.

"You want to talk more about what went down with your parents?" he asked.

"Not really." Dane ducked his head for a kiss, and Alex

evaded.

"But they weren't behind Ryan changing the test. At the airport, then after with them here, you did all that—came out—for nothing?"

Dane tugged him over to the bed, bringing Alex tumbling down with him. "Not for nothing." He rolled so Alex was underneath him, forearms braced on either side of his head. "For you." He stared down, blue eyes swirling with a devotion that made the question nagging Alex hard to ask. But necessary.

"Where does this go, Dane, after Madrid?"

"You and me, in Colorado Springs, if you'll have me. I don't plan on spending another decade without you." Dane's thumbs played with the hair at his temples. He seemed so calm, so at peace, even as they talked about uprooting his life.

"Just like that, you'll leave everything, for me?"

He smiled, small, a sudden sadness creeping in. "What's there to leave? I live at home with my parents. I swim for a club five miles from my house."

"One of the best clubs in the country."

"*One* of the best. But as you said, any club would be happy to have me. The question is, would you?"

"Would I what?"

"Be happy to have me, for good?"

Heart pounding, Alex ran his hands up Dane's arms, over his shoulders, and to his neck, finding Dane's own racing pulse there, betraying his outer calm. He'd offered himself to Alex, afraid he might be turned away.

"This is real, isn't it?" Alex said, marveling at this new road he found himself on.

With Dane.

"That's what I've been telling you."

Alex smiled, and took that first step. "Yeah, Big Red, I'd be thrilled to have you with me." Before Dane could kiss him, he took another step, hoping Dane would follow. "Though maybe not in Colorado."

Dane's happy face fell. "I get it. It'll take some time to get used to. I can wait."

Alex cupped his cheeks. "That's not what I meant, babe." He rubbed his palms against the red scruff there, reassuring both of them. "I've been thinking, when Mom's recovered from this round of chemo, that I might make a change."

"What kind of change?"

"California, if I can swing it financially. I miss it, and Bas is there too. I'm sure his club would take us, if you'd want to go there, with me?"

Dane dipped his head, giving him another one of those kisses so full of promises Alex thought the world possible. "I'll go anywhere with you, Alejandro Cantu."

ON HIS STOMACH, head pillowed in his arm atop a soft pillow, Alex thought this was a much better way to wake up than yesterday morning. Sunlight streaming in around the edges of the window blinds, warming the side of his face.

Body sore from yesterday's hard practice in the pool and last night's hard workout in the bed. His partner in both endeavors a heavy weight draped over his back and side, his light snores ruffling the hair on the back of Alex's neck.

Dane Ellis.

In his bed, in his life, and hopefully on the same team together again.

Alex turned his head and opened his eyes, happy to find he hadn't woken in an alternate reality. Dane's freckled face glowed in the morning sun, his shining red-gold hair stuck out in every direction, and a hint of a smile played on his lips, even in sleep. The world had gone to hell around them the past week, and Dane seemed more relaxed than ever.

If someone held a mirror to his own face, Alex suspected he'd see the same this morning. Sure, there were plenty of problems to tackle, but he felt lighter, fuller. Because he'd let someone else, his teammates and Dane, help carry the load. No matter the outcome this morning, no matter whether he added more medals to his case or not, Alex was in a better place, with the trust and respect of his family, team, and coach, and with the love of his life at his side.

"You're staring," the sleeping giant mumbled.

Alex chuckled. "Yeah, I am."

Dane opened one eye, pupil shrinking in response to the bright light, the blue of his iris translucent in the morning's rays. He grinned wider. "You're smiling too."

"Yeah, I am."

Dane's other eye popped open. "We get word from Coach, yet?"

Alex snaked an arm out from in between them and brushed the hair off Dane's forehead. "No, but I've got all I need right here."

Mo was right. There was more to life than medals. And Alex's more was Dane.

Hand diving under the sheet, Dane threw it over Alex's waist and hauled him closer. "You saying you don't want that gold medal anymore?"

"Oh, I still want it."

Dane forced a thigh between his, spreading Alex's legs and making room for other parts of them to meet, to bump and glide, both half-hard already. Dane dipped his head, licking a path up Alex's neck to his ear, breathing hotly there. "I bet I know what else you want." Dane's sun-warmed hand slipped off his hip and around to grasp their cocks, gathering their slick and using it to ease the glide of his fist around them. "That round four we didn't get yesterday morning," Dane said, and Alex groaned his agreement, arching into the tight, hot grip.

Definitely a better morning.

He made to fall back, but Dane kept him on his side, even as he slid down his body, kissing a path from neck, to nipples, to belly button, to the place that craved his attention most. Those full lips closed around Alex's tip, tongue teasing his slit, and Alex braced a knee on Dane's broad shoulder to stay upright.

Dane moaned as he swallowed his cock down, as if there was nothing he liked doing more. His fist at the base moved with his mouth, and he slipped a finger along Alex's length, wetting and teasing, heightening the sensation.

Preparing Alex for what came next.

Hooking an arm under his leg, Dane palmed his ass, steadying him, then trailed that slick finger down his crease and over his rim, circling the edges but never pressing in. Alex was forced to thrust after his mouth and chase after his touch, a back and forth where both directions were mind-blowing pleasure.

Alex clutched the sheet with his outstretched hand while the other dove into Dane's hair. "Babe, please," he begged, hips so far back, so wanton for more inside his ass, that he'd brought his tip to Dane's lips. Dane circled his tongue around it, and Alex didn't know which way to go. "Gonna fucking kill me."

"Gonna fuck you," Dane mumbled, then took all of him down again, tip bumping the back of his throat, at the same time two fingers pushed inside.

Senses overloaded, Alex didn't know which way was up; all directions pointed to Dane. His fingers in his ass, his mouth around his cock, and his leg thrown over Alex's, Dane's dick hard and wet against his calf, humping in time with his mouth and hand.

Alex flattened his hand in Dane's hair, turning it into a caress that tunneled in and out of the strands with each pitch of their bodies. Heat all around, both of them still hungry for every touch, every connection, they were at the edge in no time flat. The speed of Dane's rutting escalated, hips snapping on either side of Alex's leg, and he homed in on the spot inside Alex, stroking with single-minded focus, until

Alex spilled down his throat, shouting all manner of Spanish obscenities as he came. Dane's release followed in short order, coating Alex's leg.

Teetering on his side, Alex finally fell back and Dane rolled with him, hand still under his ass, face nuzzling his groin, like he was perfectly happy to stay right there all morning, in spite of their mess.

Alex hummed, likewise content. "You comfy down there?"

"Very," Dane said. "You mind if I stay here?"

"Go right ahead." Alex slung a leg over Dane's back, caging him in. "I enjoyed round four."

Dane tilted his head, chin resting on Alex's hip bone, grinning up at him. "I know you did. Though technically, it's round five, counting last night. Give me a few to recover, then I'll treat you to round six."

Alex was going to ask what that entailed, but then their sex-dazed bubble was burst by someone pounding on the door.

Dane's tortured groan was loud enough to be heard outside. And unmistakable.

"Go away," Alex hollered at the unwelcome intrusion.

Bas's deep laughter floated through the door. "Stop fucking like rabbits for two minutes, and open up."

A curse-laden version of his previous order was on the tip of his tongue, but Dane beat him to it. "Give us a minute." Alex glared down at his bedmate. "He might have news," Dane said, pushing up from the bed.

Alex growled in frustration. Dane was right; his dick

didn't care. Dane laughed and slapped his ass. "Up, Cap."

They rolled out of bed, Dane grabbing a hand towel out of the bathroom so they could clean up before pulling on clothes. With each piece, the morning's lightness faded and Alex's nerves crept in. He wasn't lying, all he needed was Dane and the future they'd talked about, but it would still sting to lose the other thing he wanted most.

The chance to compete again with his team. And now with the man he loved.

If nothing else, though, they'd done everything they could to make that happen.

"Hey," Dane said, at his side. "They're going to let you back on the team." He held out his hand. "Come on, let's get the official word."

Buoyed by his confidence, Alex slid his hand in Dane's, marveling at how much easier this was now that he wasn't doing everything on his own. Dane dragged him toward the door, opening it to reveal Bas and Jacob standing in front of the rest of the team.

"Tell me," Alex said. Perhaps his last order as captain.

Bursting into a smile, Bas withdrew his hand from behind his back, holding up a plane ticket. And it wasn't back to Colorado Springs.

Alex's relieved exhale was choked off in a gasp when Jacob hit him square in the chest, wrapping him up in another bear hug. "Welcome back, Cap."

Alex smiled big, but it was nowhere near as big as the heart expanding in his chest. The road opened back up in front of him, full of all the possibilities.

Dane hugged him from behind, whispering in his ear. "Now I get to kiss my boyfriend in Madrid when we win the gold."

"If we win the gold."

"You bet your ass we're winning," Bas said, piling on as chants of "Al-ex" and "U-S-A" broke out in the hallway.

If Alex had to guess that morning, he'd say they were going to win too.

Not the silver this time.

Gold.

ACKNOWLEDGMENTS

Thank you, Readers, for joining me on leg one of this Changing Lanes journey! As a huge fan of second chance romances, I loved telling Alex and Dane's story and bringing them back together. I hope you enjoyed it too, and that you'll join me again as the Olympic competition and romance heat up in Bas and Jacob's story—*Medley*!

Special thanks to Tera and Mirna for the beta and Spanish reads, to Jeff and Maxym for their swimming input, to Kristi for the editorial assistance, to Victoria for the invaluable feedback, to Garrett and LC for the cover and layout, and to the amazing authors in my various writing groups, online and in-person, who help keep me on track and are always there with helpful advice.

There are not enough *Thank you*s and *I love you*s in the world for my dear husband, who's been a super trooper and A+ coffee-and-donut delivery service this past year as I've launched a second career and worked two full time jobs.

Finally, much love to my Lushes, whose excitement for my books, characters, and words has been a truly wonderful and humbling gift. I can't wait to bring you more stories in the year ahead!

ALSO BY LAYLA REYNE

Changing Lanes series
Medley

Agents Irish and Whiskey series
Single Malt
Cask Strength
Barrel Proof
Tequila Sunrise

ABOUT THE AUTHOR

Author Layla Reyne was raised in North Carolina and now calls San Francisco home. She enjoys weaving her bi-coastal experiences into her stories, along with adrenaline-fueled suspense and heart pounding romance. When she's not writing stories to excite her readers, she downloads too many books, watches too much television, and cooks too much food with her scientist husband, much to the delight of their smushed-face, leftover-loving dogs. Layla is a member of Romance Writers of America and Kiss of Death, and Rainbow Romance Writers chapters. She was a 2016 RWA® Golden Heart® Finalist in Romantic Suspense.

You can find Layla at laylareyne.com, on Twitter, Facebook, Instagram and Pinterest as @laylareyne, and in her reader group on Facebook—Layla's Lushes.

CPSIA information can be obtained
at www.ICGtesting.com
Printed in the USA
LVHW080006270319
611968LV00010B/178/P